# THE MAJOR'S WIFE

## *The Witness Tree 2*

**Beverly Sims**

**MENAGE AND MORE**

**Siren Publishing, Inc.**
**www.SirenPublishing.com**

**A SIREN PUBLISHING BOOK**
IMPRINT: Ménage and More

THE MAJOR'S WIFE


ISBN-10: 1-60601-718-7
ISBN-13: 978-1-60601-718-0

First Printing: July 2010

Cover design by Jinger Heaston


Printed in the U.S.A.

**PUBLISHER**
Siren Publishing, Inc.
www.SirenPublishing.com

# DEDICATION

To Jerry and Tom.

Many thanks for the jokes and fun (at my expense) which never cease to amuse me. Hugs to both.

# THE MAJOR'S WIFE

***The Witness Tree 2***

**BEVERLY SIMS**



## *PART I*

## Chapter 1

*Here I stand, as I have for many human years. Things have changed here on the Plains and I am not sure these were good changes. Even after my tall mother died, a long time in the past, I grew at her craggy side, offering shelter and shade for all who sat beneath my spreading branches. I now suffer from the same cancer of rot that took her life, so my days are numbered. Until then, I will tell my stories...and there are many.*

*As a seedling, I watched Summer Swan and her tribes of strong Indians hunt their buffalo, fight their enemies, and love one another in every way. The Indians are here, too, at the time of this story, but Summer Swan lies on her platform where the gods can see her, with her husband, Soaring Eagle. Yes, she did marry him, but only as he lay on his deathbed in her arms. It was his last request and she cried as she remembered his countless proposals in the past. However, that is another story...one already told.*

*I am watching yet another column of wagons crossing the river in the distance, heading west. I have learned new words, such as homestead, wagon master, mountain men, cavalry, trading post, forts, and such. You will probably already know them, so no need to say more.*

*In these times, there has been much killing. So many useless deaths, both Indians and the whites, and I hate it all. I think the gods are testing the people, but I have no idea why. It is so sad.*

*Right now, there is a pretty young woman on a buckboard, heading for Fort Mason, just a short jaunt from here. As they pass beneath my boughs, I see a man in uniform is driving and eight soldiers surround the wagon...two in front, two in the back, and two on each side. Later I will learn her name is Lucretia Lucinda Sawyer, known as Lulu to her friends and family. The old woman with her is her Auntie Liz.*

Corporal Dryer was smitten with the young woman sitting beside him. She looked to him like a ray of sunshine this cold winter morning. Her yellow hair glistened in the sun where the curls escaped her pink fur-lined bonnet, which matched her cloak, down to the ribbons that tied both garments. Her face glowed as the frosty air took its toll on her fair skin.

In all truth, Corporal Dryer had never been this close to a real lady before, and never anyone as beautiful as this woman nor one who smelled so good. Had the lady known he thought she smelled good, she would have laughed aloud. After that long train ride and a night in that sad little hotel, no one could smell good.

*Actually,* he thought, *I have never been this close to any woman, but for the ones in bars and brothels, and they were nothing like Mrs. Sawyer*. He enjoyed himself under the sheets with them, but could not imagine this angel doing those things to him or with him. Or with any man, for that manner. The major was a lucky man.

He drove the wagon as carefully as possible, considering the ruts in the two-track road. "Sorry, ma'am. There are just too many bumps for me to miss them all."

"Well, I suppose you are doing the best you can, considering. I hope I never have to travel this way again. A stagecoach would be so much better," she replied. Corporal Dryer did not have the heart to tell her a stagecoach would be worse because its speed gave no relief, as drivers had no time to avoid hazards. Nor did he tell her that the only other transportation was on the back of a horse. He wanted her smiles, not her frowns, as he had seen plenty of those since she stepped aboard the best buckboard the fort had. Lord, what would he have said if the major had not sent this one instead of any of the rest?

Behind them, huddled down in her fur ensemble, was the older woman, whom the lady had introduced as her Auntie Liz. Auntie Liz appeared about fifty, but to Corporal Dryer, anybody much older than he…well, they were all about fifty, or older. After all, Corporal Dryer was the ripe old age of twenty-two and proud of his rank.

## Chapter 2

Auntie Liz pulled the back of Lucretia's lap robe. The young woman leaned back and listened to the whisper from her aunt. They did not speak again until she asked, much like a petulant child, "Sergeant, how much longer? You told me hours ago, when you picked me up at the hotel in Cottonwood Creek, that it was a long way, but it has already been that long and I see no sign of life anywhere." Lucinda pouted prettily as she cocked her head to look at the man on the seat beside her. She had fidgeted for the past few minutes, letting his embarrassed mind know that she had a nature need.

"*Corporal*, Mrs. Sawyer. I am a corporal. Corporal Jed Dryer. The major told me to stop whenever you wanted or every hour if you did not ask. It has been an hour, ma'am. I will stop."

"Whatever for? I need a necessary and there does not seem to be one here. We can go on for a few more minutes until you find one."

Corporal Dryer was the fidgeting one now. "Well, ma'am, er…er…" *Perhaps the best way,* he thought, *is just to blurt it out.* "There are no necessaries between the train station and the fort. You can find a sheltered place to…" Again, he could not picture this woman doing such mundane things as relieving herself.

"Surely you joke, Private."

Ye gads, an instant demotion, and he still had to deal with the problem. Her anger was apparent, but he had no choice. The major had been very clear on this matter. "Ma'am, your husband said…"

She cut him off. "My husband must not be aware of the lack of necessaries, Private. Do you expect me to simply climb down from this back-breaking pile of wood, traipse off into the weeds, pull up my skirt, and tinkle in front of all of you?"

"No, ma'am, we will turn our backs. We do have some manners, ma'am." He did not tell her that the major had ordered them to give her privacy, knowing that these men would take advantage and peek at any female. "I will come around and lift you down, if you like."

"Yes, you will, and do it now." As he rounded the wagon, Auntie Liz stood. *Dear Lord,* he thought, *I do not think I can pick up that heavy woman without dropping her.*

"Corporal Dryer, I will assist this lovely lady." Sergeant Michael O'Brian shoved him out of the way. The sergeant was tall, rotund, and strong as an ox. He bowed to the lady and reached up, taking her by the waist to set her gently on the ground beside Lucretia. "There you go, Miss Liz."

Liz turned to him. "First of all, we have not been properly introduced, sir. My name is Mrs. Elizabeth Harold. I expect you to address me as such until…and *if* I ever give you permission to do otherwise." She stared at him until he dropped his gaze, unsure of what he had done so wrong.

The men laughed aloud at her words, but the sergeant just grinned. "That is some woman," he said. "Mark my words, laddies, and watch. I will be a-marrying that one." This time, hoots and hollers greeted his announcement.

# Chapter 3

Once on the ground, the women walked rapidly into the bushes under the trees. Sergeant O'Brien's words carried to them. "How dare he make such an assumption?" growled Liz. "The nerve of that man." Lucretia smiled but made sure her auntie did not see it.

Corporal Dryer knew it must be dreadfully cold as the ladies lifted their skirts and removed the layers of clothing they wore. It took a great deal of time and effort, slowing down their progress, but he also knew they had little choice. Neither was smiling as they returned to the wagon and were lifted to their seats. He carefully avoided Lucretia's eyes as he stood her in front of the vehicles. Sergeant O'Brian was bolder and held the robust woman around the waist, looking into her stern face as he lowered her plump form onto her blankets. He reached inside and tucked them around her, only to receive a slap to his hands. He laughed and smiled, very content with himself.

Jed tried to speed up the team, but when he did, he could not miss the holes and bumps, so he slowed back down. He looked around him quickly, trying to see things from Mrs. Sawyer's eyes. Lord, it must look forsaken to a lady from the big city, from a life of wealth and culture. He had been to St. Louis himself once, and remembered the busy streets, and the colorful dresses and austere suits on the ladies and gentlemen there. Himself, the city had scared him so much he never wanted to go there again.

However, to such a lady…from that to this! How would she abide the endless grass and wind with nowhere to go, the howling animals at night instead of gala evenings on the town, and her tiny, drafty cabin instead of a large home? What would she do with no shops or churches, no promenades in the park with her friends, and the few friends she could make with only two other women, plus her aunt, on the post? Not to mention the cold winters, hot summers, the bugs and snakes, and the perpetual tension created by Indians and outlaws. No, this was no place for her.

He asked her awhile later if she wanted to stop again, but she did not even answer. The third time, she told him to stop. The same the fifth and seventh time, when they stopped again. It was much later when he said, "If you look ahead, ma'am, you can see the fort towers ahead. We will be there within the hour."

"Another hour? Is this the fort?" Her face drained of color as she looked at the rough timbers and through the gates that opened for them. "Dear God, this cannot be. This is little more than a corral with barns. Where are the houses and meeting hall?"

"Yes, ma'am, it is. It is all right here." All aboard the wagon were silent until they reached the gates.

"I do believe I see the major heading this way. Thank you for letting me drive you here." Jed Dryer was so sincere, Lucretia had to smile.

She looked at the eight men who rode guard for them, taking in each face. It had been the longest day of her life, but she knew manners were still important. "Thank your other men, as well. While their presence was unnecessary, it was nice to know we were well protected in the event that something did happen." She nodded to each and returned their smiles, until she saw the stern face of the man who had ridden a distance in front of them. He was tall and dark, with brown hair, high cheekbones, and eyes like obsidian. While the other men dismounted, he remained on his horse, looking down at her with an unsmiling, disinterested face, much as he might look at a dung beetle. She turned away to race into arms of her husband.

# Chapter 4

Major Jeffrey Daggett Sawyer held her stiffly and kissed her forehead, much as a doting uncle might. Lucretia pulled back and looked up into his face. She grinned. "Is that the best you can give your bride who has missed you so much for these past months?" She stretched her arms up to encircle his neck, pulled his head down, and kissed him full on the mouth.

His men applauded and shouted encouragement when he finally responded by removing his hat, taking her into his arms, and returning the kiss. He felt his cock stir as she slipped the end of her tongue into his mouth. He felt that if he did not stop this now, he might throw her to the ground and take her body right there.

He drew away, well aware that his penis was now at full alert and that it was obvious in his tight trousers. He dropped his arm with the hat to shield his erection and offered his other arm to Lucretia. "Come, dear wife, let me show you around."

Her tiredness forgotten, she grinned at him and then whispered toward his ear, "That can wait. I want to be alone with you. Right now. Which building is yours?"

He nodded toward one of the ramshackle dwellings. She pulled his arm, forcing him to walk to it. The men laughed and cheered as he gallantly opened the door. In an attempt to cover his embarrassment, he said loudly, "Yes, of course. You want to see where you will be living. Any woman would."

Before the door even latched, Lulu pulled him to her, kissing him the way he loved. Jeffrey knew that nothing could stop him from taking her and nothing did. She pulled his jacket back over his shoulders and helped him shrug it off without breaking the kiss. His suspenders were next, followed by his trousers. His cock stood straight, but hardened even more as she dropped her skirt. He pulled her "littles" down and pushed her back against the edge of the bed until she fell backward. He spread her legs and stared down at her exposed pussy.

"Are you ready? I cannot wait," he moaned. She held out her arms. He dropped between her spread thighs and shoved himself into her. She was wet, to his amazement, so wet that in three or four jabs, he came. He felt ashamed, knowing that her wetness meant she was ready. "God, Lucretia, you are so…I am sorry. I have not come that quickly since I was a young lad. Please forgive me." He wanted to cry in his embarrassment.

# Chapter 5

"Now you stop that, Jeffrey. I know how long it has been, as well as you do. In addition, as I recall, you found other ways to please me, besides just your cock. Now, before I have to beg you, please give me what I need."

He helped her remove the rest of her clothes and lay down beside her. He kissed her deeply, letting his tongue explore first her mouth, then her nipples. He moved his mouth up again to nibble on her ear, then down her neck. She closed her eyes and basked in the wonder of sensations his lips gave her. When his tongue flicked first one nipple, then the other, she moaned and whispered his name. His mouth took command of her breasts, kissing and tonguing her everywhere.

"Bite my nipples, darling. Not too hard. Yes, perfect. More! God, how I love you." Her whispers incited his ardor and his cock began to stir again. He ran one hand down her stomach and then spread his fingers to completely cover her riot of yellow curls. He cupped her tightly before allowing one finger to move into her wetness. She moaned again to his touch. Her hips began to move as he rubbed and teased the tiny button. It grew as he manipulated it between two fingers. It grew as his penis grew.

He pushed his hard dick against her hip, rubbing it as he rubbed her clit. When she exploded, he stifled her cries with his mouth. Her hips still moved as he buried his cock in her hot wetness. This time he moved in and out at a slower rhythm and his moans told her he was enjoying every stroke. She continued her heavy breathing against his neck, but its tremor changed. Her lips moved up to lick his ear, which induced whispers of his love for her.

"Now, husband, I am ready for some heavy fucking." Her words—ones he never expected to hear from any lady—excited him even more. She wrapped her legs around his hips and met his every stroke. He felt her tightening as a sign she was ready to come, so he increased his rhythm, bringing them both to incredible climaxes. Then they slept, and he dreamed.

# Chapter 6

Major Jeffrey Daggett Sawyer was twenty years older than his bride, who he wed last summer on her eighteenth birthday in June. She was so beautiful it had taken his breath away as he watched her and an elderly family friend walk up the aisle toward him. The dream faded and resurfaced as he carried her over the threshold of the Grand Palace Hotel into the Bridal Suite, where in actuality, they spent only two days together.

As dreams do, his jumped from thing to thing, place to place. First, the bed and then the floor, where their clothes jumbled together, and finally he saw them making love for the first time. Her face was a blur in his surreal world and he wondered in his dream if it was Lucretia he was fucking. Surely, a virgin bride should be meek, embarrassed, and afraid. The woman under his body acted anything but like a virgin, although he knew she was when he broke her cherry. The woman he saw on the marriage bed demanded and gave as good as she got from him.

He saw her body for the first time, naked and pink with dark areolas, big tits, and a yellow juncture between her legs. Suddenly the yellow grew bigger and bigger as he backed away. Next, he saw her touching herself. His dick throbbed as he watched. When he tried to put it in her, another cock slid in ahead of him. It was bigger, darker, longer, and seemed to grow to fill her pussy, which was enlarging again as it had before. He watched her lift her hips to meet the cock sliding inside her body. She cried out for more, more, more, and the cock gave her more before the scene slipped away.

Where had she learned the words that she had whispered when they fucked? Who had taught her the things she did to him? Was she a whore instead of a lady…one who lay smiling at him, exposing every inch of her nudity for him to see and want? Next, he saw her in her white wedding gown, standing outside among the flowers. The gown had a big hole in front for all to see her cunt. The top of the gown dropped away, leaving her tits bare, but only long enough for two men to cover them with their mouths.

"Honey, Jeffrey, wake up. You are moaning. Please wake up." He realized his beautiful wife was shaking him, pulling him back from the horrible place where cruel dreams come to life. He was soaking wet with sweat and terribly thirsty. He pushed her hands away and jumped up naked, looking around as if still somewhere other than his major's quarters at the fort.

# Chapter 7

Jeffrey shook his head, found the water pitcher, and drank deeply from it, not taking time to pour a glass. Lucretia sat up with a blanket wrapped around her hips, but her breasts exposed. Her nipples felt the cold of the room and hardened, causing little bumps to arise on her areolas. His voice came out raspy. “Cover yourself, woman.”

She stared at him, but did as he said, slowly. She was confused—no doubt—from the way he spoke to her. His dream loomed heavily in his memory. He knew it was a dream, and yet…yet, it was so real. He shook his head again and sat on the edge of the bed, head in his hands.

Lucretia moved closer to him, touching him gently on the shoulder. “It was just a bad dream, Jeffrey. Just a nightmare.” When he did not move, she pressed her torso against his back, careful to keep the blanket up. She kissed the back of his neck and held him close. She felt him start to relax.

He turned to her, gently pushing her on her back onto the bed. He lay down beside her and lifted her to lie against him, head on his shoulder. “I am sorry, my darling. It seems like all I do is apologize. I am truly sorry. It was a nightmare. Lord knows I have not had one since I was a child. Even out here, where death is so common and cruelties are an everyday occurrence, I have slept soundly.”

She placed her fingers over his lips to silence him and smiled as she looked deeply into his eyes. “Maybe it was because you are not used to sharing this little bed with anyone. It is barely big enough for a big man like you—let alone two people. Maybe we will have to sleep in shifts, or stacked.”

Jeffrey appreciated her attempt at humor and responded with a grin. "Great idea, sleeping stacked. Like this, do you mean?" He rolled her over until she was stretched out full length facing him and pulled the blanket away from her front. He put his arms around her soft body and held her tight. She licked her lips and lowered her face to his. He opened his mouth to take her kiss. "Just looking at that mouth of yours makes me horny."

She giggled. "I can tell. I feel something down there wiggling a bit." She shifted her hips until she felt his cock between her legs. With no hesitation, she raised just enough to take him inside her to the opening of her deep hole. When she felt it harden further, she lifted herself and drove her pussy down on him. He moaned his pleasure as he held her hips, guiding her. She placed a knee on each side of him and rode him, sliding up and down. He pushed her shoulders back until she was sitting on his dick. He touched her clit as she moved to take him even deeper. Their bodies gleamed with sweat as she pounded down on him. He lifted his hips to meet her and they exploded together.

This time when they slept, he had no nightmares, but his last waking thought was, *how did she learn to fuck like that?*

# Chapter 8

Outside their small house, the troops found dozens of reasons to wander by, hoping to hear what was going on. Some were rewarded with sounds of lovemaking, some with the major snoring. Lucretia's cries brought many a cock to a standing position and resulted in more than one young man taking longer than normal in the latrine.

Lucretia awoke before Jeff and sat with her back against the wall behind the bed, wrapping herself tightly in one of the blankets. She watched him and enjoyed the softness of his face, unguarded in slumber. She tried to find something positive in the place he called a house, and his face was the only thing she could find even remotely positive.

The house—if one could call it that—was cold, probably the same temperature as outside. In June, in their bridal suite, he had described the heat of the prairie, the endless waves of wind blowing the grass, the shimmering sunlight, and nights so hot no one could sleep. That was the opposite of what she felt now, in mid-winter.

*Hot in summer, cold in winter,* she thought. As she looked around, she saw that the cabin was little more than a large garden shack, only not built so well. The cracks and chinks in the rough boards comprised the walls and roof were so big that light came through. The floor was packed dirt and their clothing was in piles where they fell in their lust for each other. A small unlit woodstove sat in the far corner near a crude counter with a dishpan sitting on it. Above the counter were three makeshift shelves which contained three—yes, three—small pans and a coffeepot, along with a few dishes and eating utensils. A filthy-looking skillet hung from a nail beside the stove.

Washing facilities appeared to be a pitcher and cracked bowl on a remarkably nice chiffonier beside the bed. She would have to ask him how the chest got here. She presumed it contained her husband's personal items, as a spare uniform and hat hung from nails in the walls. A rickety table, two chairs, and a chamber pot under the bed completed the furnishings. Nowhere did she see towels, soap, or any such necessities.

Lucretia closed her eyes and tried to talk to God. "Lord, did you know where you were sending me? Even when my trunks arrive, today perhaps, where am I to put everything? This entire cabin is smaller than my closet at home. If Father were alive and could see me now, he would shoot Jeffrey on sight and both he and my mother would turn over in her grave." God did not answer.

# Chapter 9

"Good morning, my beautiful wife. Are you praying?" His voice was barely a whisper and the hand that touched her face was gentle. Lucretia smiled without opening her eyes and slid down to lay beside him. Jeffrey felt her warmth and smelled her woman scent, which gave him an instant boner. He moved his head to her chest and began to nuzzle her tits. Her nipples hardened under his mouth. She moaned softly when he bit them. One hand moved down her stomach and into her womanhood. He probed and caressed only a minute before spreading her thighs to accommodate his need.

He was surprised when she stopped his entry with her hand. "Wait, please. I am not ready yet. Kiss me, Jeffrey, and tease me down there first." He did as asked. Soon she moved her pussy up and down and around, indicating she was ready. She rocked up to the hand holding his penis and pushed his organ deeply inside her.

He began to move quickly before she asked, "Please slow down, darling. Give me time to catch up with you." He slowed and wondered again about her knowledge of her own body…the body he had deflowered those short months ago. How did she know that if he slowed, it would be better for her? He felt a sudden rage of jealousy as pieces of his dream came back to him.

"Oh, Jeffrey, I love you so much. I want to feel you in me today and forever. Now, yes, now," she cried. He felt the wetness from deep inside her wash over the end of his dick and he could wait no more.

Lucretia snuggled against her husband and traced patterns across his chest and around his nipples. The hair there was blond, as was his hair. *We should have beautiful, light-skinned children with golden crowns and eyes bluer than the sky,* she thought.

# Chapter 10

"Jeffrey, darling. I need a shower. Where do I go to get one?"

Her husband took a deep breath. The time of reckoning had arrived and he might as well just get it all over with at once, rather than have her find out a bit at a time. "Honey, darling, sweetheart, angel, kitten, love of my life, there are a few things I need to tell you."

She laughed. "When you start out with all those endearments, I suspect I am not going to like what I hear." Her hand continued to tickle his chest.

"I am afraid you're right, Lucretia. There was no time earlier for me to tell you about life at the fort. It has none of the luxuries of home. Actually, it is so different there is no comparison. I know I should have told you. I should have found the time, but with only two days before I had to leave, I wanted everything perfect for our marriage and short honeymoon. It was perfect, wasn't it?"

Lucretia's hand stopped caressing her husband. "Yes, it was perfect. Are you trying to tell me that things are not so perfect here?"

Jeffrey sighed. He took her hand and pressed the palm to his lips. "It is not perfect here at all. Let us start with the shower. There is no shower here, nor is there enough water to waste on showers. Actually, there is no bathtub either. We use as little water as we can because our one well is inadequate for so many people. We draw water from it every time the bucket fills. Privates Winters and Jones are assigned water duty and take turns day and night making sure the horse troughs and pails for cooking are always full. Each man—and woman—is allotted one small bucket of water a day for personal use."

She sat up, ignoring the cold of the room as her blanket fell to her waist. She did not notice her nipples immediately harden, but her husband did. If she knew that he wanted to suck them, she probably would have hit him.

"Let me see if I understand. No water, no showers, no bathtub, and one small bowl of water a day. Am I right? You expect me to wash my hair and clean my body with a bowl of water. It will take a dozen bowls like that one"—she pointed at the one on the chiffonier—"to even begin to wash away the sweat, dirt, and filth from my body. By filth, I mean dried body fluids from our lovemaking, not to mention dirty feet from this floor. And what about laundry? How do we clean our clothes?" Her eyes were flashing and her cheeks were red with anger.

"Now, honey, it is not always this bad. When we get some rain or even snow, we catch it and have more than enough water for a while. We save it in barrels, buckets, and anything else we can find. When it warms up, we can swim in the river over yonder."

*"When it rains!"* she shouted. "When will that be? Will my feet be as brown as yours are? Will my hair hang in limp strands, like yours does? Will our body odors chase people away, like your soldiers' smells? Dear God, what am I doing here?" She threw herself over on her front, burying her face in the pillow. "Even this pillow stinks. The blankets stink. Everything stinks."

# Chapter 11

Jeffrey put his hand on her shoulder. She shrugged it off. "Go away. Go out and have them hitch the horses back to the wagon. I am going home. Tell Aunt Liz…oh, dear, Aunt Liz. I forgot all about her in my…well, tell her we are going home."

Jeffrey rose from the bed and dressed in the clothes lying on the floor. He went to the door, opened it, and brought in a pail half full of water that one of the privates had left for them sometime earlier. The water had a layer of ice across the top, so he broke it with his fist. He put a scant inch in the bowl and rinsed his hands and face. He tossed the dirty water out the door and refilled the bowl. "I have left the rest for you. When you calm down, we will talk. Until then, I would advise you to dress, because if you want to eat, you will have to come with me to the dining room. Otherwise, well, you can see there is nothing here." He pulled on the coat hanging from a nail on the wall and without another word he left, closing the door softly behind him.

Lucretia turned over and stared at the ceiling. *No, it is not a ceiling,* she thought, *it is the damn roof.* A roof full of holes…well, it might be nice if it rained. Take a shower in bed. Pay no mind to the mud where the dirt is now. Stand outside in your clothes to wash them.

She heard a noise and looked over the edge of the bed. A mouse looked back at her. She screamed and stood stark naked on the bed. Jeffrey had gone only a few yards from the door when she screamed, and he was like a bullet flying back inside. Two of his men were right behind him, so when he shoved the door open, his beautiful wife in her full naked glory stood for all to see.

The two men stared, taking in every inch of her body before Jeffrey pushed them back outside. He shut the door and then noticed the mouse scurrying outside through a crack under the wall. He wanted to laugh, but the better part of his valor won out. He rushed to the bed and scooped her up in his arms, holding her close. She buried her face on his shoulder and sobbed until he sat her on the edge of the bed with his arms around her as the mouse left the cabin through a hole in the wall.

# Chapter 12

"I ain't never seed anything like that afore. It were like lookin' at an angel with no clothes. Prettiest thing I ever seed in my life. Like I already died and in heaven. Sure enough, like an angel." Private Jones, one of the well men, stood just outside the cabin door, repeating over and over what he had seen. Corporal Jed Dryer, the wagon driver, had seen her too, but he was speechless. He closed his eyes, trying to bring back her image, but felt what he wanted was a sin. Sin or not, he knew as long as he lived, he would remember the pink and blond beauty on the bed. Her round tits were globes like summer melons, her hips were smooth and silky, and her womanhood…well, she was for sure yellow-haired all over.

Corporal Dryer finally heard Private Winters mumbling. He grabbed Winters' arm and spun him around. "Listen and listen good, you rock-for-brains. You will never tell anyone what you saw. That is the major's wife, not some slattern you visit above whatever bar you crawl into. Do you hear me? Not a word."

"Oh, yes sir, Corporal. I hear you. Not a word."

"If I hear one word about her from *any* of the men, I will know where they heard it and I will come looking for you. You know those two front teeth you be missing?" Winters nodded. "Well, it will be four missing if you say one word about Mrs. Sawyer. Do you understand?"

Winters nodded again and the men turned away to return to their duties.

Within minutes, Jed Dryer heard Private Jones let out a hoot. "Blond all the way. Wow, the major is one lucky man." Jed turned away from the horse he was currying and walked quickly toward the well. Private Winters never saw the fist that collided with his face in the split-second it took the corporal to spin the private to face him. Private Winters hit the ground, spitting blood out his mouth and nose. He sat up, shaking his head. When he opened his mouth, two teeth fell out.

Men ran from all directions to the well, hoping for more fighting, but Sergeant O'Brian arrived first and stood between the two enemies just as Captain Grant walked toward them. "Now, what was this all about? I want to know. You, Dryer, why did you hit this man?" Corporal Dryer simply looked at the sergeant and refused to answer.

"All right, Winters. What have you to say for yourself?" The private, too, refused to answer. "Well, seems the cat has your tongues, so I guess a night in the brig might get the cat to return a tongue or two. So, up with you, Winters. Both of you, let's go. You know the way."

The sergeant tipped his hat to Mrs. Liz Harold, who had come outside the small room where she slept. The sound of the fight—short though it was—drew her, as well as Lieutenant Deke Carter and his wife, Molly. Deke was tall and black as coal, with hair so short it looked like a mat. He was a strong man, with muscles that strained against his uniform. Molly, while not as black as her husband, was pleasantly pretty and barely reached to his shoulders. Her hair was dark and carefully braided into long rows that reached her shoulders.

Liz nodded to Molly and walked over to meet her. Molly seemed hesitant and shy, but Liz failed to notice. In no time, Liz had the younger woman laughing as they walked together into the small house the Carters shared. Molly made strange-tasting tea, but Liz ignored its flavor and thanked her generously. Soon they were chatting like old friends.

Molly was too polite to ask about the newcomer, who had not been seen since her arrival on the buckboard, and Liz volunteered little information. She told of St. Louis and their home there. Of the train ride to Cottonwood Creek, where they left the railroad, stayed the night at the questionable Cottonwood Hotel, and the bumpy ride to the fort. Personal things went unsaid for the moment.

When everyone was out of hearing range, Captain Grant asked, "Sergeant, what was that all about? I thought those two men were friends."

"They are, sir…or were, I guess. Nothing like a naked lady to drive a wedge atween two comrades."

"What lady, Sergeant?"

"Oh, I thought everyone heard her scream. She was loud enough to avalanche the snow on those there mountains. Anyway, a mouse was all it was, but the two of them rushed to her rescue before the major got there. Our pretty Mrs. Sawyer was standing on the bed as naked as a bride on her wedding night. Dryer told Winters to keep his mouth shut, but Winters being Winters was describing it in careful detail to the rest of the troops as soon as he had a chance. Jed did not take kindly to that, and that is what happened."

Captain Grant nodded and walked away. He wished he had been one of those men, or at least heard what Winters had said. She had found a wedge somehow, somewhere in his mind, and would not go away. Under his breath he said, "Get over it, Grant. She is another man's wife."

Inside the house of the major and his wife, Lucretia had stopped crying. She listened to her husband's soft voice, crooning to her that everything would be all right and that he would find a way to make a better place for them to live. She was not sure she believed him, but feeling his hands on her soft skin as he rubbed her shoulders and back pushed away her panic over the mouse.

His dick hardened when she pressed her tits against his chest. He moved his mouth to capture hers and found it willing. Just as their tongues touched, a bell rang outside, catching her attention. "What was that, Jeffrey? I think I heard it last night, too." Jeffrey sighed, knowing the moment was lost.

"That is the dinner bell, calling us to breakfast."

She giggled. "A dinner bell for breakfast. Wonderful, I am starving. Filthy dirty and starving. We will just have to make sure no one gets too close to us, the way we smell. Oh, but I have nothing to wear. My gown on the floor is disgusting and so are my littles. Maybe I should just wear your shirt instead."

He picked up her dress and shook it out. A dust storm descended on everything, making them both cough. "I like that picture, my darling, just you in my shirt. I would wager the men would love it, too." She stepped into her dress and waited while he tied the tiny bows as best he could, fumbling. "I like untying them better than tying them." He laced her shoes too, letting his fingers caress her legs. "After breakfast, we should come back here and I will comb out your hair." She grinned, knowing full well what he had in mind.

From her tiny handbag, she took a comb and pulled at the knots in her hair. "Liz usually does this for me. Poor Liz, I have abandoned her somewhere and I do not even know where. We must find her, Jeffrey."

"Come, my dear. I think finding her will be no problem." He helped her into her coat and bonnet. He opened the door and offered her his arm. They stepped into the bright sunlight and walked toward the group of tables inside three walls under a partial roof, beneath leafless limbs of three small trees near one wall of the fort.

They knew every eye was on them. Lucretia saw Liz walking with a little black woman and forgot her embarrassment at being the subject of close observation by so many men. Not that she did not like it, but after all, she was a married woman now and flirting was a thing of the past.

# Chapter 13

Jeffrey watched his wife run to her Auntie Liz. She looked fetching, with her skirt rocking as she ran across the packed dirt surrounded by high log walls. Until now, he had never really looked at the place. He had looked, yes, but he really did not see. At least he did not see it as he suspected Lucretia saw it. It was as dusty and ugly as she said. He felt despair settle in. What could he do to change it? Nothing. It was a fort and forts are forts are forts.

He watched Lucretia hug her aunt and listened to a few words the wind did not blow away. She apologized for leaving Liz to fend for herself, but the others just laughed. Something caught his eye behind them. It was a curtain over the window of a house. He thought of his own window covered with a blanket to keep out the cold.

Like a slam on the side of his head, an idea formed. He could at least fix up the cabin, as he now saw that Deke had done. The chinks and holes looked as if they were filled with an adobe made of clay, hay, and water shoved in the gaps. He called to one of the men just leaving the breakfast table and gave him curt instructions. The man nodded, then shook his head as if trying to understand, but immediately went to work as instructed.

He walked to where his wife still chattered. "Let us get some breakfast before Greta feeds the rest of it to the dogs." Jeffrey offered one arm to Liz and the other to Lucretia. "I doubt either one of you has ever eaten anything quite like what Greta makes. She originally came to stay to do the laundry—when we have water—but Private Jones, who was the cook, did so badly that she ran him out and took over."

"Greta, my sweet Greta, I would like you to meet my beautiful bride, Lucretia, and her aunt, Elizabeth Harold, both from St. Louis. Ladies, this is Greta Stormah."

The women nodded to one another, but when Lucretia stepped forward to kiss the older woman, Greta stopped her. "Sorry, missy, I ain't smelling like anything kissable. Lordy, I keep praying for rain, or even snow, but the Lord be ignoring me. Now sit yourselves down." She filled three tin plates with mountains of food. Scrambled eggs from the hens that ran freely everywhere, thick slices of ham from one of the hogs that had been in a pen outside the fort, and milk from one of the cows in the barn near the hog pens. A guard posted twenty-four hours a day protected them from predators.

"You are right, Jeffrey," said Liz. "I have never tasted food like this." She smiled at Greta, who grinned at the compliment. The major did not know if Liz was serious or just being kind. Either way, he got the sense the praise gave the woman a sense of worth that feeding only men seldom did. Soon they were chatting like old friends.

Sergeant O'Brian spoke from behind them. "Miss Greta, may I have a cup of that wonderful coffee of yours? Good morning, Mrs. Harold. Mrs. Sawyer. Major." He nodded to each and took a seat across the table from them. "Did you sleep well, Mrs. Sawyer?"

"How she slept is no business of yours, Sergeant." Liz's cold voice matched the look she gave him.

Lucretia smiled at him and patted her aunt's hand. "I slept fine, except for the cold. Thank you for asking." The small talk continued as Liz scowled and ignored the man who had so carefully removed his hat when he greeted her. Lucretia and Jeffrey exchanged smiles, knowing that fun was ahead for these two.

Jeffrey gave the women a tour of the fort, starting with the stable, where Frank Grogan was shoeing a horse. He was courteous, but clearly uninterested in anything but horses.

Liz said, "He and Greta have different last names. Perhaps they are brother and sister, she being a widow." It was her way of snooping, albeit with finesse.

"Auntie, it is none of our business."

Jeffrey smiled. "I am afraid they are not related and, to my knowledge, not married. They do share a cabin, but beyond that, there is nothing I can tell you."

"Humph" was the reply.

They saw the storerooms for food and the munitions depot, set far away in one corner; the privy and a small chapel; a store of sorts with tobacco and such; the barracks, with a separate room for the sergeant; a room for card tables and the like; and a room with desks for the major, Lieutenant Deke Carter, and one for the man who was a guard from their trip to the fort.

"Captain, I do not believe you have met my wife."

"Yes, I did. I was part of the unit that escorted her here to the fort." He nodded at her before returning his eyes to his paperwork.

Lucretia was unaccustomed to being dismissed like that. She resented him for making her feel unimportant. "No, Captain, we have not been introduced properly. I do not know your name." She extended her hand. Courtesy forced him to stand and take it. He bent over as if to kiss it, but his lips made no contact.

"Darling, this is Captain Black Eagle Grant."

"How do you do, Captain? It is nice to have a name for the face that is so stern. I have the distinct feeling that you actively dislike me. Do I offend you in some way, or do you just dislike women in general? Or is it officers' wives? Perhaps women with yellow hair? Or is it my clothing? Maybe the way I speak. What, Captain, do you find about me to be so distasteful?"

# Chapter 14

No one spoke. Jeffrey looked stunned by her questions. Liz looked at Lucretia carefully, wondering why she was being so rude. Captain Grant regarded her without expression. "No, ma'am. I do not dislike you in any way. I do not think about you at all, except to say you sure do talk a lot."

Lucretia never took her eyes off his. When he spoke, she detected a glimmer of a smile deep inside him.

They continued to stare at each other until even Jeffrey could feel the tension between them. "Well, come now, darling. Let us go see what all the noise is outside. I think it is the other wagon back from Cottonwood Creek with your trunks. Corporal Dryer told me they were delayed en route, so he had it wait for your luggage and start out as soon as it arrived. They were to travel all night, or stop to camp as they preferred."

Lucretia did not even hear his words, as she was so engrossed in her dislike of the captain. At the door, she stopped and turned. "Captain, I am sorry if my talking is offensive to you. I will endeavor to say nothing in the future when in your presence."

"Mrs. Sawyer, do you make it a habit of having the last word?"

"Yes, Captain, I do." Then she was gone.

Liz trailed behind them, but stopped at the door. She turned back to the captain. "I will reckon no trouble from you, sir. Be certain of that."

If Lucretia had been asked why she was so rude to him, she would not have been able to answer. For all her sexual activity with her husband, she was extremely naïve in other ways. A mature woman might have sensed the raw magnetism the man gave off and would have been awed by it, either pleasantly or it might have frightened her. That was not the case with Grant and Lulu…at least that day.

# Chapter 15

Captain Black Eagle Grant understood the aunt's words and he knew why she spoke to him that way. He and the major's wife were two of a kind, although he doubted the young woman, barely more than a girl, knew it. The old woman knew it and was afraid of it. He knew enough to be afraid of it, too. She was nothing but trouble. Just looking at her made his cock begin to rise.

That and the odor of sex on her were impossible to ignore. He was Indian, or at least part, and his keen sense of smell was part of his heritage. He doubted if any of the white men detected it, but it was there on her and the major. He closed his eyes and allowed his imagination to picture them in the throes of passion. He saw them entangled, crotch to crotch, moving in the age-old rhythm of sex. The picture changed and he was the man fucking her. Her legs were around his waist, her hands pulling his head down to her swollen tits. He forced his eyes open and the pictures out of his mind. Damn her to hell.

A breath of fresh air and a long ride would help clear his head. Eagle left the building and strode to the stable, where he quickly saddled his horse. The gates were open as the wagon from the depot came through. He ignored the excited chattering from the women and the orders the major gave. Even Lucretia's voice was enough to make him catch his breath. He spurred his horse out onto the prairie, letting it choose where it wanted to run. His thoughts took him back to the time when he was no more than a sapling, playing under the tall trees on the hill.

*I watched the young boys at their games. They considered themselves more than boys and took their games seriously. They were warriors, in their own world, out to best one another. His grandfather, Soaring Eagle, had named him Black Eagle after himself, the year before he died. The boy's father, Iron Eyes, took a white woman as a wife when the matriarch of the tribe refused to allow slaves in the village. Their union produced only Black Eagle, as the white woman died in childbirth. The boy knew nothing of his mother, not even her name.*

*Black Eagle never considered himself anything but the smartest, bravest, most courageous of all the young ones, but his white blood made him different. Even his brown—not black—hair had set him apart. He bested all comers in shooting, hunting, and everything else, but the elders had never considered him worthy of being their chief. Jealousy of his talents spurred them to point out to their sons that a half-white should never be superior to them in any way. More than one boy felt a switch or a backhand when he failed to defeat Black Eagle. Thus, their resentment of him grew.*

*Only when he became an adult did he begin to understand and begin to hate the woman who lost her life giving him his. He did not hate women of his tribe, but passionately hated the pale-skinned females of the white men.*

*I watched him with one of those women from the wagon train as they fucked under my boughs. She followed him when he moved away from the group that he had escorted to trade their blankets and herbs with the women of the train. She came up behind him as he relieved himself. He heard her long before she neared him. He stood with his back to her, waiting to see what she would do. I wondered that myself.*

He could smell her white woman odor, but also the odor of a female in lust. He was not surprised when she slid her arms around his waist and took his cock in one hand. He stood still, letting her caress him until his rod hardened. It had been a long time since he had been with a woman. Was he no better than his father was? Lusting for a woman not of his world? By now, it no longer mattered. She was there and he would give her what she wanted.

He seemed to take her as he might an animal, hard and savagely. He turned around, took her by her shoulders, and leaned her forward over a log. He pulled up her skirt, moved into her, and took her with thrusts that could not have been pleasant for her. She complained and begged him to be gentle, but he ignored her. Before they ended their joining, she cried out for him not to stop.

*This is another thing I do not understand about women. First a no, then a yes. Who can comprehend how they think?*

*Nor did I understand why he would mate with her, knowing how much he hated those females. I decided it gave him power over them in a way that was like a small death. When he finished, he just walked away without a look backward. To an Indian woman, he was gentle and loving, making sure she enjoyed what they had done. The women of the tribe who offered their favors to him were older ones, widows and the like, but never maidens. They waited for a husband. Later they might come to him, but he showed no desire for a wife. He had fears the white woman might say he attacked her, but nothing came of that.*

His father, Iron Eyes, called him to his side one evening.

"Come, my son, let us walk. You are a man now, but you are an unhappy man. I know the others care for you, as they do for one another, but you are different. No matter what I say, nothing can change that. I should have given you this advice as a child, but I was proud of you and your coups. I have done much thinking about this and now tell you how you can change things.

"Let others win. Do not always kill more buffalo or defeat more enemies. Do not outride them or beat them in wrestling. It will make them feel superior to you and soon they will forget what you are and accept you."

All the years of knowing that brought anger neither Iron Eyes, nor Black Eagle himself knew he felt. His rage suddenly broke over the dam behind which he had held it his whole life. He turned to face his father and yelled at him, as he had never done before.

"Why, Father? Why did you have to fuck a white woman? Were your own people not good enough? Was her cunt different or better than our women? You should have killed her, instead of bringing her here. Or you should have killed me when I was born. I can never forgive you for letting me live this life with no hope of ever being a warrior in the eyes of our people. Oh, yes, I hunt with them, war with them, fuck with them, but I am not one of them. Nor will I ever be. I will leave here in the morning and will never return. Tell my grandmother, Summer Swan, that I love her and thank her for the life she tried to make for me. She will understand, but you will not."

He turned from his father, gathered his robes and weapons, and mounted his horse. Morning was too far away to wait to leave the place he had loved as a child. As an adult, he knew he had to go, but where to, he had no idea.

*Black Eagle rode up the hill and sat in his saddle, overlooking his village, the river, and the plains. He looked at the flickering fires in the distance, where wagon trains had camps, some south of here and some north. Far off on the western horizon, with the mountains behind it, stood a fort the army had begun to build. Finally, he dismounted and sat at the base, leaning back against my trunk. All night he stayed there. Did he sleep? He knew not. Did he dream? I hope he dreamed and talked to the gods.*

*At first light, he arose and mounted. For a minute only, he surveyed the world once his, now belonging to the white man. I know I heard him say, "Good-bye, Grandmother. Good-bye, my dear Summer Swan."*

# Chapter 16

Major Sawyer watched Captain Grant ride away without a word. He did not notice that his wife watched the man from under her long lashes. With her head bowed, her bonnet covered her eyes so no one was the wiser, except Liz, who elbowed her in the side gently. She raised her head and ignored her aunt.

The troops unloaded her trunks, tied to the top of the fully laden wagon. Auntie Liz made certain they took care with each piece. She instructed the men to carry them to the room where the officers had their desks, the only place she deemed large enough and suitable to put them.

*At least it has plank floors,* thought Lucretia. Plank floors. Large, with windows. Warm. *That is it,* Lucretia thought. *I have money in the bank in St. Louis that came from my parents. I will have lumber made and sent here. The men can build us a suitable home, with a second bedroom for Liz.* Why had she not thought of that before? Moreover, why had Jeffrey, her husband, not thought of it, either? Especially since men are supposed to be so much smarter than women are. Ha! And why did he not have a fire in the small stove in their room? Why had he not realized that the tiny cabin was too small for two of them? And closets…did he not think of closets? And water…why did they not haul water from the river and warm it for bathing? Was there not firewood in the forests to the west?

For the first time, she looked at her husband with thoughts other than physical desire for him. That was important, too, but other things were important as well. Why had she never considered anything but being together in bed?

# Chapter 17

When Lulu first met him at the June Ball, a dance of high importance in her crowd, she instantly desired him, although what she wanted from him, she was not sure. They walked in the garden outside the plush hotel and when he tried to kiss her, she did not bother to play coy. He pressed his lips gently to hers, while one hand held her and the other touched her face. Her response was all he needed to push her back against a light post to hold her while his tongue slipped into her mouth. It astounded her and when he stopped, she wanted him to kiss her again, but she knew it must stop now or…or what she was not sure, but she would have been happy to kiss him all night.

He apologized profusely and she nodded, but forced her eyes to fill with tears. "Sir, I have never been kissed like that before and your ardor surprised me and frightened me a bit too, I think. Your apology is accepted but I think we should go back inside. I promise you the next dance."

In the two weeks before he was to leave St. Louis, they spent every possible minute together, always with Auntie Liz to chaperone. The first night of the last week, while returning to her home in an open buggy, Liz was apparently asleep in the front by the driver. Their lips met for an all-consuming kiss that did not stop until Liz barked at them, "Major, you do that one more time, and I will insist my niece's reputation is ruined and you will be forced to marry her."

He laughed and pulled Lulu to his chest, kissing her again, but this time he slid one hand down to cup her breast inside her low-cut dress.

"I say, Major. You are a rascal. I shall call your commandant and report you for attempted…attempted…"

"Yes, Mrs. Harold, as you should. I will be drawn and quartered for kissing the woman I love and for touching her most delectable breast. Or you can give me your blessing so I can marry her within the week."

Lucretia hardly heard the conversation. Her entire being was in the palm of his hand. His touch was like a strike of lightning. She moved her hand to cover his, hidden under the fabric of her dress, holding it tightly so he could not take it away. They both felt her nipple tighten into a tiny hard bead that pressed against his skin. She closed her eyes and let her desire take over. She wanted him the way he wanted her.

They were married three days later. They spent their short time locked away in the hotel, ordering in food, and sleeping between passionate loving. Never once did they make plans or think about their future. There was no time for anything but making love, over and over again.

# Chapter 18

Lucretia followed her trunks into the officers' office area. How could she approach Jeffrey with her ideas without hurting his manly ego? Liz taught her, years before, just how a man's self-worth depended on a trusting wife who worshiped him in all facets of their life. She also taught her the importance of making him think any idea she thought to imbed in his mind had come from him originally. Liz did admit that her husband, Clarence, was not too bright and convincing him that he considered every problem and solution to be totally his was an easy task.

Jeffrey was too bright to maneuver that way. A frank discussion would have to do. Before or after sex? She would have to work that out later. Either way, sex was the key.

# Chapter 19

Liz and Lucretia opened one of the trunks and found some clean littles for each of them. "I never expected to get excited over fresh under things," commented Liz. Jeffrey worked at his desk while the women chatted. He smiled to himself, thinking of the projects he had assigned to several of the idle troopers. He would have to keep the women here until late today, but he was unsure how to do it.

These well-laid plans went awry in the next minute. Captain Grant came inside. "Sure is damn cold out there, Major. I shot a few rabbits and a deer and dropped them off with Greta. Any report from the crew in the forest?"

Jeffrey sighed. So much for secrecy. "They should be back before dark. I told them I wanted the dry wood and to chop it before they returned. Easier to transport after dark than chopping in the dark."

"Dry wood, Jeffrey. How wonderful! To be warm again at night. You are so thoughtful." Lucretia ignored the man who turned to give her that "dung beetle" look. She rushed to her husband and bent over to plant a resounding smack on his cheek. "Some warm water would be nice, too. But just to be warm will be wonderful." She hugged him around his shoulders, snuggling her face in his neck.

Jeffrey was a bit embarrassed by her open display of affection, but rather enjoyed it, too. "I guess I might as well tell you the rest of it, Lulu," using the nickname only family ever called her.

"What? What? There is more? Tell me, darling. Please tell me." She snuggled closer to him and pressed her breasts against the back of his head. His cock wiggled its awakening, but he wanted to stop this before it got out of hand and before he lost control of the situation.

"Yes, Lucretia. Let me go and I will show you. Come, both of you." He led them outside where a wagon laden with buckets and barrels rolled in and stopped before him. The four men on board grinned as Jeffrey spoke. "So, my ladies, you shall have water to wash with tonight. Tomorrow and every day hence, as long as we can break the ice, we will bring water from the river. Does that make you happy?"

Lulu jumped up and down like a child, before throwing herself into his arms. "Oh, my husband, you are…you are…I cannot think of a word for how good this is and for you, who thought of it. I must think of a reward."

Her face was so innocent that he forced himself not to smile. "I am sure"—he whispered in her ear—"that you can think of something."

Every one of the four on the wagon knew exactly how they would like to be rewarded, but would have to settle for their hands and visions behind their eyes. They did the work and the major got the reward. Such was life in the army.

Inside the officers' room, Captain Black Eagle Grant heard the exchange. He thought she was nothing but a cock tease. She would do whatever it took to get what she wanted. God, he hated her and her kind. Even more, he hated the stirring of his always-ready pocket snake.

# Chapter 20

Mrs. Sawyer was not the first white woman he had lusted for. However, he suspected she would be the only one he would never fuck. The others were so easy. Carol Winthrop was a barmaid with a room upstairs in St. Louis and a lust for any man different from others. For him, she was free.

The only other one he remembered by name was Mrs. Clarkson Wade, known as Bibi to her friends. Her carriage careened around a corner in St. Louis, hitting him as he crossed the street. The impact threw him into the air, causing a broken leg when he fell. One of the horses fell, forcing the other to stop, but not before the carriage tipped to its side. He heard the scream inside. Although in terrible pain from the bone pushed through the skin, he crawled to the carriage. Leaning against it for support, he stood on one leg, opened the door, and lifted the petite woman out.

By that time, a large crowd had gathered, including some of her friends' husbands. Once on her feet, Mrs. Take-Charge Wade assured everyone she was fine, but insisted a doctor be called for the man who she said had saved her life. Biting a stick he found on the street to control his pain, he limped through his fog, as two men he did not know carried him to where an old man lived as Mrs. Wade led the way.

Black Eagle could only think of his own stupidity. How could he have let the carriage hit him? His reflexes had been dulled by the city. He would return to the land as soon as he could.

That did not happen, at least not the way he had intended. The old doctor, with the help of several men to hold Eagle down, pulled his leg until the bone slid back inside. Once the old man was satisfied that it would set, he stitched the leg, thanked the men for their help, and disappeared from the room.

# Chapter 21

The next years raced through Eagle's mind as he sat behind his desk at Fort Mason. He recuperated at the home of Major General and Mrs. Clarkson Wade. He bedded the woman who taught him to speak their language like a gentleman. He rode with the man who taught him the white man's ways and who suggested he would make a great military man. He enrolled to attend West Point as Black Eagle Grant. The general convinced him to take a white man's name to add to his own, so he chose the name of the big White Chief. Years later he would wonder why he had done those things, but at the time, all seemed right.

Much as he hated to admit it, he had grown fond of both the Wades. He felt at ease with them and secure in a way he never had before, even in this white man's world. The night before he left for the academy, the three of them had celebrated with a fine meal and much too much wine. Bibi had taught him to dance, saying all officers must have that social grace, among the many others he learned.

After the second bottle of wine, Clarkson suggested he play the piano while his wife and Eagle danced. So it was that inebriated Bibi snuggled close, rather than the expected inches between them. She pressed herself against him and licked his ear, sending a shock down his body. Her husband watched them as he played on. Even in his alcohol haze, Eagle tensed, expecting his host to attack him.

Instead, Clarkson smiled as Bibi pressed her lips to Eagle's, whose cock leaped to attention when her tongue began to tease his. Clarkson nodded to them before standing to ring for a servant. He opened the parlor door only a crack and said, "You are not needed any more this evening, Mrs. Bigelow, nor are the others. Please lock the house when you leave. See you in the morning."

Eagle did not understand, even when Clarkson locked the door and carefully circled the room, closing each window blind. Bibi giggled and let her hand drop to the front of Eagle's trousers, as she had done so often to entice him to her bedroom. In front of her husband…well, this was incredible.

Even more so was what happened next. Clarkson came up behind his wife and slid his hands down the front of her gown, cupping each breast. She tilted her head to smile at him. She reached behind her to rub his cock as she rubbed Eagle's. "I do not understand," he whispered.

"You do not have to understand, my lover," Bibi said. "Just enjoy." She unfastened his suspenders under his jacket and slid her hand down inside his trousers to grasp his throbbing cock. Her husband opened her dress top, pushing it down to expose her hard-nipple tits. "Kiss them, Eagle. Nibble my nips." She laughed at her own joke.

"I cannot. Clarkson…" Whether it was a question, a plea, or something else, he wanted her but was afraid to continue.

"Ah, young man. I see you are confused. I know you have fucked my wife many times and hearing about it excited me a great deal, giving us some wonderful nights. I suggested that, since you are leaving us tomorrow, tonight I join you. Believe me, Bibi can handle us both. Actually, she can take care of three men at a time with no complaints. There is no need for you to be self-conscious. She says you are incredible in bed. Would you prefer to go upstairs or is here fine?"

Eagle looked from face to face, seeing only lust in their eyes. His tribe had these couplings, but he never considered white men doing it as well. He stepped back and slowly removed his clothes to stand proudly naked for both to see. His scar was still white against his dark skin, his chest was muscular, and his arms were hard as tree limbs.

The thing that interested them most was his huge cock, standing up and throbbing.

"Oh, you do have a big one!" said Clarkson. "Bibi was right. It is the biggest I have ever seen. No wonder she could not get enough of it." He removed his uniform as he spoke.

Both men were soon naked with the partially garbed woman between them. "Oh, I cannot wait." She pushed Eagle backward into a chair, where she knelt between his legs and took his dick in her mouth. She ran her tongue around it and sucked it gently at first, then harder.

Behind her, Clarkson lifted her skirt up to expose her bare ass. He spread her thighs and ran his hand under her to tease her pussy. Her body began to move with him as he shoved his hardness into her. Eagle watched them as his cock hardened even more. Bibi looked up at him with a face full of want. Her mouth continued to love him, even as her cunt loved her husband. Eagle felt his cum rising and could not stop. He grabbed her head and held her mouth over him as he spewed his seed. At the same time, Clarkson moaned and pushed his last jab into her. The men both watched the actions of the other, adding an excitement to it that Eagle had never felt before.

It was an orgy of lust—nothing more—but a night Eagle would always remember. Bibi could handle them both, with not a problem. It was the men who finally gave up, even as she demanded they finger fuck her together, one in her cunt, the other on her clit.

Eagle carried his own water for a bath that night, but left the next morning, still not feeling clean. His hosts did not arise to wish him farewell.

He forced his memories to recede until he stared at the dark boards of the room and the ornate trunks sitting open. On top of the piles of clothing, he saw daintily stitched undergarments and for a split-second saw Lucretia stand before him, wearing only those silken white pieces. He closed his eyes and lifted his face upward, praying to his gods to erase this woman from his mind.

# Chapter 22

The four women watched as troopers carried cut firewood to set outside each cabin. Lucretia clapped her hands like an excited child. Liz smiled at everyone, including Sergeant O'Brian for a moment or two, before remembering she did not like him.

"Oh, Jeffrey, can we go build a fire now?"

"Not yet, my dear. Wait until you see what is on the wagon heading this way now." Everyone looked until Deke hugged his Molly close and whispered to her. She bounced up and down and kissed his face all over as she held it in her hands.

Greta smiled at the two young women. She and Liz stood apart from the married couples, giving them space to converse in low tones. Liz looked up, as startled at what Greta told her as if she had found a pile of gold at the end of a rainbow. "I ain't ad no bath since the summer. Lice from the straw sure do make a body itch. Hell, I can just go sit in the horse trough until the little buggers drown or hop off. We can have two troughs in the stable filled if you want ta join me."

The ever loquacious Elizabeth found herself without words for the first time in years. She stuttered a polite refusal and turned away as Greta smiled and strode toward the barn.

"Water, water, water." Lulu giggled. "I see barrels and buckets. Water and ice. From the river, Jeffrey? You had the men break the ice for fresh water." She stood on her tiptoes to kiss his lips before running to watch the wagon pull through the gates toward the area where Greta cooked.

When he caught up with her, he said, "Now, little wife, let us go build that fire you want." He offered his arm and escorted her proudly across the compound to their door, where troopers had set two buckets of water and a pile of wood. This time, Jeffrey picked up his wife and carried her over the threshold…or what would be the threshold, instead of hard clay.

He set her down, although it was more fun to hold her in his arms while she planted kisses all over his face. When she fastened her lips to his, he wanted to forget the fire and build one of his own on and in her sweet body.

"Enough of that for a minute, my dear. Woodstove fire first, Jeffrey fire second." He opened the door in the front of the stove and a dozen mice of assorted sizes spilled out to the floor, running every direction. This time when she screamed, she did not jump up on the bed, but instead ran to the door to open it, hoping they would find their way out.

As before, everyone came running. When they saw the mice scurrying out the door and Jeffrey standing in front of the open stove, it became clear what had happened. Soon, the tiny cabin held as many men as was possible to squeeze into it, all in search of any elusive mice. They bumped into one another, trying to look under the bed and table.

A short trooper jumped off the chair where he stood to chase two mice off the top of the pathetic cupboard. He landed on a big foot, and a big mouth yelled in pain before taking a punch at the littler man. He connected, knocking the unfortunate guy into the back of another man, who lost his balance and fell on the bed, breaking the frame and sending it to the floor.

"Stop it, all of you. Look at what you have done," Lucretia shouted and almost immediately, all fighting stopped. "I think the way you are acting…well, I prefer the mice to this ridiculous display of chaos. Out with you. All of you. Out, out, out!"

Red-faced from embarrassment, and blood in some cases, they all left quietly after picking up their lost hats. No face looked at her or the major. She strode to the door and closed it quietly behind them before bursting into near hysterical laughter. Jeffrey looked at her in amazement and joined her. He scooped her up and laid her carefully on the now floor-level bed. She wound her arms around his neck and met his kiss with an ardor that always took his breath away.

# Chapter 23

A knock on the door forced them apart. Jeffrey rose and opened it, motioning Frank Grogan inside. He carried a metal bowl smaller than the horse troughs, but big enough for a small woman. He set it on the floor beside the cold stove. "Need some help, Major, getting that fire started?"

"No, thanks, Frank, I can do it myself." The man left and Jeffrey waited at the door before he turned to his bride. She sat on the bed with eyes wide and tears running silently down her cheeks. She stood and walked slowly to him, into his waiting arms.

"Oh, Jeffrey, you are the most wonderful man in the world. To think how I hated you just yesterday makes me so ashamed. I love you!"

"Honey, I know you do and you can show me later. First, I want to show you how to build a fire in this contraption, then we will heat some water, and I will sit here and watch you bathe. How is that idea?"

That is exactly what they did. She quickly got over her squeamishness about the bugs and creepy crawlers on and in the wood, even though she hated to touch the wood that contained them. Once the fire was hot, Jeffrey carried in buckets of water to warm. "We will heat several buckets full and add cold as we need it. From now on, a bucket on the stove at all times is the rule. How about that, pretty one?"

They embraced, kissing sweetly at first. Jeffrey pressed her closer to him so he could feel her breasts against his chest and his hips against her. Her hand stole down between them to rub his cock through his trousers. He groaned and pushed himself harder against her hand before stepping back to open his pants for her. She kissed him and slid her tongue into his mouth and her hand over his throbbing shaft. She shoved his trousers to the floor with her other hand, lifted her skirt, and pushed down her littles.

There was nothing stopping him from rubbing her smooth stomach and down into her curls. When he touched her clit, she whimpered and opened her legs. There they stood, masturbating each other until their organs exploded. He sprayed his cum into her hand, where it dripped to the floor, sinking into the packed dirt. She rocked back and forth while her wetness came forth onto his moving fingers before she stopped moving to cling weakly to him.

"Jeffrey, why is it that all you have to do is kiss me and I am nothing but a ball of butter in your hands?"

"Because, my dear, I am an incredible lover!"

She laughed and pushed away from him. "I would hardly call what we did 'incredible loving,' but it was nice. However, so is a bath nice. How about it?"

He poured two buckets of nearly boiling water into the tub after one bucket of cold water, to keep the metal tub from getting too hot. A third bucket of hot and one more of cold filled it. Lucretia tore off her clothes like a child opening gifts at Christmas. He held her hand for balance as she stepped into the water. Although it had been only minutes since he had emptied his balls, he began to stir again, just looking at her. *Lord, she is so beautiful,* he thought, *and all mine*. For a split-second, he remembered parts of his nightmare, but shoved those thoughts away. He knew she was his.

# Chapter 24

Jeffrey watched his wife wash her head and body. He laughed as she scrubbed her feet until they were red, trying to get the dirt off them. She stood, pink and yellow, drying herself on a huge towel from one of her trunks. "Come on, the water is fine," Lucretia said, as she wrapped her body tightly in the towel.

She loved watching him as he finished undressing. His shoulders were wide, his arms long and muscular, his stomach flat, and his penis erect. She looked at it, shaking her head as if she could not believe it was ready again. She stepped out onto her discarded clothes to keep her feet clean, at least for a minute.

Jeffrey stepped into the tub, kissing her as he passed by. She laughed aloud at how funny he looked with his knees pulled up as he scrunched himself into the small tub. He began to sing a nameless tune as he scrubbed his body clean. "When the weather turns warm," he told her, "you will have a shower outside where the sun keeps the water hot. I know you find this hard to believe, but like I told you before, sometimes the water is too hot, even."

"You are right, Jeffrey. I do not believe it ever gets warm here, let alone hot. You are just making it up to reassure me that it will not always be freezing. Showers are nice, but I still prefer a bath so that I can lie back in the water and soak."

"Sure, look at me soak," he replied sarcastically.

"Well, how about I wash your back for you, since you can't lie in the water?"

He leaned forward. She jumped back to the pile of clothes and bent over to soap him. Her towel dropped a bit in the front, giving him a clear view of her tits. He could not resist pulling the towel to his face so he could lick the globes that immediately responded to his tongue. She did not stop him, but rinsed his back and said, "Stand up. I will help you dry off."

He stood, but instead of a towel, she pressed her breasts against his chest. He reached for her, but she dropped to her knees to take his hard-on into her mouth. She felt him jerk away in surprise. Nevertheless, she held him tight and moved her mouth up and down his shaft while sucking it. She ran her tongue around the tip. She knew he was ready when he gripped her shoulders and held her tightly as she continued her movements. He tried to push her away at the last second, not wanting to drop his seed in her mouth, but she held fast. She took it as he came, a burst that dripped out her lips and down over her chin into the water below.

He shook with spasm after spasm until he drained himself into her mouth. She smiled up at him as she rubbed the last few drips over his softening penis. "I never knew before just how much you have inside of you. Inside my body it is hard to tell, but this way, I know exactly."

"Why did you do that, Lucretia? It is not right." His face reflected his words.

She said nothing, just rinsed her face with a cloth before reaching to wash him. He grabbed the cloth from her hand and dropped to his knees in the tub to wash himself. Lucretia did not understand his apparent anger. She stood, pulled the towel tighter around her, and jumped back to the bed, where she sat watching him.

He took his old towel from a nail and quickly dried himself. He reached for his clean trousers and shirt, and he quickly dressed. Boots were next, without socks. He did not speak until he dragged the tub through the door and outside. "The others are waiting their turn." He closed the door behind him, not to return until dark.

Lucretia had no idea what she had done wrong. Her friend Ruby told her last summer that whatever men and women did together, if they both liked it, was right. Had Jeffrey not liked it? Of course, he did. He came, shook, and moaned, just like every time. So, what was wrong? She sure wished she could talk to Ruby now.

# Chapter 25

"May I sit here?" Lucretia asked the young woman on the park bench. She knew Auntie Liz, her guardian since her parents died two years ago, would disapprove, but the other benches were all taken. Auntie Liz would be upset in the first place because Lucretia had ventured across the street to the park by herself. That in itself was unheard of, and now to sit with a woman Auntie would consider unworthy.

The woman looked up, startled. "You can, but are you sure you want to? I am not what most consider respectable company for a lady such as you are."

"Poo," answered Lucretia. "I am a newly married lady and I can make my decisions myself now. My name is Lucretia Sawyer now… Mrs. Jeffrey Sawyer," She said the name proudly and Ruby realized the young woman was little more than a child.

"It is nice to meet you, Mrs. Sawyer. I am Ruby Clanton. I saw you cross the street. Is that big house where you live?"

"Yes, but please call me Lucretia or Lulu, which is what my friends call me."

"Perhaps a bit between. I will call you Miss Lulu. How is that?" Lucretia rewarded her with a warm smile and offered her hand.

Their meeting led to a strange relationship over the next couple of months. Liz was horrified when she saw Lulu's new friend for the first time. "Lucretia Lucinda Sawyer, you will not associate with *that* woman. She is…she is…well, she is unfit for your company."

Seldom had Lucretia ever disagreed with her aunt, whom she loved so dearly, but this time she held firm. "Auntie, Ruby is my friend and I am proud to say so. She is a nice person, although I will admit sometimes that I am amazed by what she wears and her loud laughter. Oh, yes, and that wild bright red hair. I think she dyes it. Nevertheless, if I decide to bring her home for tea, I shall do so."

Lulu was sorry her aunt was hurt, but she was so old-fashioned and overprotective of her ward. Now that Lucretia was a married lady, Auntie would just have to accept that she would make her own decisions. Liz only said one more thing on the matter: "I certainly doubt if your husband would approve either."

# Chapter 26

Ruby refused the offer of tea, as horrified by the idea as Liz had been. Lucretia did not understand, but accepted the refusal. Instead, they agreed to go to a small tea parlor a few blocks away. Lucretia had no idea that Ruby hoped no one there would see them together, so afraid of hurting Lucretia's reputation and standing in the community.

As often happened, one afternoon conversation turned to the marriage bed. "Ruby, there is nothing I would not do for or with my husband, if he asked me to. I love him so much that if he told me to stand on my head naked in the middle of the street, I would do it."

Ruby's loud laughter turned heads, as usual. "Honey, I doubt he would ask that, but there are things he might ask that…well, things you probably have never heard of. Believe me, I have done them all. I think you are so naïve and sweet, you have no idea what I am. What I do."

"Well, I have thought about it and decided you serve drinks somewhere, probably in a place I have never been."

"Oh, honey, it is far more than that. Lulu, have you read in the Bible about harlots?" Lucretia nodded. "I am one of them. I am a whore. I make my living by selling my body to anyone—man or woman—who wants it enough to pay me. I get paid very well, because I am good at what I do.

"Many high-quality people come to me. I see many of them when we sit here watching the carriages in the street. Sometimes a man or woman who is my customer will bring their children or grandchildren here to play."

Lucretia hid her amazement as best she could, but Ruby saw it on her face and the way she suddenly looked around as if someone might be wearing a sign that read "I am Ruby's customer."

Ruby stood and nodded as if to leave. "Wait, Ruby, where are you going? Sit right back down here. Do you think that changes anything? You are my friend, period."

Ruby looked up to see tears welling up in the green eyes that looked at her so gently. She sat, smiling through her tears. No one but her Johns and Janes had ever accepted her for what she was, and even they used her and considered her their lesser. "Lulu, if ever in this life I can do something for you, I promise to do it."

"Do you mean it? Will you tell me how to keep my husband happy forever? I can cook and clean and such, but I know so little about the…the …"

"Sex. It is sex. Sometimes good, sometimes bad. Bad if anyone gets hurt in any way by it. Good if you enjoy it and so does your partner. Tomorrow I will bring you a book that can answer your questions. It has a lot of actual pictures of people fucking. There, did that word bother you? Because if it does, I will not bring the book. What we do with our genitals is fucking, in one way or another. Do you like what you do with your husband?" Lulu nodded. "The book will give you ideas."

Ruby brought the book the next day, carefully wrapped in bright paper and carried in a shopping bag. Lucretia entered the house, glad to find no one around. She crept up to her room to slip the package under her mattress, way to the middle so if the maids changed her bed, they would not see it. When night finally came, she yawned in pretence that she was tired and went to bed.

She slipped into her nightie, fluffed her pillows, and slid the book out. It was called *The Kama Sutra.* The pictures astounded her. They left nothing to the imagination. She wondered at how some of the positions could be accomplished, as she knew she could never twist in those ways. She read every word and looked at the pictures again. Her body responded to what she saw and she ached for Jeffrey to satisfy her need. Without him, she did the best she could and brought herself to climax with her fingers. It was not the same as when Jeffrey did it, but she enjoyed it.

In the days that followed, Lucretia asked more and more questions about the things Ruby did with men. She dismissed the women seeking other women as something too far-fetched to even consider. She made a little statement one day that caught Ruby's attention. She said, rather offhandedly, "I think I would like to see what men want from you. But then, again, how silly of me."

"Why is that silly, Lulu?" Ruby asked.

"The men would never do it in front of anyone else, and you would have to be naked in front of them, too, I suppose."

Ruby's loud laugh was deeper than ever. "Listen, my little friend, I do not care one whit who looks at me or sees me naked. Hundreds already have. If you really want to see, we could hide you in a closet or something. Not only that, some of my johns like to be watched. It is as if they think they fuck better than any other guy and want to show off. We could put a costume on you and cover your face. But, you could not talk. That would give you away in a second as a lady."

"Could we do that?" Lucretia could barely contain her excitement.

"Yes, I can think of no reason we cannot. I will figure it out. How about Monday afternoon when my Big-Nosed Banker comes to put his teenie peenie in me?"

# Chapter 27

Jeffrey quietly opened the door. Through the shaft of moonlight, he could see his wife asleep on the bed, still wrapped in her towel. The fire had died down and the room cooled off fast. He knelt in front of the stove to stoke it back to life and feed it more wood. He stood and looked at her in the twilight. She was awake now, watching him as a mouse might watch the cat ready to pounce.

He cleared his throat. "I came to see if you would like some supper. You have not eaten all day."

"No, thank you. I am not hungry." She slid under the blankets and turned her back toward him.

"Lucretia, I think we need to talk. I am sorry I yelled at you. What you did…I never expected you even knew about those things, let alone how to do them. Besides that, you did it with so much expertise, it was as if you had practiced it many times before." When she did not reply, he sat on the bed beside her back. "Honey, talk to me."

She sat up, pulling the towel up to cover her breasts and shoulders. "Talk? You want me to talk? Okay, I will talk. Yes, I had lots of practice doing that. I practiced on long squash and stuff like that. Ruby showed me first; then I understood how to do it better after I watched her and a couple of her johns."

Jeffrey shook his head in confusion. "You practiced? Why? Who is Ruby? You watched her suck some cock?"

"Yes." Her reply was matter-of-fact. "I wanted to learn to do it to please you. I learned a lot of things I thought you would like and some things I thought I would like. Ruby is my friend." She slid back down under the blanket and turned her back to him again. "Now, go away."

Jeffrey felt his anger building. "I am not through talking to you. Sit up and look at me." She did not move. He rolled her over on her back and roughly pulled her back into a sitting position. She struck out at him, catching him on the side of his neck. He grabbed her hands and pinned them with one of his above her head against the wall. "Answer me, Lucretia. You will answer all my questions. Let us start with who Ruby is."

Her face froze in a mask of anger that aroused him as much as it fed his fury. He dropped his pants. His cock was erect and throbbing. He would show her who the man in the family was. Before he was done, she would tell him everything. He jerked the blanket and towel away and spread her legs, but before he could enter her, his penis began to shrink.

His anger turned into self-loathing. He turned toward her. "Baby, oh, I am so sorry. I do not know what came over me. I would never hurt you. You know that." He tried to take her in his arms, but she flew from the bed, dragging her towel with her.

"If that is how you want sex in the future, please give me warning so I can at least grease up my hole for you. Bear grease or whatever you have handy, will be fine." She stepped into her filthy dress on the floor and, barefoot, ran out the door without another word.

She ran across the compound to the cabin where Liz lived. She knocked quietly. When the door opened, she rushed inside into her aunt's open arms.

Jeffrey dropped to the bed, ashamed, with no idea of what to do or say to her. She had been right, but she had been wrong. He loved her to distraction and the idea of her even looking at another man's body filled him with fear and anger again. What if she liked the looks of the other naked men and compared them to Jeffrey? What if he failed in comparison? What if she desired the others? Ruby and her johns…Ruby must be a prostitute. How did Lucretia even know such a person? And to watch them…how could she?

He had no answers and until she was ready to share with him, he would not know. He doubted that Liz knew about any of it, so he saw no reason to upset her as well. Therefore, it boiled down to Lucretia and Lucretia alone to tell him. First, he had to get her back. But how? His mind roamed through the day and he remembered the lumber in the bottom of the wagon from the depot. He had ordered it months ago to enlarge his cabin before she arrived.

His commander at Fort St. Louis was the one who suggested it when he asked permission to take his wife with him to his new command. He received permission, but with the stipulation that he spend four or five months putting things in order after his predecessor had died of pneumonia. After ordering the lumber, his mind let it slide with his new responsibilities.

The lumber was here and she was not. What a perfect time to rebuild. That surely would bring her back, and it was the perfect excuse to explain her absence from him and his bed.

# Chapter 28

The eyes that watched Lucretia run to her Auntie belonged to Eagle Grant. He tried his best to ignore her and when he did have to acknowledge her existence, he did so like the officer and gentleman that he had become. At those times, he wished he had remained the savage he had been.

Eagle would have been both amused and irritated that she considered herself a dung beetle in his eyes. He did not know that her aunt laughed when Lucretia told her that was the way she thought he pictured her. No, how he really pictured her was naked under him. He could not get her out of his mind. Never had he wanted a woman the way he wanted her. The fact that she was white made it even worse. Maybe he should take a leave and visit his people to the south for a few days to get himself back in perspective.

Yes, that is what he would do. He moved toward the major's house when the door opened. "Ah, Captain," the major said. "Just the man I wanted to see. Did you see the lumber that came in today?" Eagle nodded. "It is to enlarge my quarters. They are very small for two people, especially one who came with a wagonload of trunks. So I am asking—not ordering—you to help me with the building. I am thinking of knocking out the wall this afternoon and starting the work tomorrow. Lucretia has gone to stay with her Aunt Liz until we can move back in. How about it? Will you help?"

"Of course, Major. However, help is all I can do. I know nothing about carpentry. Our homes are of trees and buffalo hides. Muscle I have, so yes, I will be glad to help." That was a blatant lie and he knew it. The last thing he wanted was to build a cozy home for two with a bed for their nights together. And days, too, considering how much time Major Sawyer spent with her, locked away together. It was not an order, but it might as well have been.

Black Eagle was not the only one who lied. The major had not sent his wife to stay with her aunt. She had run away from him to Liz. Eagle wondered if the major thought this might bring her back. Maybe it would, maybe not. Build he would, either way.

The major strode away and returned almost immediately with four troopers. They carried out everything, from the bed to the clothes hanging on the wall, and stored it in the officer's office. What were a few more things, along with the pile of trunks?

As far as Eagle could see, the only way to get this over with was to get it started. He joined the major as he began to tear the walls apart, carefully saving the lumber to reuse. Deke Carter wandered over and with his muscle, things went twice as fast. Sergeant O'Brian, with six young men in tow, showed up and no one complained when they understood the building was for Mrs. Sawyer.

By dark, the entire structure was down and stacked in neat piles, according to the sizes of the salvageable lumber. Jeffrey called it too late to continue and thanked them all for their help, noting that if they so chose, he would welcome them again in the morning. Again, not an order, but again, it might as well have been one.

Eagle grew up where conversation was only when needed or with very close friends. Idle talk was difficult for him, so much so that at the Academy he was considered aloof and distant. That was fine with him, although it did cause a few occasions where he had to defend himself against those his own age. Later it was upperclassmen, until they learned that he could best three at a time with no problem. After that, he returned to his solitary life. He made no real friends and that, too, suited him fine.

His final year, he did find a closer relationship with Daniel Crockett Boone, a distant relative of the famous Indian killer, Daniel Boone. The friendship grew from a discussion in class of the hero who had died at the Alamo. Daniel begged to differ with the professor. He said his relative was no hero, but rather a man who drank heavily, killed without reason, deserted not one, but at least two families, and cared for no one but himself. The professor turned twenty shades of red that a student—even a relative—would talk that way about the revered Boone. The younger Boone was invited to leave the class and banished from it forever. When he rose to leave, Eagle stood and together, they left the lecture hall. Their punishment was hours of marching, both a written and verbal apology to the professor, and a warning that any further infractions would result in expulsion.

They graduated with honor and were assigned to Fort Wayne, Indiana, where they enjoyed the lives of modern young lieutenants, partial to demon rum and easy women. Once such woman was a Mrs. Delpha Glasgow. The Mrs. part of her name was always a question, but for sure, Mrs. Glasgow liked young men like the lieutenants. As dark as Eagle was, Daniel was the total opposite…as bright and pale as a summer morning. She especially liked to take them to her bed at the same time, and the men found it equally interesting.

The men always undressed and waited for her to make her grand entrance. It was never the same. One time, she was wrapped in a sheet with a ribbon for them to open, like a birthday present. Another, she was a harem girl. Still another, she was a schoolmarm, complete with glasses and a pointer that she knew how to wield. This particular night she dressed as a queen in long robe and crown. Under it, she wore nothing at all.

"Ho, Your Majesty," said Daniel, keeping with the play she had set up for them for the evening. "You are so beautiful, I cannot keep my hands off you. Do I have permission to kneel at your feet?"

"Yes, you do. And you," she pointed to Eagle, "have permission to unfasten my cape and admire my tits." Eagle did as ordered, enjoying her hardening nipples with his lips and tongue before biting them the way he knew she liked. She bent her torso backward until her back met the bed. She spread her legs for Daniel to worship between them, first with his mouth and then his cock. The men changed positions several times over the course of the evening, enjoying her as she enjoyed them.

They paid her and wandered back downstairs to the bar for one more drink before returning to the fort. They were pleasantly tired and in no mood for any sort of altercation. That ended with one comment, "Hey, half-breed, that bitch will fuck anything. Might as well be a dog as an Indian."

Eagle's knife pressed against the man's throat so quickly that witnesses would later say no man could move that fast. In his rage, Eagle had let his guard down and had not sensed another man move up behind him until he felt the other's knifepoint jab into his side. He swung around, killing the man with one stroke of his own knife across his throat.

Daniel moved forward to protect Eagle's back, just as the first man stepped forward, knife raised to bury it in the Indian's back. Daniel jumped forward and the blade came down in the side of his neck. Blood spurted everywhere, covering the four men and a dozen or more spectators.

Eagle dropped to his knees beside his wounded friend and pressed his hands into the gushing wound. "Get a doctor. Give me a towel or shirt or something. We have to stop the bleeding."

Mrs. Delpha Glasgow, naked in all her glory on the balcony above, yelled and threw a towel to Eagle. Everyone knew that nothing was going to stop this amount of blood, and while Eagle pressed his hands into it, the heart stopped pumping, and Daniel was dead.

The murderer made it no further than the door before being stopped by the angry crowd, made up of many troopers from the fort. Others forced Eagle to stand and pushed him outside to the horses. They mounted and raced to the stockade, followed by several townsmen who were friends of the murderer.

Inside the fort, Eagle was safe, at least for the moment. The fort commander himself rode into town with his major and a few troopers. They were just enough to deter the murderer's friends from making any kind of hostile move. Once at the sheriff's office, several witnesses stepped forward and all told the same take, of the murderer of Daniel Crockett Boone and the retaliation to protect his own life by Black Eagle Grant. The sheriff dismissed the charges, but quietly suggested to the officers that in his opinion, the best way to put a lid on the potential boiling pot was to remove Lieutenant Grant from the area.

Before dawn the following morning, Eagle was escorted to another fort to the west, then another, and another, until he arrived at Fort Mason. He mentioned to no one that if he could have requested any post, this would have been his choice. When he received his final papers with his assignment near his former home, he could not have been happier.

*By the time the soldiers reached the hill, Brave Eagle was the ranking one. He called a halt under my branches and ordered break. As the horses rested, he turned to the others and announced, "The fort is just over yonder. You have done your duty and now are to return to the train and your last assignment. I will go by myself from this place onward."*

*Someone started to argue that their orders were to accompany him to the fort. He reminded them that he was the senior officer, and that he was releasing them from that duty. No one argued and, within a few minutes, turned to return east.*

*I was pleased, as a tree can be pleased. I am pleased with warm sun, birds in my boughs, and a man I admire within my sight. Black Eagle appeared very different to me in his blue uniform and short hair. Not short by army standards, just cut much shorter than his tribesmen. I wished I had been able to tell him of things since he left. I would have warned him of the buffalo hunters sent here by the army to kill for meat for the soldiers in forts across the plains. The kill was of thousands, sometimes in one day, dropping the herds so much that the Indians had little to hunt.*

*The hostility toward white men had festered into what was now a full hate. Those living around the fort here were not hungry, but by the snows...well, who knows? As long as there are deer and such, they can get by, but without the buffalo, they will have no new blankets, teepees, clothes, and the countless other things the bison provide.*

*I should warn Black Eagle and hope he can stop what I know is ahead.*

# Chapter 29

Lucretia ran into Auntie Liz's arms, sobbing. She still cried as the noise started. Liz peeked out the door from the windowless cabin to see several men taking down the major's house. "Lulu, you have to see this. Did Jeffrey tell you he planned to dismantle your home? Is that why you are so upset? I should think you would be delighted to see it gone, and you know you can stay with me forever if you want. I think it is best you tell me what is going on, or I cannot help you."

Lulu peeked outside, too, and shut the door. Amazed, she turned to her aunt and nodded. Since there was no furniture in the room, they sat side by side on the edge of the cot that served as a bed.

"We had a fight. At least Jeffrey had a fight. He got mad at something I did and he tried to…to…but he could not at the last minute. So I ran here to get away from him. In the morning, we will start back to St. Louis. Marriage is not a fine thing after all. Being a bride was fun at first, until I found out that I did not know my husband at all. There is no reason to delay."

"I think you are leaving a lot out of your explanation, honey. What did you do that upset him? Jeffrey is such a mild-mannered man, it must have been something dreadful for him to do what he did."

"Auntie, I do not want to talk about it. It was too horrible for words."

"Lucretia, the best way to handle the unmentionable is to simply mention it. I figure that he tried to have his way with you and could not. That is good. But what did you do?"

The girl started to cry again. Through her tears, she whimpered, "He was getting out of the bathtub and I put my mouth…"

"You put your mouth on his penis?" Lulu nodded and cried harder. "Honey, you are not the only woman who has ever done that. I found it stimulating to both your uncle and me." Lulu stopped crying, looking at her aunt with eyes wide.

"Yes, my dear. That is part of a marriage bed and nothing to be ashamed of—as long as you both want it."

"Oh, Liz, that is the problem. Jeffrey was so angry when he finished. He told me it was not right and asked where did I even hear of such a thing. I felt humiliated and ashamed, so I lashed out at him. I told him I watched Ruby do that and learned how by practicing on a long squash. Why are you laughing?"

"Honey, I wish I had thought of a squash myself. I was not good at it for a long time. Now, I, too, want to know about Ruby. I think perhaps Ruby will be a problem for you two until you tell Jeffrey about her. I cannot imagine any woman letting another watch her do what couples do unless she were…oh, Lulu, wherever did you meet such a person?"

Lucretia felt exhausted from crying and hiding her secrets from everyone. Telling Aunt Liz lifted a cloud and cleansed her fear of talking about it. Actually, Liz at first was horrified and then began to calm until she was asking questions, one after the other. Soon they were laughing at some of the tales Lulu related.

Lucretia refused to share the tiny bed with her aunt, instead laying a blanket down on the dirt floor and covering herself with another. Sleep was impossible for either of them, with the sounds of laughter and demolition on the other side of the compound. Only when it was too dark for the men to work did the noise stop. Lucretia wanted desperately to know why Jeffrey was doing that, but she suspected it was to eliminate her from his life forever by destroying the place where she had done the unthinkable. Yes, St. Louis was best.

## Chapter 30

At first light, the noise started over again, but this time included sawing and hammering and not a few swear words. They took turns peeking out the door, but with no idea what it was until the roof went on.

"Oh, Auntie. I have it figured out. He tore down the old cabin to build a new one that has no memories of me in it."

"That is utter nonsense, Lucretia. Get dressed and let us go for breakfast. I am famished."

"No, you go. While you are out there, tell Jeffrey to arrange our transport to Cottonwood Creek. This morning, if possible."

"I will not! If you want transportation, then you will have to arrange it yourself. Do you want me to bring you something to eat when I return?" Lulu shook her head. She sat on the bed with her back to the wall and let her tears run as soon as Liz closed the door behind her.

Lucretia told herself that she loved her husband, but the fact was that now she was not sure. Oh, yes, she loved the sex, but beyond that…well, what was to love? They talked about nothing. She listened to his tales of battles and running the fort while daydreaming. Her fashions and plans were of no interest to him, as he always changed the subject. Actually, they did enjoy walks together, which gave them things to notice and discuss. Otherwise, they did not talk at all.

She knew she resented his not telling her about the fort and how they would live. In truth, all she wanted was the physical part of marriage. That was the only level on which they communicated, but that was not enough for a marriage.

Lucretia did not understand why he had become so angry with her for doing something she thought he would love. She knew that he enjoyed it as she had. She could feel his cock harden even larger as she slid her mouth up and down its length. It throbbed, he moaned, and yet still, he pronounced it wrong.

Ruby said the same thing her Auntie did…if they both liked it, then there was nothing wrong about it. Therefore, the problem was Jeffrey, she decided. She was wrong only because she did not mention it before doing it. Jeffrey was the problem, for sure.

Liz ate a leisurely breakfast before wandering over to where the men worked. "Good morning, all," she said pleasantly. "You gentlemen made such a racket last night, we did not get to sleep until way into the night. Will you be doing the same tonight?"

"Yes, Mrs. Elizabeth Harold," answered Sergeant Michael O'Brian. He bowed to her in a courtly manner before taking her hand to kiss the back of her glove. "It is a fine morning, but cold, so it is good that you are dressed warmly. Later today, if the major approves, would you care to join me in a buggy ride onto the plains? I promise it will be a proper ride, and if you prefer, I can find a chaperone for us. Your niece, perhaps?"

Jeffrey heard the conversation and grinned. "Sergeant, if the lady agrees to ride with you, I see no reason you cannot take a bit of time off. Surely, the lady will be safe with you without a chaperone."

"I suppose that will be fine, Sergeant. But I think my niece needs some air, too, so I ask for her to accompany us."

"More than fine, Mrs. Harold. I shall call for you at fourteen hundred hours in front of your home. I am looking forward to this ride, madam." Michael bowed again before bursting into song as he nailed yet another board to the cabin door he was building.

Lulu did not want to go with them, but found she had little choice. Leaving the cabin would mean she and Jeffrey might see each other, and that she did not want. When it was time to leave, she rushed to the wagon and climbed into the back without looking anywhere but the conveyance itself. Had she looked around, she would have seen her husband walking toward the wagon, but by the time she realized he was joining them, it was too late for her to escape gracefully.

Michael and Liz sat in front and Lulu and Jeffrey sat in the back. Conversation was strained at first, but with Liz around, that could not last long. "Tell me," demanded Liz, "what was all that racket about last night and today? Cats got your tongues? Sergeant? Okay, Jeffrey Sawyer, I am talking to you. I have never known you to be so uncivilized as to ignore a lady's question, so do not start now."

"I was trying"—he started slowly—"to surprise my lovely wife with a new home. I guess in my excitement, I did not think of the noise and chaos." He turned to Lucretia. "Darling, I am sorry I upset you the other night. For all the world, that will never happen again. I promise. I am a lout and beg you to forgive me. I love you."

He looked so pitiful that Lucretia felt her heart melt. She slid over to him and welcomed his arms with a long, deep kiss. She whispered, "I promise to do nothing like that again. I forgive you and beg you forgive me. I love you, too." Deep in her heart, she wondered if it was true.

The next hour was pleasant for all. The newlyweds held hands and whispered love words while the older couple finally arrived at the first-name basis of their relationship. The plains were desolate in the winter sun, in a cruel but wonderful way. Liz pointed out a fox ahead and moved slightly closer to her companion. They spotted some rabbits, a pair of wolves in the distance, and some deer who regarded them with disinterest. When their breath turned visible, Michael turned back to the fort, taking a shorter route.

To the west, they spotted a group of carrion feeding. Without a word, Sergeant O'Brian urged the horses into a run, stopping several yards away. The buzzards made their displeasure known as the two men ran to the remains. They both removed their hats and knelt to examine what they found. Lulu climbed down from the wagon and followed them. Jeffrey turned to stop her from coming, but not before she saw what they did not want her to see.

# Chapter 31

The remains were of a man badly damaged by the carrion. Jeffrey pulled Lucretia's face to his chest to block her view, but she struggled away. She approached the body of the man, seeing that he had no hair on his head, only a bloodstained skull. "Is this what a scalped person looks like? The poor man! Dead is bad enough, but all the worms and bugs… God has strange ways of making us feel useless and small. Not much left of him to identify, but does he have anything in his pockets?"

Her calm voice broke their shock. She sounded much as if she might be discussing a past tea party or a book she had read, but one look at her face told otherwise. She was white as the proverbial ghost. She shook, but stood firmly as Michael stooped to search the pockets. He dropped his finding on the frozen grass, finally rising.

Liz took the reins and allowed the horses to move forward until even she could see the corpse. Always in command, she called out, "Here, take this blanket and wrap him up. He deserves a decent burial. We can put him under the backseat and hold our noses until he freezes solid again tonight."

Back at the fort, they placed the body in a coffin Frank Grogan had made when he first arrived. He mumbled something about never knowing when one might be needed. The dead man's personal effects gave little information, other than some paper that said he had gold in an account in a St. Louis bank. It was money from the army for payment of buffalo meat. His name was James Adcock. That was all there was.

The discovery of the body brought a pall over the fort. Work on the house stopped as the sun set. The roof was on the house and the windows in, so it was complete enough for the stove to be put in place temporarily. The men dragged the bed back inside for the night and planned to complete the house the next day.

Once the fire was blazing, Jeffrey put buckets of water on it to warm while they ate supper. There was little conversation, as if no one felt like talking with the dead man so close. Actually, the men did not want to discuss it in front of the women, but the problem of the man's death spoke volumes. Indians—not men who pretended to be Indians—had killed him. White men would have left no identification.

Jeffrey carried the little bathtub with them as they returned to their warm cabin. He set it down, filled it with water just the right temperature, and took his wife in his arms. The kisses were sweet to start, but soon turned passionate. He unfastened each piece of her clothing until she stood naked in front of him. He nibbled on her nipples until they were tiny points.

"Now, into the tub. I want you clean enough to eat, because tonight, that is what I am going to do to you." He stripped off his clothes and dropped to his knees beside the tub. He dumped water over her head and soaped every inch of her body, head to toes. He rinsed her again. His teeth teased her breasts again as she stood to give him the bathwater.

Now it was her turn. He quickly washed his head and face and waited for her to move the soap slowly across his chest and under his arms. She made suds to wash his neck, shoulders, and arms before returning to his body. Her hands were gentle and exciting as she moved them between his legs while bending over him.

She soaped his hard cock until he stopped her hand. "One more minute and I will explode in your hand." He stood and dried himself carefully, never taking his eyes off her face. "Lucretia Lucinda Sawyer, you are the most perfect wife in the world. What you did the other night…I cannot get it out of my mind." He watched her smile slide away. “No, listen. It was wonderful. I was so amazed and shocked that my sweet virgin bride would to that. Now I am begging you to do it again.”

She moved closer to him and placed his hands on her dangling tits. He watched her mouth and lips close in on him. Her tongue darted forward and licked the tip. He groaned and moved his hips closer to her face. This time she took his shaft by the head and ran her tongue around it, teasing him even more. He could stand it no longer and gently pressed her so that his ramrod went inside and she sucked it deeply. “Now, oh God, darling. Do not stop. Yes, more.” He jutted his hips toward her and away until the last drop of his cum shot into her waiting mouth and dripped down her chin into the water. He held her head for balance, feeling so weak that he might fall.

She washed her face and rinsed her mouth before standing to kiss him again. He held her close, murmuring into her ear that he was going to return the favor. Lulu knew what he meant. She had seen several men do that to Ruby, who claimed it was better than an actual fuck. Even better done by a woman, Ruby said, because a female knew exactly what and where to lick and bite.

They lay together on the bed, facing each other, kissing endlessly. She caressed his chest, pinching his nipples lightly. He liked it, he said, but moved her hand down to cup his balls. Jeffrey felt a stirring and knew it was time. He turned her over onto her back and spread her legs. He knelt between them, rubbing gently inside. When he found her clit, he bent down to take it between his lips, touching it with his tongue. He knew it was right when she lifted her hips, moaning his name and pushing his head into her. His cock hardened and throbbed.

Lucretia had never before felt anything as wonderful as this. She writhed on the bed, crying out her explosion and then begging for more. Her clit grew larger and seemed to slide out of the tissue holding it in place. The more he sucked, the larger it got, until she reached a mountaintop where she had never before been.

When she dropped her hips back to the bed, he slid up on her body and planted his rock-hard prick as deeply into her as he could and then began to move slowly. She wrapped her sweaty legs around his waist and met his every stroke. He cried out his climax as he jabbed into her slippery cunt. He collapsed on top of her and then rolled to the side.

"Let me touch you again, Lulu. I want to feel my juices running out of you." She opened her legs slightly, but it was enough for him to finger fuck her vagina and feel himself in her. When his finger brushed her button, she jumped again. He laughed as he gently rubbed her again, bringing her to another cum.

Satisfied for the time being, they washed and climbed back into bed. She was asleep in seconds. He rose quietly and dressed. He had a meeting with his officers when the women were asleep. He smiled as he looked at her. He knew she would sleep until morning. *Dear God,* he thought. *Thank you for such a wife.*

# Chapter 32

*I know that the death of the buffalo hunter weighed more heavily on Eagle Grant than any of the others, because it placed him in a dubious situation. He did not know the circumstances that led to the murder of the man, but even without the facts, he considered it from the Indian point of view. The loss of buffalo could lead to starvation and destroy their lives. On the other hand, the army did need the meat to feed their personnel. Once the white man came into the lands of the Indian, it was only a matter of time before there would be conflicts. This was most devastating for the natives.*

Eagle sat at his desk, as did the other officers. Sergeant O'Brian found a straight-back chair, which he leaned back against the wall. Major Sawyer asked if anyone had any ideas and at first, no one answered.

Eagle finally broke the silence. "My best guess is that the scalping was done by members of the tribe that has a camp about five miles south. On one of my reconnaissance missions, I visited several villages within a thirty-mile radius. Those farther away from the railroad were much more prosperous than closer tribes, like the one near here, because the buffalo hunters had farther to go with their meat and pelts for transportation east. The village near us is a poor one, obviously lacking essentials like new robes and hides to repair their teepees and, most importantly, food."

Deke looked around the room into each face. "Major, do you want me to take a party to check out this village? I would consider it an honor, sir, if you would trust me with this mission. I have done nothing since I got here but sit behind this desk or watch the troops on parade. My wife thinks that is all there is to being a lieutenant."

Eagle felt he should be leading that party, but said nothing. It was right to grant the young man's request. In his heart and head, he knew it was not the best thing for an inexperienced man who might run into hostiles, who by now did not care if the enemy was a buffalo hunter or an army officer. Still, he remained silent.

"If you want the duty, Deke, then it is yours. Nevertheless, as you admitted yourself, you have no experience, so Sergeant O'Brian will accompany you. Before you say anything, this is no longer a request, it is now an order. Be prepared to leave at first light. Oh, yes, one other thing. You are not to engage the Indians under any circumstances."

Eagle finally broke his silence. "Major, may I speak?" Jeffrey nodded. "I do not think it is a good thing to forbid engagements if the company is attacked, and that seems like a real possibility. The death of the man out there and the stealing of his supplies, including his gun and ammunition, will not be the last. It is the beginning."

"Captain, I understand your thinking, but I will not rescind that part of my orders. Fighting will only encourage more bloodshed and that is what we must stop before it advances. Now, good night, gentlemen." He rose and the meeting was over.

Eagle caught up with the major as he crossed the compound to his new cabin, where his soft, loving wife warmed his bed. "Major, I know you have the command. But this time, sir, I think you are wrong. I know these people. I am one of them. I know how they think and what they will do. Unless your God feels especially protective of the men you are sending out, you might be sending them to their deaths."

Jeffrey felt mild irritation at his captain. "Yes, you made your thoughts clear, but I stand behind my orders."

With no further discussion, he opened the door to his cabin, leaving a frustrated Eagle outside, clenching his hands. His frustration was twofold: one was because he knew the major was wrong and the second was because the major was going to the bed of the woman Eagle wanted as much as he wanted air to breathe.

Black Eagle was fourteen when he claimed his first scalp. His tribe was a peaceful group most of the time, but if forced into battle, they were as ferocious and relentless as the worst killing tribes. A wandering group of renegade Apache from the south was plundering their way across the plains. They stole, raped, killed, and burned their way from village to village.

Scouts looking for buffalo saw them at a neighboring village in what was once a peaceful group, now a place of slaughter. The scouts raced home to report what they saw.

What happened before would not happen again. Once the hunters left the village unguarded and a rogue band attacked it, killing everyone but small children and young women. The women were used, as women always are by ruthless men. Those who survived, if any did, along with the children, would be sold into slavery. The hunters returned to find a burnt village; they hunted down the marauders, and life went on, but the memories never faded.

Instead of waiting for the Apache to find them, his people armed themselves and set out to surprise their enemy. It was a great success. It was Black Eagle's first coup. He had used his knife as if he had taken scalps for years to take the hair of the man he killed. He waved it in the air, as did the others, shouting their chants and thanks to their gods. No Apache survived the surprise attack and only one of Black Eagle's tribe died.

Now, standing in the center of the fort, he remembered the horror and excitement of that first battle. He had experienced bloodlust for the first time then. The sounds of the killing and cries of the wounded rang in his ears as if it were yesterday. Only this time, it was his first people who would kill his present people.

# Chapter 33

Three mornings after the party left led by Lieutenant Carter, Liz did not come out of her tiny cabin as usual. Her voice was weak when Lucretia knocked. "What is wrong, Auntie? You are so pale."

"Oh, honey, I hurt fiercely. Here." She indicated her right side. Lucretia felt the spot and Liz cried out in pain.

"That is where I hurt when I was little. Remember? It was my appendix and you took me to the hospital where they cut me open and took it out. Oh, dear God, if it is your appendix, what shall we do?"

Lucretia ran outside, calling Jeffrey's name. He came running, as did several other men. "I think Auntie Liz has a bad appendix. Come, see for yourself." He did as bade. He suspected she was right. There was no doctor for hundreds of miles. He sent for Greta, who agreed.

Lulu could not conceive of life without Liz, who took in the orphan child after her parents drowned in a boating accident on the Mississippi River when Lulu was only six years old. Liz loved the child and had raised her as her own. Lulu had helped to fill a void in the life of the newly widowed woman. Their relationship was as mother and daughter. It was a bond that only death would break. Now she might lose the woman who had been her mother.

After a few minutes, Captain Eagle Grant stepped into the cabin. Without a word, he stepped to Liz's side and felt the swelling himself. This time he looked directly at Lucretia and said, "Yes, her appendix has exploded inside her and she will die if we do not take it out."

Lucretia's voice was so low, it was hard to hear. "How? We have no doctor. Is there a doctor in Cottonwood Creek? Do we have time to get her there?"

"No—to both questions. Her only hope is to have it out of there immediately."

Jeffrey asked, "Eagle, can you do it?"

"Major, I never have done it, but I have watched it done. Perhaps someone else…"

Liz spoke for the first time. Her pain caused her state of mind to haze in and out, but she understood some of what was said. "Captain. Please, you do it. I trust you. Please hurry, because I do not know how long I can stand this. Otherwise, someone put a gun to my head."

Eagle took her hand. "If that is what you want, I will try, Mrs. Harold. I cannot promise I can do it right, and you might die under my knife." Liz squeezed his hand and nodded her understanding. "I will need water—lots of hot water—and some whiskey. Give her as much of the whiskey as you can get down her. It will help deaden the pain. Get clean rags and a couple of bowls.

"You"—he pointed to Greta—"will have to help me."

"Not me, Captain. I faint from the sight of blood unless it is some hog, steer, or chicken heading for my frying pan."

"Then you." He nodded to Lucretia. "And you will not faint, do you understand? None of those wimpy lady things. You will do what I tell you, when I tell you."

"Now, wait a minute, Captain, you will not talk to my wife like…"

Lucretia touched his hand. "It is fine, Jeffrey. What is important is that we try to save Liz. All right, Captain, let us do it."

The whiskey worked its miracles on Liz, sending her into a stupor only a lifelong teetotaler would succumb to. Eagle spoke. "Now, everybody out but Mrs. Sawyer and Corporal Dryer. Jed, you will hold the lantern as close as you can without getting in my way."

Jeffrey opened his mouth to object, but said nothing. He knew it was best for him to leave with the others.

"Here we go. Mrs. Sawyer, help me remove her garment. I want her lower body completely exposed. We will then wash her with soap and water, several times. I learned this at the Academy, as I am sure your husband did as well. We learned to do some field surgery when no medics were there.

"Call her name. If she does not respond to you, she is probably unconscious." Lucretia did as instructed and Liz remained silent. "Good, are you both ready? Mrs. Sawyer, there will be a lot of blood when I cut, so be ready to catch as much as you can with the cloth and squeeze it out in this bowl, and then do it again and again."

Blood welled up from the incision he made on Liz's torso. "Damn it, Mrs. Sawyer, faster. I cannot see with all the blood." Jed held the lantern with one hand and used the other to soak up the blood until Eagle had packed the opening with as many rags as he could. "There it is. Now, when I cut it out, Mrs. Sawyer, do you think you can put a bowl under it so it does not drip back into the cut? Can you do that?"

"Damn it, yourself, Captain. There is no need for your sarcasm and snide remarks. Unless you had a doctor or nurse here, I doubt that anyone could do better." Her voice was soft, but emphatic enough that he lifted his eyes to hers for a moment, surprised again by her iron will. Jed chuckled under his breath, but it was enough to draw a dirty look from Eagle.

They continued with no further conversation. The infected gland removed, Eagle carefully removed the bloody rags and rinsed the wound with clean water before he stitched it closed. He sighed with relief when the last stitch seemed tight enough to satisfy him before looking up, first at Jed and then at Lucretia. "You both did well and can be proud of yourselves. I have seen full-grown men faint away and vomit at less. Now, let us wash our patient and ourselves. Mrs. Sawyer, can you find something clean to dress her in? Jed, a clean blanket or two. I will lift her and you replace the bloody ones."

Together, Eagle and Lucretia dressed the comatose woman and covered her tightly. "Corporal Dryer, you are free to go. Mrs. Sawyer, a moment, if you do not mind."

Lucretia stood beside the cot and waited for him to say something mean again, but instead he asked kindly, "Are you tired? I know I am. There is a bit of whiskey left and I would like to share it with you." He handed her the bottle. She took a deep drink, coughed, and grinned as some of it ran down her chin.

Eagle actually smiled at her. "I can see you are a heavy drinker. Probably get snookered every night." Lucretia laughed with a merriment he had never heard before. It grabbed his heartstrings the same way her smiles did.

Outside, Jeffrey heard her bell-like voice for the first time since she had arrived at the fort. He remembered it from their wedding day and nights in the hotel, before realizing that she felt no reason to laugh like that anymore. That it was in response to something said by some other man caused a shock to run through his body. He pushed the door open to see Eagle handing a whiskey bottle to his wife. "What is going on here?" The jealousy was so clear in his words that they both looked at him in amazement.

"Nothing, Jeffrey. We are just celebrating our success. It appears that Liz will be fine, if she does not get an infection or break the incision open again."

"Thank you, Captain, on behalf of my wife and myself for saving her Auntie. That will be all. Good night." He waited until Eagle closed the door behind himself before he spoke again. "Come, it is time to return to our cabin. We have some things to discuss."

"That was rude, Jeffrey, and uncalled for. As far as I can see, we have nothing to discuss right now. It does not matter anyway, because I am staying with Liz until she awakens." She turned her back to pull a chair close to her Aunt Liz's head and took the woman's hand. She gave him one glance, as if in dismissal, before she began to bathe the wan face of the woman she loved more than anyone on earth, including her husband.

Black Eagle left the cabin and retrieved his horse from the stable. He mounted and rode away from the fort as fast as his steed could run until he knew it had tired. He dismounted under the tree on the hill and hit its trunk in fury. The damn major had ruined the only pleasant moment Eagle had ever had with the woman whose lips promised a million nights of love. He beat the tree until his hands hurt. He did not know how or when, but someday she would be his.

# Chapter 34

It was later that day when a ragtag line of five men returned to the fort. Fifteen had marched proudly away, but there was nothing proud about this quintet. All were wounded…two seriously, one semi-seriously, and two with minor afflictions. The seriously hurt would die, Major Sawyer was sure, because they had no doctor and insufficient medicines to treat them.

The women rushed to help. Molly Carter stopped as they moved the men into the enlisted men's quarter that would be the infirmary. "Where is my husband?" When no one looked at her nor answered, she screamed and covered her face. Lucretia ran to her, holding her small black head against her shoulder, whispering useless comfort words. Molly was inconsolable, even as Lulu walked her back to her cabin. Suddenly, Molly pushed her away. "Your husband did this. He killed my Deke. Get away from me. I hate him and I hate you." She ran into her cabin, followed by Greta, who closed the door behind her. It was hours before the young woman quieted.

Sergeant O'Brian was semi-seriously hurt, but in good enough condition to rant, rave, and swear as he related what had happened. Quite simply, they rode into a trap. They expected to arrive at the same peaceful village they had visited on earlier occasions. Instead, in a narrow trail by the river, they met an ambush of both rifle and arrows. "It was like shooting ducks swimming in a pond," he reported. "I know he was too experienced to see the things he missed. I pointed them out to him, but he reminded me that he was in charge and he would make the decisions. His decision led to Lieutenant Deke Carter himself being the first killed."

Eagle Grant's black eyes moved from Michael to Jeffery. Major Sawyer felt them even before he looked at him. They were full of fury and admonishment of things better left unsaid. Eagle saw pain and guilt in the eyes and face of his commander.

Sergeant O'Brian was a wise man who gained knowledge not from books, but from life itself. He saw the exchange between the two men and understood them both. "Ain't no reason for getting upset now. Ain't nothing going to change what happened. If there was, I would go back and flat-out take the command away from the lieutenant, but I did nothing. So I ain't feeling any better about it than you. The thing now is to plan what we do next."

Eagle nodded. Jeffrey replied, "You are right, Sergeant. Since you were there and we were not, what is your feel of the situation?"

"That those damn redskins out there are full of hate and anger at all white man for what a few did. We are too few men here to do anything about it, except to warn the settlers and wagon trains to turn back until we get reinforcement to put down this here uprising. First thing is getting the women and wounded out of here. Right now, if it was not so close to sundown."

"Yes, you are right on all counts. Eagle, will you arrange for transportation to the depot to leave at sunup in the morning? Do you, in your knowledge of the enemy, think they will attack our caravan east? Will our women be safe going?"

Eagle thought a long time before answering. "Yes, perhaps, if they leave now. Sergeant, you need to know that Mrs. Harold must be transported immediately, as her appendix went bad and we removed it this morning. I do not like the looks of it. It appears to have some swelling and dripping that is not good. The sooner she gets to Cottonwood Creek and the train, the better. We will put her in a wagon to look like it is empty, hopefully of no interest to our enemy. The driver will be alone, which should indicate he is of no consequence."

"Wait a minute. I want Lucretia on that wagon, too, and Mrs. Carter. And Greta, if she wants to go," said Jeffrey.

"Then you might as well put up a sign that says, "Come get our women." Eagle looked at his commander with unmoving eyes and no expression. "Tomorrow would be better. No, I do not think they will be safe, but they will be safer on the move than staying here after tonight."

Later that afternoon, Black Eagle went once again to see the comatose woman. He was not surprised to find Lucretia sitting by the bed, bathing her aunt's face. She looked up as he entered the room and said, "She is hot. Fever. Is there anything we can do?"

He looked at her face, seeing pain for her aunt and exhaustion for herself. It was not like him to feel sympathy, particularly for a white woman, but he did at that moment.

"There is nothing here that will help her, but perhaps out in the prairie there may still be some plants that might help. My grandmother Summer Swan relied completely on the things she found in there to help her tribe's people. There were no other medicines then, at least no white man's medicines. Sometimes, from what I have seen, her medicines were just as good, if not better, than what is available now."

Lucretia jumped up. "I will get my coat. You get your horse. The buggy will take too long. Hurry, Captain."

"Whoa, whoa. What are you talking about?"

"The prairie and the plants. We need to go right now." Without another word, she ran out the door and into her own little cabin, appearing immediately in her coat.

"What are you waiting for?" she asked as she ran into Black Eagle, who was standing in Liz's doorway. "Get your horse. I will tell Jeffrey. And hurry."

She ran to the officer's office and appeared almost immediately with her husband at her side. The major looked at Eagle and said, "If you think you can find something to help Liz, you have my permission to go look for it. However, I don't think it is necessary for Lulu to go with you, unless I go too, and I can't leave the fort with you gone."

"I agree, Major. I will go immediately."

"Wait, you two. I am going too. Two people can collect faster than one. Liz is too hot, Jeffrey, she will surely die if we can't get her fever down, and this is no time for silly rules of city society. No more arguments. I am going as soon as the captain gets his horse." Lucretia looked pointedly at the man, who shrugged and ran to the stable. His horse had no saddle when he stopped in front of her.

"Madam, unless you can ride bareback, you will have to stay here."

"Of course I can ride bareback. Give me a hand, Captain, and a boost, Jeffrey."

Feeling as if they had been stonewalled, each man did as bid. She sat behind Eagle with her arms around his waist. "Now, let's go."

Jeffrey nodded at his captain, who turned the horse and galloped out the gate.

His destination was the small river, now covered with ice. Along its banks grew willow, which Eagle recalled used for fever. The bark was boiled until it changed color, cooled, and given to the ill person in the form of a tea. Beyond that, he recalled nothing else his grandmother had done.

He dismounted and lifted the pale woman to the ground. She weighed no more than a child, he thought. She smiled and thanked him before turning serious again. Her smile hit him like a rock to his chest. The smile lit up her face, shining in her eyes and showing her small, even teeth. It was something he had seen as she looked at her husband and aunt, but no one else. Until now, when she smiled at him.

Brusquely, he walked away and motioned her to follow. "I will cut the bark and you roll it up. Try not to let it touch your clothes or it will stain. I will tie it when we are done and put it on the back of my horse. You will have to sit in front of me."

It started snowing, lightly at first, and suddenly it was a blizzard. "Damn," he said, "I'm sure it will stop in a few minutes, but you are getting soaked. I know of a cave close by where we can go until it stops." He jumped onto his horse and pulled her up in front of him. He did not even think that she could ride behind him because the willow was still on the ground and was sure to knock her off the back of the horse.

The cave was a small hole in the ground with a rock for cover. Eagle slid from his horse to prod into the space with his rifle butt. He grabbed his blanket from his bedroll and spread it on the ground under the overhang. He lifted her from the horse and carried her to the mouth of the cave.

"It is small, but it will provide protection. Crawl inside and sit. You will be dry."

Lucretia did as told and sat quietly for a minute before saying, "Aren't you coming in? You are getting soaked, too."

"In case you haven't noticed, Mrs. Sawyer, there is no room for two."

"Nonsense. You sit first and I will sit on your lap."

"I feel that is hardly proper, madam."

"Proper, be damned." She rose gracefully and walked out to stand beside him. "If you don't want protection, then neither do I."

"You are the most stubborn female I have ever met," he said.

"Then you have not met many females, have you?" She stood firm, leaving him no recourse but to do as she wanted.

He crawled into the cave. It was so short, he had to bend his head to keep from hitting it on the overhang. "Now, get your white butt in here before you melt."

She laughed, letting his "white butt" comment pass. "What makes you think I will melt, Captain? I am tougher than you think. Why, I have wrestled bears, wrung the necks of wild birds, and outrun a vicious bear, too."

Black Eagle laughed, a full rolling display of amusement, for the first time in her presence. "I bet you have, Mrs. Sawyer. Now, sit down. I will have to bend over you a bit, unless you want to have me bleed all over you from hitting my head."

"Bend as you wish, Captain Grant. Now, isn't this cozy?" She snuggled down as low as she could to give him more room. "Now, tell me about yourself, sir."

"This is hardly a tea party for small talk. I joined the army just to avoid those things. And now, here in the middle of nowhere, in a cave no bigger than a child's bed, you want to chat about nothing. Lord, you are something incredible."

"Hardly incredible, I think. Just trying to make the time go faster. But, if you prefer silence, then that you shall have." She closed her eyes and within minutes, he felt her muscles slacken and her breathing change. She fell asleep.

He wrapped his arms tighter around her, telling himself she was cold, but in truth, he wanted her as close as he could get. She sighed in her sleep and turned her head to press it against him. He bent his head to rest on the top of her head. He breathed in the woman smell of her. His fingers touched her cheek, feeling the smoothness. His fingers curled in her hair, which was so soft and silky. Suddenly, he realized what he was doing.

This was another man's wife, not for him, even if she should want it. He doubted that would ever happen, but a man could hope, couldn't he?

She awoke, grumbling about a stiff neck. "I must have slept like a pig's tail to get this sore." She rubbed her neck and shook her head. "Ooh, I forgot not to talk."

Again, he laughed. "Have you ever been quiet for more than five minutes, unless you were sleeping?"

"Probably not," answered Lucretia. "And why ever would I want to. Talking, if both parties participate, is the best form of communication, don't you think?"

"There are other forms I like better," he answered, trying to erase the vision of her naked under him from his head.

"What might that be, Captain? Oh, look, the snow is stopping."

She was right and he was relieved that he did not have to come up with an answer to her question. She climbed off his lap and went outside. She turned to face him, extending her hand. "Here, let me help you. You were all curled up like a cloth doll and you must hurt all over."

"Thank you, Mrs. Sawyer, but I am fine." As he slid on his butt out of the cave, his joints made little noises.

Her laughter was like bells ringing. "Yes, sir, you are fine. For an old guy." She laughed again and started running.

Before he realized what he was doing, he found himself chasing her. He caught her around the waist causing them both to fall. He looked into her eyes as she lay under him and saw only her innocence there. He stood and took her hand. "Next time, I will give you a head start," he said. "How about a mile head start."

She laughed and he joined her. In that moment, something changed.

They gathered the willow bark, now covered with snow, bound it to the horse, and rode at a full run back to the fort. Inside the gates, they found Major Sawyer mounting his steed. "We were just on our way to search for you."

Lucretia slid from the horse and ran to her husband, giggling. "How were you going to search when your scout was not here? Actually, Jeffrey, Captain Grant found a cave where we sat out the snow. And we got the willow bark, too. Now, I have to go boil it for Aunt Liz." She turned to look up at Black Eagle, who was still on his horse, and said, "Thank you, sir, for keeping me from the storm and for finding a something that will help for my aunt." With that, she turned and ran toward the cooking shack.

The two men looked at each other for a long time before Jeffrey spoke. "Yes, my thanks too. Now come, let us go inside and you can tell me all about it."

Morning came too soon. Lulu forced the smelly tea down her aunt's throat and was signed happily to find the fever dropping. Outside there was turmoil.

"I am taking Liz to Cottonwood Creek myself," insisted Sergeant O'Brian. "I can easily drive a pair of horses, even with my little sore shoulder. Besides, if we do not make it, I would rather be with her than back here wondering." No one argued with him. Instead, they helped him mount the wagon after they padded the back, and lay the prone woman under a half-torn tarp that looked like it covered nothing.

"Here are your papers, Sergeant," said Jeffrey as he handed them to the man on the wagon. "You are on furlough for as long as it takes. Keep me abreast of happenings by telegraphing Cottonwood Creek." Michael nodded and urged the horses into a slow walk to make sure the ride was as easy as possible for the woman in the back.

A few hours later, Liz awoke. She was in pain, but aware that she was in the wagon. "Where am I going?" she asked in a ragged voice.

"Oh, my darling Liz, I have been so worried about you. Do not sit up, or even try to. We are heading for Cottonwood Creek to the train. Captain Grant took out your ailing appendix, but you are not healing right. Major said to take you back to St. Louis, and whatever the major says is what I do. Now you go back to sleep, my wonderful Liz, and let me take care of you." Whether she heard him or not, he did not know, because she did not answer. Sergeant O'Brian had not been to church since he was a child, but this night he prayed, begging for the life of the first woman he had ever wanted to marry.

# Chapter 35

At daybreak, the second wagon was ready. "I ask permission to lead the group, sir," Eagle requested, but knew he would be refused.

"I would feel better, Captain, if you stayed here at the fort and oversaw preparations for the attack I think is coming. I would like to take my wife myself to safety, and the others as well."

The decision made, they separated. Jeffrey found his wife bandaging one of the dying men. He slid his arm around her waist, pulling her close to apologize for his behavior. Lucretia wanted to accompany Liz, but understand why she could not. Her heart was so full of pain, she let him embrace her.

Eagle stood in the shadows, watching. He knew that once again, the major was wrong, but he would follow orders. He listened to the quiet words the newlyweds exchanged, not feeling any guilt for eavesdropping. One did not learn by feeling guilty.

He heard Jeffrey say, "Lulu, listen to me. We are leaving first thing in the morning. All the wounded and women will be taken to the depot for safe return to St. Louis. No argument. I will escort you myself and you know I will never let anything happen to you. I love you, darling, more than life itself."

Eagle watched Lucretia turn in her husband's embrace and put her arms around his neck, hiding her face in his shoulder. Eagle could not hear her words, but her body alone expressed her pain. *I hope someday to have a wife and love like the one they share.* He turned away, no longer able to watch without guilt.

Lucretia heard her husband's words, but refused to accept them. She was not leaving him, no matter what he said. Things were not as bad as he said. He led her from the stable across the compound to their cabin. So close to completion, so very close. He lit a fire and put a couple of buckets of water on to warm. Slowly, he kissed her mouth, letting his tongue touch hers. He moved his tongue up to lick away her tears. He pulled off her bonnet and released her cascade of curls before running his fingers through them.

She lifted her hands to the sides of his head, pulling it down to her mouth. Her kiss was urgent and full of desire. He responded as she hoped he would. They quickly undressed each other, kissing and touching everywhere.

Things did not go according to her plan after this. She planned to extract a promise from him during sex, allowing her to stay in her safe new house and not go with the others. She rolled on top of him, pressing her tits, swollen with desire, against his face. He licked her nipples, taking one and then the other in his teeth, nibbling gently.

She felt his cock searching for the opening between her legs. "Are you ready, darling? Do you want me to spread my pussy wide for you? Do you want me to sit on your cock? Do you want to fuck?" She knew that sex words excited him, so she teased him with them as she teased him with her body.

"Lulu, please. Yes, I want to fuck you. Open yourself for me. Sit on my cock. Let me feel your wetness. I need you." He groaned as she did as he asked. Slowly, she slid her slick pussy down over him and began to ride him. First, she moved slowly, watching his face as his desire built. She increased her rhythm. She took her hand and touched her clit, making sure he watched what she did. He groaned and squeezed her tits as her own need mounted.

"Oh, Jeffrey, how can you send me away? Think of yourself alone in our bed. Will you jack yourself off, dreaming of me like this?" She bounced up and down with her hair flying in abandon, as she knew he liked.

He grabbed her waist and held her down over his cock tightly. "If I have to jack myself off, then that is what I will do. You are leaving and that is the end of it." With his terse words, he arched up and shot his cum into her, not waiting for her to finish.

She lay back down atop his body to kiss him again. Instead, he rolled her off him. "Jeffrey, what is wrong? What did I do?"

"Lucretia, you know exactly what you did. You tried to bribe me with sex to get your way. Have you thought about dying here in this place that you hate? Because that will happen if you do not leave, and I do not want you to die. Sometimes I think you are never going to grow up. It is time to stop being a child and become a sensible woman."

Lucretia lay unmoving, stunned by his words. "Grow up? I am a woman already. Would a child fuck you the way I do?"

He interrupted her. "That is the only thing you want from me. Just sex, pure and simple. Is that the only reason you married me? No, do not answer…I know it is. You should have stayed in St. Louis with your friend Ruby and joined her and her johns."

Her anger needed venting, but he did not allow it. "Do not say a word. I am not finished yet. I think you do not even know how selfish you are; that is the sad part. I love you, but there is more to marriage than one-sided love and great sex. Now, be honest with yourself and me. Have you ever loved me, even a bit?"

# Chapter 36

Instead of anger talking, it became guilt, knowing he was right. "How could I have married you if I did not love you?"

"That is not an answer. It is another question. Try the truth." He pulled her close and pushed his mouth down on hers, hard. She struggled, trying to break away, but he held her tight, forcing his tongue between her teeth while his hand moved down into the juncture of her legs. His fingers found her clit. His caresses were not gentle this time. Instead, he pushed it hard and moved quickly. She fought him, trying to push him away, but he held her firm.

Her body took control, even while her mind wanted him to leave her alone. She could not stop her hips from pushing even harder against his hand as her convulsions began, one after another, giving her a climax like none before. When she collapsed back against the bed, her body throbbed still and her mind refused to admit that she wanted this kind of sex. Hard and raw. Lord, what kind of a woman was she?

Jeffrey stood naked, looking down at her, his cock at half-mast. "Is that the way Ruby liked it? Did you have sex with her and her johns? I think you did. Otherwise, there is no way you could have learned the things you did to me. I thought I was marrying an innocent girl, but instead I got a whore. Never mind, Lucretia, I shall take you to the train depot tomorrow as planned and you can return to your previous life of daytime lady and nighttime harlot."

Now her anger took over. "How dare you say those things? You know I was a virgin. I watched Ruby, but I never had sex with anyone but you, before or since we married, and I did it to learn to please you."

She stood beside him, grabbing his penis in one hand and his balls in the other. He tried to push her away, but she held firm and dropped to her knees. He had hardened while playing with her pussy and it had not gone away, even during his tirade at her. She took the cock into her mouth and moved her tongue around it. She felt his response, even as he tried to pull himself away.

He could not stop his desire—which she knew—as he began to move with her. When he came, he cried out while spewing his seed into her mouth. The look he gave her was filled with pain and loathing. Had she done the wrong thing again?

He stepped away from her. "Lucretia, we cannot have a marriage based on sex alone. Dear God, forgive me, but I cannot resist you and you know it. What kind of a man would I be if I let you control me like a puppet?"

"Am I allowed to say anything, Jeffrey? I did not marry you for sex. I did not even know what it was until you took me on our wedding night. You taught me so much in those two days. You taught me well and made me want it, and you, even more. Apparently now you wish you had not done so. Well, I will do as you say, only because I do not want you embarrassed by anything, including having a harlot for a wife.

"Hell, Major. I might start jumping every man here soon, so it is a good idea for me to go away. Unless you would like to watch. Or participate? That is a great idea, husband. Go find someone to join us in our sweet marriage bed. Find someone with a big cock you can enjoy seeing me fuck."

Jeffrey had never hit a woman in his life, but he wanted to now. She had goaded him too far. He raised his hand, but stopped when he realized what he was doing. At that moment, he understood why men strike out in anger without thinking. Lord, he was not one of those!

He looked down at her soft, smooth, sexy body; he knew he still desired her and always would. "Yes, I bet you would like that, would you not, Lucretia? Well, I will see what I can do for you. I am sure I can come up with someone to fuck you. Any special requests? I know there must be at least a dozen men out there who caught your eye." He dressed with his back to her. "Be ready to go when I return for you. It might be a good idea for you to clean up now and get ready for your next man. No, wait! I will bring your bathtub and you can give us both your 'Lucretia Bathing' seduction scene." He closed the door softly as he left.

# Chapter 37

She had goaded him until his rage had taken over his common sense and she did not know why she had done it. Was it because he was right? She was a slut hungry for a cock? No, not really. She only wanted *him* and *his* cock.

However, she had hurt him dreadfully, for no apparent reason. As she sobbed into her pillow, she remembered all the hateful things they had said to each other. Her words cut, as she had intended them to. His were in retaliation. Suddenly, as if a light came on, she realized that it was because she did not love him that she was trying to punish him for her own faults. He deserved more than that. She knew him to be a good man, one who really did love her, and who asked only for her love in return. All she could give him was sex, because she felt no such love.

But then again, maybe he really did want to see her fuck someone else. Ruby said most men like that. Lulu had watched two of Ruby's customers share her one afternoon. Was that what Jeffrey wanted? Well, if he did, then she would oblige. Would he enjoy it? Or was he just trying to hurt her? Either way, she would do it. She closed her eyes and tried to picture someone else with her and her husband. The other person was a blur, but she felt her pussy dampen and her body soften in anticipation.

Common sense took over as she wiped away her tears and washed her reeking body with the lukewarm water on the stove, emptying the bowl in a corner of the room. Dirt floor be damned, she thought. She dressed in the gown on the floor, not caring if she looked disheveled and messy. She did not bother to comb her hair, but tied a bonnet over her head. She tossed away her torn undergarments and slid back into the soiled bed and was asleep in minutes.

* * * *

Outside, the wind was picking up as Jeffrey walked quickly across the compound to the officers' office. It was not even five in the evening, but the sky was black with clouds and the only men outside were the sentinels, huddled against the walls overlooking the prairie. He had changed the watch times for the night to give the men shorter periods out in the bitterly cold night.

Through the window, he could see Black Eagle at his desk, lantern glowing as the captain worked, bent over whatever he was reading. Jeffrey's anger had not lessened, but rather built, as icy fingers of the dark night surrounded him.

*I should be warm,* he thought. *In my cabin. Damn woman! She drove me to hitting her. She is not the sweet little virgin I thought I married. She is a manipulative, brazen female with the morals of her friend Ruby. She could not have learned what she knows by just watching. How man cocks sampled her soft pussy? How many mouths have suckled her tits? How many cocks has she teased with her lips?*

Even as his anger grew, he felt desire. Desire to see her do the things he imagined. What was wrong with him…wanting to watch his wife fucking as he ran his own hands over her body? The picture sharpened as he opened the office door.

Eagle looked up, surprised to see his commanding officer come in from the cold, windy night. "Major, what brings you out? I was just ready to retire myself, but if I can do something for you…" He let his voice trail off as he looked at Jeffrey's face.

"Perhaps there is. But let's just talk awhile…man to man, not as officers." Eagle nodded, sat back in his chair, crossed his feet on his desk, and waited.

"Have you ever been married, Eagle?" A shake of the head told him no. "Do you like women? Do you like fucking them?" This time a nod. "When I was young," continued the major, "one of the things I liked best with the whores was going with my best friend and taking one of them together, just the two of us. Well, I liked two whores with me alone, too, but that meant twice the money. So my buddy Charlie and I would pool our money, and in the end sharing one saved us a lot. We both liked it that way and we made sure the woman liked it, too. Have you ever done that? Did you like it?"

Eagle nodded again. "Yes, several times. My friend Daniel and I had an older whore, almost past her prime, but she knew all the ropes and taught us a lot about women and what they like. So, Major, what does this have to do with anything?"

"Have you ever fucked a woman with her husband there?"

Eagle was slow to reply. "Yes, I have." Where was this going? He could not be asking…he could not be suggesting… God, if true… He felt himself harden just thinking of the woman who shared the major's bed.

Jeffrey sat for a long time without speaking. "This is hard for a man to say, but say it I will. I want you to join me in fucking my wife."

Eagle looked into the other man's eyes, trying to read his thoughts. All he saw was pain mixed with a plea. "Are you sure that is what you want? Men have killed each other for less."

The major stood and laughed. "I promise I will not harm a hair on your head…which, incidentally, is past due for a cutting." He stuck out his hand and Eagle slowly rose and took it, shaking it with a firm grip.

"I wondered when you were going to get around to the haircut. All right, as soon as I can. But what are you doing, offering your wife to me? Does she know about this and agree?"

Jeffrey closed his eyes for a moment, remembering their argument. His anger grew again and the need to punish her grew again as well. Normally he was not in the least vindictive, but this time he wanted her to hurt like he hurt. He did lie as he answered, but told a tale as good as any lie. "There are women who…you know…just cannot get enough. No one man can ever satisfy them. My uncle told of one woman who finally said 'no more' after the sixth guy finished her…for the second time. My uncle said she was great. She was ready again after every one of them and they claim she came with every one of them, each time, but needed more."

"Are you telling me that your wife is one of those women? I cannot believe it."

"No, only that she wants more, even if we've done it four or five times a night. She is never really satisfied and I feel like a failure. Tonight I knew she was not satisfied, so I asked her if she wanted another man, too. She did not answer, which I took as her answer.

"I could hardly get one of the enlisted men, now could I? You are an officer and a gentleman and I know I can trust you. I love my wife and she needs…well, I want her to do it. Will you help?"

Eagle was unsure, but picturing her blondness for his taking was more than he could refuse. He nodded.

"Good, I have one stop to make before we go to the cabin. My lovely wife always wants a bath before fucking and I promise it is a sight you will enjoy. So, come, my friend, let us spend a few hours with the beautiful Lulu."

# Chapter 38

The wind rattled the cabin so intensely that it woke Lulu. She felt beside her…no Jeffrey. A flash of memory and their fight overwhelmed her. He was not back. How long had she slept? She closed her eyes and lay still as the door opened. She had not lit the lantern and the candle had burned out, so she could not see a thing. She heard a wrestling of boots being removed as a weight sat beside her on the bed. A hand touched her head gently and a form stretched out beside her. The hand caressed her cheek, then her lips, tenderly, and then were replaced by another pair of lips.

Softly the lips moved over hers, then down to her neck and throat. She put her arms around the shoulders that pressed down on her, now kissing her again. This time, his tongue slid behind her teeth and moved in a way she had never felt before. Suddenly she realized the man was not Jeffrey.

Who was it? Had Jeffrey really made good on his threat to bring someone else to share her body? She pressed her hands to the chest and tried to push him away, but he held her firmly and continued to kiss her until she weakened. One hand slid down to her breast and the other lifted her skirt and ran up and down her leg.

"Stop. Please stop. Who are you? What are you doing in our cabin? Please let go of me." She felt tremors of lust up and down her body and felt a wild disappointment when the caresses stopped. The man rolled away as the door opened.

"Damn, Lucretia, what happened to the lantern? You might have thrown some more wood on the fire, too. Christ, woman. Now, girl.

Can't you do anything without being told? Can't you do anything for yourself?"

At Jeffrey's words, her anger roared to life again. "I will not have you talk to me like that. I was asleep when this—" She stopped to look at the shape in shadows on the bed beside her. "Are you responsible for this person being here? Did you bring him to…like you said you would?"

"Yes, my sweet wife. My sweet virgin wife. My chaste angelic wife. And not only that, I brought your bathtub, too, so that you are clean as a baby for us both. Hell, Lulu, I am hard already, just thinking about it. And I bet your pussy is wet, too."

"What kind of husband are you? What kind of man wants his wife covered by someone else? If you really loved me, you could not let this happen."

"Ah, just the opposite, my dear. I want you to have everything you need." He lit the lantern. "Are you not going to welcome your second lover?"

She turned to look into the face of the man she detested. The man who hated her as well. But this time, his eyes were soft and full of desire, instead of eyes looking at a dung beetle. He touched her hair gently, but looked at Jeffrey. "Major, it appears to me that your wife is unaware of your plan. For me to go any further—well, that would be rape. I have never raped a woman before and I don't intend to start now." He reached for his clothes without taking his eyes from her strained face.

"Mrs. Sawyer, I am sorry to have offended you. I thought this is what you wanted, and only a saint would pass up the chance to lay with you." He dressed quickly and left the cabin without another word.

Jeffrey swayed as he moved toward her. He lost his balance and fell to the floor, where he passed out. She threw a blanket over him and returned to her bed, but she did not sleep immediately. She remembered the soft kisses and caresses in the dark with the man she presumed hated her. She admitted to her own response and knew that if her husband had not entered when he did, she might have gone on with it. No, not *might* have, but probably, surely, definitely she wanted to give in to the lust he created in her. She knew she had desired him and that he wanted her, too.

In the darkest part of night, Lulu felt her husband climb into bed with her. She feigned sleep, but his voice by her ear whispered, "Darling, I know you are awake. I am the biggest lout in the world. I have no excuses but my own jealousy. I was so hurt that I wanted the whole world to hurt, too.

"But, darling, much of what I said was true, I think. You are more woman than I can handle. I know I have let you down—"

She started to speak, but he stopped her with his fingers. "It was not fair for me to think I could take you from the city and drop you in the middle of nowhere and expect you to be happy. I gave no thought to your wants and needs. All I wanted was you here in my bed. And even that was not enough, because I was so involved in my job and the fort that I forgot about you."

"That is not all true, Jeffrey. I—"

"No, let me finish. I have no right to be jealous of your friendship with Ruby. I should have appreciated her keeping you occupied, even if it was not what I would have liked for you to do. The things you learned from her have certainly surprised me and made me wonder if you wanted to do the things you saw.

"Now, I am sure you would like to do more and I can't blame you. And to tell the truth, I like what we do. No, more than like, I love what we do.

"When I threatened to find you a second lover, the truth of the matter is that it excited the hell out of me. I could picture your face in the throes of ecstasy as you twisted and turned and moaned under two mouths, two cocks, two of everything."

He stopped to take a breath and found his lips covered by hers. She moaned as she took his tongue in her mouth and sucked it.

As they joined their bodies and moved toward a climax, he asked, "Would you like that, Lulu? Would you like to do the things you watched Ruby do with those johns?"

Her hips lifted to meet him. "Yes, yes, yes, I would."

"I love you, Lucretia. Oh, God, how I love you!"

"Just Jeff here, Eagle. No major or captain here. Just two horny men and one incredibly beautiful and talented woman who can fuck our brains out. Can you not, Mrs. Sawyer?"

Lucretia watched her husband pour hot water into the tub he had pulled inside the cabin. "No one will hear a thing with the wind. Makes it kind of eerie and special, doesn't it, my wife?" He moved to the bed and took her hands, pulling her up. Without a word, he pressed his mouth to hers and forced his tongue inside. His hand began to undress her slowly, the way they both liked. "Oh, God, Lucretia. I want you. I always want you."

He tore her shirt off and pulled her skirt up. His mouth dropped to her naked tits, suckling one, then the other nipple. She knew she was his to do what he wished, just as every time he took her like this. She moaned as she dug her fingernails into his muscular shoulders.

* * * *

Eagle reclined on the bed, watching, aching with his desire to be the one holding Lucretia. He forced himself to stay still, instead of leaping up and pushing Jeffrey aside. He wanted his mouth on her tits and his hands on her legs. He wanted her moans to be for him.

His cock was harder than it had ever been, of that he was sure. He watched his commander wrap his wife's curls around his hand and run his tongue down her neck. Her head bent back as she pressed her hips closer to her husband, clearly inviting him to do as he wished.

Jeffrey moved away from her and turned to Eagle. "I will finish preparing her bath now. She is ready—I think—if you want her. Lucretia?" he asked. "Are you ready for Eagle?"

Eagle watched her face as she turned to him. His heart jumped up into his throat when she nodded. He arose from the bed and took her into his arms, with his eyes never leaving her. "Lucretia?" It was a question that she answered with her lips, as she opened them slightly and pressed them together. The kiss was soft until she ran her tongue between his teeth, exploring him and inciting him into a storm of desires and emotions. He moved his hands to her breasts, squeezing them gently before his fingers took the nipples between them, rolling them back and forth in a way that was new to her. She moaned again and this time he knew it was for him and him alone. He fought within himself to keep from taking her right then, but felt her retreating. That forced him to let her go, but he was rewarded and rewarded well.

* * * *

Lulu looked at one man, then the other. Slowly, she untied her skirt and let it drop away, exposing the rest of her naked body. "Are you sure about this, Jeffrey?" He nodded as he sat on the bed to remove his boots. "All right then, Eagle, you should get naked, too. But listen to me, both of you. If we are going to do this, then I decide what we do and do not do. Understood?"

They nodded. She moved to the tub, pulling each by one hand. She kissed first Eagle, deeply, and ran her hand down his chest. Then the same with Jeffrey. Still holding their hands, she stepped into the tub and sank slowly into the water. The men could see her body clearly through the water as she began to soap first her face, then her body. She lifted each full breast and moved the soap almost lovingly over each one.

The soap began to cloud the water, but neither man cared. She smiled at them, knowing that her teasing was making them even more horny. She lifted each leg and soaped it before moving her hand into the curly yellow mound between her thighs. Lastly, she soaped her head into a cloud of suds before she rose and settled onto her knees to rinse her hair.

Deliberately, she raised her heart-shaped ass for them to see, moving it slightly. She heard Jeffrey's intake of breath and realized she was aroused herself. She wrapped her head in a towel, then lifted a breast in each hand, offering them to the men. "Anyone want to lick them dry?"

A mouth covered each and began to tease her as she was teasing them. She reached behind them to squeeze one ass cheek. Suddenly hands were all over her…her ass, her legs, even inside her thigh. "Stop now. It is time for you two to get clean. If you want the things I think you will want, you must wash." She felt them reluctantly release her and let her climb out of the tub.

Jeffrey bowed deeply at her, then Eagle. "You first, sir, as I get clean often, as required by my lady."

"In that case, Major, I defer to the cleaner man."

Lucretia thought the whole exchange to be asinine, especially with the incredibly huge erections they wore. She did not say a word, just toweled her hair as she watched first Eagle, then Jeffrey, kneel in the water to wash. Eagle was heavier and taller than her husband and his penis was stouter, but not longer, than Jeffrey's. Ruby said that size did not matter; it was what a man did with it that counted.

She dropped the towel and walked into Eagle's waiting arms while Jeffrey watched from the tub. Being naked against another man was frightening and exhilarating. In his eyes, she could see Jeffrey felt the same way. She raised her lips to Eagle as she put out her hand for her husband. He climbed out of the tub and stepped toward her and let out a gasp as she curled her fingers around his hard cock. She slid her other hand down to grasp Eagle's equally hard penis.

From that point on, it was hard to know what man was doing what to her. The mouth kisses she knew, but those to her body were different and the same. Not knowing was even more arousing. She kept her eyes closed and let the caresses take her into a world of incredible sensuousness that seemed to have no bounds.

She knew the cock that entered her first was Eagle's. His movements felt different, but no less wonderful. Initially he set a slow rhythm, but it built rapidly as she met his every stroke. So different but so much the same, she loved his throbbing cock and how it made her feel. His lips moved down to her neck, where he whispered soft words of love that blew away with the noise of the wind. Not only did she feel lust, but tenderness as well. She wanted it never to end.

Jeffrey knelt beside her head and put his dick on her cheek. She turned her head and took it into her mouth as she squeezed his balls. He moved to lie beside her, with her head on the inside of his thigh so she could suck him while he watched her hips bouncing to meet the man fucking her. She cried out as Eagle thrust into her while holding her legs wide apart. Jeffrey could not stop, arching himself into her open mouth. Eagle was the last to come because he held off until Lucretia dropped back to the bed, indicating her finish.

Lulu watched Eagle's face as he exploded inside her, his eyes closed. Her husband's eyes were also closed where he had collapsed beside her.

# Chapter 39

Lucretia awoke lying between the two men. Both were watching her sleep, lying on their sides, propped-up elbows and heads in their hands. They had stared at each other for a long time before Jeffrey offered his hand to the man he had given his wife to. They smiled at as they clasped one another, hands around wrists. Now she opened her eyes, momentarily confused until recollections of the night before raced through her mind. A blush crept across her face and she reached to pull the blanket up over her nude chest.

"No need to do that. We like you just the way you are, my sweet wife." Jeffrey moved his head lower to flick his tongue out to one nipple before raising it again to press his lips to hers. "Hmm…you taste a bit like the little virgin who loved me on our honeymoon, but I like this taste better. Now you taste like a woman who knows how to please a man and herself, too." His fingers were teasing her nipple, making it harden.

"Jeffrey, do you hate me? I am sorry…"

"How can I hate you for doing what I—no, *we*—all wanted? It was my idea. Maybe I should ask you if you hate me for it."

Slowly, she smiled. "Of course I do not hate you. Either one of you. Honestly, it was incredible. I have never felt so many…so much…so…*everything* ever before. Eagle, I thought you disliked me, but now I think you at least like my body. But, now you two, I need to use the bedpan." She scrambled over Jeffrey's body. "Do not look, either one of you."

Jeffrey's laughter filled the tiny cabin with merriment and Eagle snickered aloud. "What?" she asked.

Her husband said, "After the things we did and felt and saw, how can you be so modest as to need privacy to pee? Only you, Lucretia Lucinda!" Again they laughed, but this time she joined them.

She moved to the tub and intended to step into the cold water to wash. Eagle spoke. "Wait. How about some warm water?" Both men stood. Eagle went to the stove and added wood, while Jeffrey poured the tub water out the door, letting the wind suck the warmth outside.

Immediately the chill caused her nipples to harden into points that actually hurt. "Ah, Eagle, look. Our lady is cold." Jeffrey bent to take one breast in his hand while he sucked her nipple. "Come, man, there are two and one is still cold."

Eagle had waited, obviously, to see how Jeffrey would react to his touching the other man's wife again, but he did not need a second invitation. "Hey, pretty lady," he said. "We will warm you all over." He sucked the other nipple until the hardness changed from pain to pleasure. Lulu sighed contentedly as two hands moved to cup her buttocks. She pushed them again gently and pointed at the tub.

"I want us clean again. Remember, I am in charge now." They nodded and then made the tub ready.

As she stepped into it, Jeffrey said, "If the one in charge is happy, Eagle, I think we will be happy again, too."

Lucretia washed hurriedly, noting that both men were already showing huge erections. She teased them as she cleaned her pussy and breasts, slowly now. When she stepped out, Jeffrey stepped in behind her, but she stopped him. "You men watched each other do whatever to me. Now I want to watch you wash each other. Not full baths, just clean your cocks and that area. And lots of soap."

"Now, wait a minute…" Eagle spoke first. "I have never touched a man's…"

Lulu interrupted him. "Well, now is a good time to try it. I bet you will both like it and I want to watch." She giggled, but they knew she meant it. "No wash, no fuck!"

"We might as well humor her," said Jeffrey. "After all, she does have a point. Seems only fair and it does not make us queers, just horny men."

Each soaped the other as Lucretia smiled at them. "I bet it feels good, too, doesn't it? Come on, admit it."

"I will show you, woman," said Jeffrey as he splashed himself to remove the soap. He jumped to the bed, still wet, dragging her with him. He pushed her to her back and spread her legs. Within seconds, his face was buried in the junction between her legs.

And show her he did. His tongue found her little button. He teased it until she started to move, then put his lips around it and sucked. She cried out as her climaxes exploded, one after another, lifting her hips into the air. Her head rolled back, then from side to side. Her hands dug into his shoulders. She moaned, "More, more, more," until she fell to the mattress, unmoving except for a heaving chest as her breathing slowed.

* * * *

Eagle's cock hurt with desire. He knew that this was really all about the married couple and their need to love and hate each other. He was here as part of that love and hate...he was only a pawn in their game. But to possess Lucretia, he would play any game they wanted. He moved to her side and worshiped her breasts until she opened her eyes again and captured his cock in her hand.

"Jeffrey, fuck me. Fuck me deep and hard. And Eagle, put your cock in my mouth and let me pleasure you, too." Neither man had to be told twice. Eagle felt the tip of her hot tongue flick the end of his throbbing dick; then her wet mouth began to move up and down the length of him while her hand caressed his balls. He watched her wrap her legs around her man's waist to match his movements.

Both Lulu and Eagle knew it was his time. He tried to pull out of her mouth, but she kept him entrapped, even as his cum shot out of him. She swallowed quickly, but still did not release him until every drop was gone. Even then she teased him again, until unbelievably, his cock stirred again.

Jeffrey, who had been watching them, closed his eyes, but Eagle kept his open. He did not want to miss one second of this time with the woman he now realized he loved, totally, no matter what.

# Chapter 40

They slept, briefly, as if some inner clock woke them. Morning was still hours away. The wind still raced in the cracks, chilling their sweaty bodies. Jeffrey leaned over his wife to kiss her bruised lips. Eagle rose to light a lantern, which he set on the floor to give a dim light over them.

"Lucretia," Jeffrey said softly as his lips ran down her neck to her breast. "If you want to sleep, just say so. We can quit, if you like."

As Eagle returned to the bed, she took his hand in one of hers and one of Jeffrey's in the other. Slowly she looked from one to the other. "Will we die tomorrow?" Her voice was low and trembling as she tried to read their faces.

"It is a possibility, Mrs. Sawyer," Eagle answered.

Lucretia Lucinda Sawyer began laughing, at first softly, then louder as the men looked at her. "Mrs. Sawyer. Oh, Eagle, that is the most insane thing you have ever said. After the night we three have shared, you call me Mrs. Sawyer." She began to laugh again and Jeffrey joined her. Eagle smiled and gave a small chuckle.

* * * *

Lulu raised herself to her knees and pressed her lips to Eagle's as he sat on the end of the bed. He wrapped his arms around her to pull her to him. Jeffrey rose to plant kisses on her round pink bottom before moving away. Somewhat sated, he was content to simply watch for the time being.

Eagle lifted Lucretia to her feet and joined her, standing. His movements were slow, not those of a man who had been without a woman for God only knew how long. Jeffrey admired the man's self-control, knowing that just a kiss or two like the others were sharing was enough to drive him into a rush of lust. Eagle traced a line down the side of her face, across her shoulder, and down her arm. He lifted her hand to his mouth and kissed it before sliding her fingers into his mouth. He continued to suck them as his other hand lifted first one breast and then the other.

He bent slightly to pick the woman up in his arms. He began kissing her again. It was strange to Jeffrey to watch her curl her arms around another's neck, but at the same time, it excited him. Eagle laid her down and himself beside her. He continued to kiss his way down her body until he reach the joining of her legs. His fingers slid into her wetness and she let out a tiny sigh.

It was one of the gasps of her pleasure that her husband enjoyed. A rush of jealousy swept over him as Jeffrey watched the fingers moving inside her. Eagle was licking her stomach, then moved down to follow his fingers with his mouth. Lucretia cried out as he pressed his mouth down onto her womanhood.

Jeffrey's cock was swollen now. He stroked it as he watched Lulu's movements with her hips, becoming increasingly excited. Her head moved back and forth on the pillow as she gave in to her pleasures. Only when she dropped back down did Eagle move up on her. Between her spread legs, he slowly dropped his throbbing cock into her dripping wetness. His movements were slow, as if waiting for her to catch up with him.

Suddenly, Jeffrey realized that he was not watching a couple merely fucking, he was watching a man making love to a woman. The man was making love to his wife! How could he have been so blind? He should have realized the man loved her, but he had not. He had even invited him to their marriage bed and shared his Lucretia with him. He loved her more than life, but he had given her body to another. Yet even as he watched, his excitement grew so intense that he was afraid he might come in his own hand.

As Eagle brought Lulu to another climax, Jeffrey realized he was glad this night was happening. He did not understand why, nor did he care. Only that it was giving more pleasure to his beautiful wife.

"Oh, I am sorry, Lulu. I cannot wait." Eagle thrust one last time into her softness before collapsing atop her.

By now, neither could Jeffrey. He none too gently pushed the other man off of her and lifted her to her knees, spreading her legs as his dick slipped into her. "Oh, baby, I feel your wetness and Eagle's cum, too. Now you will feel mine join them."

He began to ride her, not waiting for her to meet him. He forced himself to slow. Eagle moved closer to them and began to stroke her clit again. He lifted her hair from the back of her neck and kissed her. Soon she was moving with her husband. "Oh, harder now. Both of you, harder. Harder, harder." Jeffrey could feel her muscles inside respond to wave after wave of molten lava that raced like ocean waves through her as he spewed his own seed into her.

# Chapter 41

Lucretia awoke when the wagon pulled up in front of the cabin. Both men were gone. She might have dreamed the night before if her aching body did not remind her of the incredible sex, both loving and full of anger.

The voices told her Molly was outside, as well as Corporal Dryer. She vaguely remembered Jeffrey stoking the stove and filling the pails to heat before he came back to bed. That must have been when Eagle left. Her husband had pulled her naked body to him as he lay beside her, covering them both. He kissed her head and whispered that he loved her. That was all she remembered until now.

It was time to go, she knew, but a couple more minutes would not hurt. She poured the hot water into the tub and found it cool enough to wash. She dressed quickly, opened the door, and stepped out, not bothering to close it behind her. Molly sat in the back of a wagon on blankets, with her arms around her knees as she stared straight ahead, still in pain from the loss of her dear Deke.

Corporal Dryer jumped down to assist Lucretia into the wagon, but a voice stopped him. "Help her into the back with the other women. We will cover them all to keep them out of sight and make it appear that you and the troops are making your daily run to the depot."

"Captain Grant." Lucretia turned to glare at him. "By whose orders am I to sit in back with the others? I will sit up front as I always do."

"No, Mrs. Sawyer. You will not. The orders came from your husband, who will be with the rest of the men. This is all for your own good, and that of the ladies. So, please, just do as you are instructed." Without a word, he grasped her at the waist and lifted her into the wagon.

For once, Lucretia did as she was told. She stared at him in total disbelief. Was this the same man who had made such tender love to her just a few hours before? Was he the man who had whispered love words in her ears? Was he the man in whose arms she had lost herself to the throes of passion and delight? This man was the one who once again saw only a dung beetle instead of the woman who had shared ecstasy with him through the night. Then one more memory of the night before wormed into her mind…Jeffrey saying, "I told you she can never get enough."

Lucretia lay on the horse blankets that padded the wagon bed. A tarp came down over their bodies and smelled terrible. It covered the entire back of the wagon, hanging over the sides, leaving some air space for them to breathe. Corporal Dryer lifted the edge beside him and tucked it under his butt, allowing fresh air from around the foot area to move to them as the vehicle moved forward.

"Thank you, Corporal Dryer," said Lucretia in an extra sweet voice. "You are by far the nicest, most considerate man around here." She knew without seeing that his face had turned bright red, even including his ears. "Where is Greta? Why did she not come with us?" she asked him.

"Miss Greta said she would leave if and when she was damn ready. Excuse my French, ladies. She said it is the Indians who had better watch out if they want to keep their scalps. Then she showed me a knife she had in her skirts. Ol' Jim Bowie would be proud of it. So, guess we do not need to worry 'bout her, madam." He whistled a tuneless song as he did every day on the way to and from the depot. The wagon began to roll.

Lucretia did not speak as tears returned to her eyes. The pain from the dismissal by Eagle cut deep, so she forced her mind away from him. She thought of Liz and the secrets they shared. Liz had told Lulu that Jeffrey loved her and wanted them all away before the fighting started. When it was over, she declared, they could come back. She had whispered that Michael had asked for her hand and she promised him an answer on their return. Soon, Lulu drifted to sleep.

She heard a horse move close to the wagon. It was her husband, who had not even greeted her this morning. Did he hate her for what she had done the night before? It was his idea after all, and she knew he had enjoyed it as much as Eagle had…and truthfully, as much as she had. She remained silent, trying to sort out what had changed so drastically in just a few hours.

Jeffrey spoke to Corporal Dryer in a low voice. She could not hear what he said, but the wagon began to roll faster. It woke Molly, as the wheels seemed to find every stone and low spot on the path. They bounced against each other and the sides of the wagon. Suddenly, a shot rang out and the corporal shouted out in pain, but did not release the reins. Instead, he urged the horses to an even greater speed.

More shots, more screams, and frightening howls came from those chasing them. Molly, tiny as she was, bounced and came down into the pool of blood draining from Corporal Dryer's wound. She saw the red spreading onto the wagon floor. She jumped up, screaming, and fell out of the wagon with a bullet in her head.

"Mrs. Sawyer, do not move. Stay down. Let them think our horses are runaways with an empty wagon," spoke Corporal Dryer from the front, where he lay sideways, half on the bench, half on the floor.

Lucretia did not argue. The battle raged around her. Her mind seemed to shut down when she realized that she did not know if Michael had made it to Cottonwood Creek with Liz. Liz, wonderful Liz.

In her semi-conscious state, she did not hear the change in the battle. She missed the increase in shots and the sound of horses' hooves. She did not see Captain Grant and a small group of troopers join the fight. Their arrival changed the tide, giving the army the advantage, routing the Indians.

The wagon turned back toward the fort, driving slowly through the battle scene. She stood finally, at the urging of the wounded corporal, who instantly wished he had said nothing. On the ground beside the wagon was the body of Major Jeffrey Sawyer.

# Chapter 42

Lucretia Lucinda Sawyer moved faster at that moment than any time in her life, past or future. She seemed to fly out of the wagon and to the ground, holding her husband's head in her lap. "Jeffrey, dear God, Jeffrey." Her pain radiated like heat from the sun as she sobbed, cradling him close.

Corporal Dryer dropped down beside her. He had a bullet in his shoulder and another had penetrated his hip. He felt the neck of the fallen man, detecting a faint pulse. "Mrs. Sawyer, he is alive." Then he yelled, "Help, help! The major is hurt bad!"

*I watch from my hill, knowing that the previous hour must have been little more than a nightmare for them all. The fighting was bloody and terrible. Men on both sides were shot, falling from their horses. They cried out in pain. They lay bleeding on the ground. They fought on foot with knives and fists. Some received more bullets, even as they lay on the ground, dying or already dead. It was horrible to see these young men, red and white and black, slaughtering one another.*

*It was not until later that I learned what Black Eagle Grant did.*

Captain Grant had disobeyed orders by following the major and his party. He made this choice only because he knew in his Indian half that those going to the depot were no match for the angry, misused natives. His white half, the army half, forced him to do what he could to save his fellow troopers and the women. That one woman was all that mattered to him. Even as he rode his horse at a full run, the picture of her in his arms, the sound of her pleasures, the cries as she came—all made him curse the animal for not being faster.

The men wanted to follow the retreating natives, but he ordered them to gather the wounded for their return to the fort. He picked up the inert body of Major Sawyer and jumped into the wagon, laying the major next to the other men already there.

Lucretia scrambled unaided into the wagon, dropped to her knees, and cradled her husband's head in her lap. She tore white cloth from her petticoat to press over the wound on his chest. His skin showed no color, either on his face or chest.

Eagle called his horse and tied it to the back of the wagon, carefully avoiding the wounded and dead, and climbed up front. He took the reins and started the column west on its return to the fort. He and the woman did not speak, but she did nod when he placed his hat over Jeffrey's face to protect him from the sun. Her bonnet covered her head from the sun, but did not stop her golden curls from escaping and glistening in the rays from above. He felt a keen desire to run his fingers through the curls and to kiss away the tears running from her cheeks down onto her dress bodice. Hell, he said to himself, dead husband or no husband, he just wanted her in his arms and in his bed again. He forced his mind to what he must do now that he was in charge of the fort.

He knew the major would not survive, even if they had a doctor, which they did not. He had seen wounds his entire life and this one was going to kill the man, pure and simple.

He also knew the Indians would not give up. They would attack the fort and cut off any attempts to leave it again. The depot was not an option because of its distance and the terrain through which they had to go to reach it…perfect for ambushes every mile. All he could hope was that the depot people would notice that Corporal Dryer had not made his daily run and inform the army by telegraph. He knew this was a wild hope, because they probably would wait a week or so, thinking it was just a fluke he missed a day. By then, it could be too late for them all.

As soon as the party entered the fort, he jumped down and started issuing orders. "The Indians will not attack us again today. Six of you take the wagons to the river and fill every bucket, pan, pail, or anything else that can hold water. And I mean everything that can hold water. Do not forget the bathtub and Greta's things and anything Frank has in the stable. Take the horse troughs, too. Now, get to it."

He jumped up into the wagon again, lifted Jeffrey into his arms, stepped down, and crossed the compound to the new house they had not yet completed. He pushed the door open and laid the unconscious man on the bed, carefully undressing him so as not to cause him pain. *Not likely,* he thought, as the major was so close to dead, but he took no chances.

Lucretia tore off her bonnet as she ran into her home. "What are you doing?"

"I am taking off his clothes so we can bathe his body when the fever starts."

"How do you know there will be a fever? He will wake up any minute."

For the first time, Eagle turned to look at her. "No, madam, he will not wake up. He will not wake up now or ever. All we can do now is make his death as easy as possible."

Lucretia ran to him, hitting him with her small clenched fists. "Do not say that! He will not die. He cannot." Her face was red with fury, even as her tears made rivers down her cheeks. He grabbed her hands and pulled her to him. She collapsed in spasms of grief as she sobbed against his chest.

Eagle held her, trying to comfort her at the loss of her husband, whom he thought she loved deeply. He would have been stunned to know her tears were of guilt for the opposite reason: that she did not love her husband.

He felt her breath on the hand he patted her with. He smelled her woman smell and even at a time such as this, he desired her. His penis rose and pushed against his trousers. He was thankful for her heavy skirts the cold required her to wear.

Lucretia forced herself to look up at the man she knew detested her. "Thank you, Captain, for your help and comfort." Her eyes sparkled like blue diamonds through her tears. He bent his head to kiss the top of her head, but when she lifted her face, his mouth came down onto her lips instead, hard and demanding. She pushed him away, or tried to, but her lips refused to leave his. She opened her lips to take his flickering tongue and met it with her own. She felt lost in an abyss of lust as she had never before experienced except in his arms the night before.

Eagle picked her up and laid her on the bed beside her husband. When he realized what he was doing—what *they* were doing—he jumped away from her. His cock rose to tent his trousers almost in front of her eyes. His voice was hoarse when he said, "I will get some water. Take off the rest of his clothes and cover him tightly. Build a fire if you know how."

"Of course I know how. I am not totally stupid, as apparently you think I am. Now, get out of here and leave me with my husband."

# Chapter 43

He left without another word. A private arrived with the water. Lucretia directed him to start a fire and put some of the water in the pot on top of the stove and to leave the rest outside in the cold.

Lucretia took off her heavy clothes as the room warmed, and slipped into a nightie. She started to get in bed with Jeffrey, but felt the heat from his body as she lifted the blanket. A fever, dear God. He had a fever. She reached for her petticoat and tore it into pieces. She ran to the door, opened it, and carried in the cold water. Hot water or cold water? She had no idea. Maybe warm was best…hot would not draw out the heat and cold might be too much. She poured a bit of each into a bowl and began to bathe his burning body, inches at a time.

He moaned every time she touched him. She lifted the makeshift bandage she had laid over his wound and her breath caught in her throat. The wound was oozing blood down his side. Black, ugly blood with clots. It was at this moment she knew that Black Eagle Grant was right. Jeffrey was going to die and it was all her fault. If she had loved him, she could have saved him.

*No, why lie to myself?* she thought. *For once, this is not about me. I have nothing to do with it.* Was there a more selfish, shallow woman alive than she? *Lucretia Lucinda Sawyer, you are damned to hell.*

She moved without thinking. She wet the cloth, wiped his body, and wet the cloth again. The heat he generated seemed to dry out each cloth as she stroked him. A knock on the door gave her cause to look up. “Come in,” she called, unmindful of her attire.

Corporal Dryer stepped inside, carrying a plate of food and a cup of coffee. "Captain Grant told me to bring you this." He gulped as he looked at her breasts through the thin cloth of her nightgown.

"Thank you, Jed. Just put it on the table. I am not hungry."

He gulped again. "Can I help, ma'am? I could do that for a while to let you rest. Please, I would be grateful to help."

Lucretia looked at his face and realized he was sincere. She also realized that she was practically naked. She reached for her husband's shirt lying on the floor and slid it on. It reached nearly to her knees. "Yes, Jed, I really would appreciate your help. But Captain Grant may have other things for you to do."

"No, ma'am. He said to stay and help as long as you want me."

"Then, please keep bathing his body. I think I will eat this after all." She took two bites and had trouble swallowing. The food hit her stomach like a rock and she struggled to keep it down. She arose and moved to the stove to add wood. She paced the floor, aching for the comfort of her aunt and her inability to help the husband dying on the bed. This time the ache was not for her, but for them. She loved Liz, but she knew she did not love Jeffrey. He was a sweet man who adored her, and now she felt shame for not returning his love. At this time, she would have gladly died to give either one of them life again.

Lucretia dropped back into the chair and put her head on her arms, which she laid on the table. Silently, at first, she cried, but soon she was sobbing aloud. Jed Dryer heard her and pretended not to, but it was tearing at his heart. He stood and moved to her, patting her softly on the shoulder. She cried harder. He took her hand and raised it to his lips.

She stood and he pulled her into his arms, patting her back in comfort. He did not know what made him do this, but her pain was so real, he had to help her if he could. At that moment, the door opened and Eagle Grant stepped inside. In one second, he took in the entire scene.

"Well, what a pretty picture. Could you have not waited for him to die before you found another pair of arms and another body to cover you?"

"Wait, Captain," stuttered the corporal. "It is not like that. Mrs. Sawyer was crying and I…"

"I can see, Dryer. Dismissed!" The befuddled young man rushed out of the cabin, red of face and near tears himself.

Lucretia turned to face him. "That was rude of you, Captain. The poor young man was only trying to comfort me. He certainly did not take advantage of my state, like you did."

"Take advantage of you? As I recall, Mrs. Sawyer, you were more than willing to return my kisses and everything else."

"Stop right there, Captain Grant. We are not talking about last night and you know it. That was a million years ago. We are talking about a short while ago." Lucretia was angry now. "You took advantage of my vulnerability and my grief. My husband is dying, but you are ready to step in to fill my bed before his body is even cold. You just do not understand, do you? Just get out of here." She turned her back to him and sat down on the bed to resume bathing Jeffrey's feverish body.

Eagle spoke. "I am not through talking to you and it is you who are rude, turning your back on me." He took one step toward her as a shot rang out. He turned and ran out the door, not bothering to close it behind him. Another shot, then another. Lucretia forced her mind to ignore them as best she could and focused on her husband, for all the good it would do. She jumped when she heard him whisper her name.

"Lulu. Lulu. Is that you?"

"Yes, darling. I am here." He tried to raise his hand. "No, Jeffery, do not try to move. You are badly hurt and must be still so you can get better." She bent to kiss his dry lips lightly. She found a clean piece of cloth and used it to squeeze water between his lips. He swallowed greedily, then began to cough. The water came back out, tinted red.

"Do you want more?" He shook his head no. She took his hand and held it while she continued to moisten his skin with the other. His body had gotten hotter and she could no longer deny it, even to herself.

"Lucretia, shots. Are they fighting?"

"Yes, darling. There is fighting. But you just stay calm and let the soldiers take care of it."

"I have to get out there. I am the commander. I…" He tried to roll off the bed, but his body refused to move more than a few inches before blood poured out of his wound, drenching both Lucretia and the bed before it dripped to the floor. She gently pressed him back and kissed him again.

He gasped for air. "Lulu, I love you." He took one more breath and then his body shut down, leaving her handsome husband dead.

# Chapter 44

Lucretia Lucinda Sawyer sat holding his hand while listening to the fighting outside. Finally, she pulled the blanket up over his face. She lay down beside him with her arm across his chest, her head on his shoulder. He had been so good to her, the best he knew how. She had rewarded him with selfishness and even meanness, sometimes. Would it have hurt anything to answer his questions about Ruby and what had happened then? No, it would not have. He never asked anything of her but the truth and she did not even give that to him. She wished now she had told him the story. In telling, it might have sounded sordid, but Lulu did not think of it that way.

*It was years later that I heard the tale from her own lips. She came to sit under my sprawling branches one spring day, not long after she returned here. From my hill, she could see the cemetery where Jeffrey lies. She spoke to Jeffrey as she looked upward, all those years later. I am telling it to you now so that maybe you will understand and not fault her too much. Remember how young she was, and inexperienced, and positive she loved her new husband. When she met Ruby in the park, they neither one expected to become friends, but that is what happened.*

*"We talked of many things those afternoons in the park." Lucretia spoke as if telling Jeffrey, as if he were sitting beside her under my boughs. "Mostly we talked about sex because of my curiosity and her ability to answer everything I questioned.*

*"Sometimes she asked about you and where we would be living. Rather than tell her, I said I did not know, because I did not care*

*enough at the time to even ask you. All I wanted were the things we did in bed and I could not confess that to her. Actually, I was no kind of wife at all to you, Jeffrey. I suffer even now for the hurt that I caused you, but that will change nothing now. Anyway, I always changed the subject when she asked, steering the conversation to things in the park, fashions, restaurants, shopping, and of course, sex.*

*"When she suggested I watch her with her clients, I was delighted and afraid at the same time. We went to her little room and I hid in the closet behind her clothes. We even set a chair there so I could be comfortable while I watched. It was a good thing, too, because some of her clients came in pairs or more and all that took a long time. The longer she entertained them, the more they paid her, except for the Big-Nosed Banker with his teenie peenie. He always paid her well and came to her every week.*

*"I never knew his name or the full names of any of her johns, nor did I care to. We referred to Big-Nosed Banker by that name only. Anyway, when he arrived, Ruby dressed and painted her face like a clown. He liked to take off what she wore and dress himself in it. She was right, too, about his teenie peenie. It only grew when Ruby pulled it out of the clown costume and sucked it. He would moan and groan for what seemed like hours until he blew his wad, which, incidentally, was huge.*

*"When he was done, he stood up and began to play the role of a clown, dancing and cracking jokes. Ruby would laugh gaily, even though it was not funny at all. After that, she would undress him and help him with his own clothes. He paid her, kissed the top of her head, and left. The whole thing seemed pathetic to me, but Ruby just laughed and said, 'You ain't seen nothing yet.'*

*"I swear to you, Jeffrey, that even though sometimes I got aroused, I did nothing about it. Ruby asked if I wanted to fuck any of them, but I never did. She asked if I wanted them to suck me or me suck them, and I never did. Sometimes, I did rub myself while I*

*watched and every time I would think of you, wishing you were the one rubbing me.*

*"Ruby's customers were often pairs of men or a man and a woman together. The women, particularly, liked to watch their men fuck Ruby from behind while she mouthed the woman. And the men got really excited watching that, too. The three would change positions several different ways until the couple was exhausted. I realized many times it was a married couple wanting more than they could give each other alone.*

*"One time two women came without a man. They brought a funny-looking thing that resembled a penis in a belt. One of them would strap it on and fuck the other, while Ruby used her mouth to make them come. It was disgusting. I asked her if they liked fucking so much, why not just get a man to do it? She laughed and said she did not really understand it either, but suggested that maybe it was because men do not have tits and those women sure did like sucking tits, each other's and Ruby's, too. I told her I did not want to see that again, and she really laughed. 'Maybe you should try it, Lulu. You might like it. I do like it, especially when one of them licks my pussy. Women seem to do it better than men do. If you ever want to find out, I can show you.' I told her no and she never mentioned it again. Many times, I wondered how it would feel, but I never had the nerve to let her do it to me. I think she really wanted to.*

*"The last time I watched her, there were three men doing things to her at the same time. Once they were all naked, she would tease every man with her tits and tongue. When they got hard, she would sit on her knees. One man fucked her pussy, one man fucked in her ass, and the third fucked her mouth. When they all came, they shot their cum all over her and rubbed it in. It was disgusting, Jeffrey, but Ruby said it was good money and really did not hurt her much.*

*"Then she did not show up for several afternoons, but a small boy came to me and asked if I was Lulu. I knew that something was wrong by the look on his face. He handed me a note that read, 'By the time*

*you read this, I will be gone. Do not try to find me. My john today cut me everywhere and pretty bad. I never told you about the sadists, masochists, and those with strange wants, but they are the best paying. If I survive what they do. Good-bye, Sweet Lulu. Have a good life. Love, Ruby.'*

*"I should have told you about her years ago, and to this day, I do not know why I did not."*

*It was a sad story. I hope Jeffrey heard it, because Lucretia really did need him to know, even now. She should have told him before, but humans do strange things. Did she keep her secrets to protect herself or punish him in some way? She probably does not even know that herself. How sad.*

# Chapter 45

Lying beside her dead husband, Lulu slept. She awoke to the sound of silence. She got up, dressed and opened the door and looked outside. There were bodies everywhere, both soldiers and Indians. The outside gate was open and just a short way from the entrance, she could see men digging holes. She recalled a weedy cemetery that direction and realized they were preparing graves. It was just before sunset and already bone-gripping cold.

Without a coat, she walked slowly toward the cemetery, trying not to look at the faces of the dead. She saw Captain Grant digging, along with his men. "Captain, you will need one more grave. My husband died." She spoke quietly, in a voice devoid of emotion. She turned and walked back to her cabin, where she slowly dressed her husband's body in his uniform. It was difficult, but something she felt she had to do herself.

She added wood to the stove again and sat at the table to wait for someone to arrive. "Come in," she answered a knock on the door. It was a private she did not know.

"The captain sent us for your husband, Mrs. Sawyer. He wants all the bodies in the ground before dark." Lucretia simply nodded and turned her head away as the man motioned another man inside. The two of them lifted Jeffrey's body, wrapped the blanket tightly around it, and carried it out to the wagon waiting outside.

Lucretia refused the ride offered by the private. She preferred to walk. She watched without seeing the bodies, including many soldiers, buried, with crosses placed at all heads. Captain Grant said a few words, a gun saluted, followed by a bugle playing "Taps," and then the funerals were over. She walked alone back to her cabin, where she found the mattress replaced and fresh blankets folded neatly on it. She knelt beside the bed and prayed for a long while, asking God to take Jeffrey into his heaven. She kicked off her shoes, removed her bloodied dress, and burrowed beneath the blankets, otherwise fully clothed.

Gunshots awakened her at sunrise. One of the privates knocked on the door with a plate of food and orders from Captain Grant for her to stay inside and away from the sides of the cabin. That made no sense to her, as there was no place to be in the small house but near the walls. What did he want her to do, hide under the bed? At that second, a shot came through the wall, missing her by inches. Badly frightened, she pulled the table over by the stove, followed by the bed. The mattress was heavy, but she managed to get it up on its side and slide it around her as she sat on the floor against the wall she knew connected to the building next door. That same wall held the mattress in place with the table for more support. As long as no one shot down on her, she should be all right.

After a while, she dared to crawl back out to retrieve Jeffrey's shirt and her shoes. It was cold in the cabin. She dropped a couple of small pieces of wood in the stove, grabbed some blankets to put under her on the cold, hard floor, and then climbed back into her mattress cocoon. The stove began to heat and soon she warmed, but her teeth still chattered.

"Stop it," she told herself. She knew the chattering was from fear, not cold. She clamped her teeth tightly together. "Relax, Lulu," she said aloud. "You survived one Indian attack and you can survive another. Or was it two you survived? Hell, who is counting?" She forced out a chuckle, but it sounded more like a cry than a laugh.

"Let's try to keep count of who is shooting whom by the screams and yells of those hit. Yes, Lulu, that is a great idea. I wish I had a pencil and paper to keep track, but I can use my fingers. So let us get started. Oh, dear God, I am talking to myself and answering, too.

Auntie Liz used to say that doing that was the first sign of madness. Seems right because I think I am going mad. All right, outside the walls, a scream…one for our side."

Tears formed, but she held them back, counting cries and screams. Hours passed, forcing her to leave her little protection to use the chamber pot and put more wood in the stove. She lost count of the number of killed or wounded, but she remembered that most of them came from inside the fort.

The sky darkened and the shooting finally stopped. She heard voices, but only a few. The door opened, showing an outline of a tall man reflected from behind by some small fires. "Mrs. Sawyer, where are you?"

"I am here, behind the mattress by the stove."

Eagle walked slowly into the room and peered down behind the mattress. He burst into laughter that sounded like laughter should, not demeaning or insulting. "I declare, you are more inventive than I ever would have thought. Do you have a gun down there with you?"

"No, I did not think of it. Should I?"

"Yes, Mrs. Sawyer, most definitely. You might be able to protect yourself for a while with it, or use it on yourself to prevent them from abducting you."

"Abducting me? You mean the Indians? Do you think they are going to get inside the fort?"

"If help does not come soon, it is likely they will get inside and we cannot stop them. There are too many of them and too few of us. Now, come out of there so we can talk. Here, I will move the mattress back to the bed for you to sleep tonight."

"Will they not return tonight? I think I will stay here."

"No, ma'am, they will not attack tonight. They seldom do after dark. They will come for their dead. They need rest as much as we do." He lit a lantern, moved the mattress, and put some more wood in the stove.

He stopped talking when she stood. Wearing only Jeffrey's shirt and her shoes and under things, she made a funny but exciting picture. Eagle felt his dick begin to rise and turned away so she could not see it. "Do you want me to have your trunks brought over so you can get yourself a dress or something?"

"That would be nice, Captain. I would like a bath, too, if possible. I appreciate your kindness."

"No bath. There is no water except for drinking and cooking. We do not know how long we may be holed up here, unless they torch the fort tomorrow instead of fighting. I will send over a small bucket for you, if you like."

"Torch the fort? You mean, they will light it on fire?"

"Yes, it is easier that way. They have lost so few men—if any—that they prefer the fun of killing us off a few at a time every day. I suspect that they will tire of that game and simply end it. I am surprised they did not do it yesterday, or today, for sure."

At first, their stilted conversation was void of any emotion, as they both were careful in what they said. It was as if they were standing on a fence, each afraid to be the first to fall off. The tone of their talk changed with the mention of burning the fort. Lucretia shivered, not from the cold this time, but from fear.

"Are you cold, Mrs. Sawyer? I can get you another blanket."

"Not cold, Captain, just frightened." Suddenly she laughed.

Eagle looked at her as if she had lost her mind. "What is so funny?"

"I do not want to tell you even. It is such a stupid thing." He continued to look at her, the question still there. "I just had a thought that if I am to die tomorrow, I want to die clean. I told you it was stupid."

He continued to look at her, but gave her a small smile. "Is that your way of telling me you want that bucket of water?"

"Yes, that would be nice. Thank you." Lucretia smiled in return, but it quickly disappeared when she dropped her eyes to the floor. She had not missed the triangle in his trousers. He wanted her, she knew. How could he when he hated her? Eagle realized his secret was no secret anymore. She had seen his hard-on and he was embarrassed. He turned to the door and left without another word.

# Chapter 46

`A few minutes later, Privates Jones and Winters knocked on her door. One carried a trunk, the other a small pail of water. She admitted them. "Put the trunk by the bed and the water on the stove. Thank you both."

They could not take their eyes off her. Lucretia knew she had to get into a dress soon or one of these men might decide to rape her. She did not understand what they saw that aroused them, but it was obvious both privates emulated the captain. "That will be all, Privates." She opened the door and then closed and latched it behind them.

Outside, neither man said a word and tried to erase that vision from their minds. It would never do for anyone else to see their rock-hard cocks. Or else they would need to find a place to masturbate, which was the option they picked. They walked to the stable and stood watching each other skim their penises. "Wanna bet who lasts longest?" one asked but received no reply. It did not matter to either as they rocked back and forth, even more excited by watching the other. When their semen shot forth, each still pictured the beautiful, half-dressed woman.

Had Lucretia known, she would have been horrified and embarrassed. What she did not know was that they were virgins, both of them. They were only seventeen and had joined the army from the farms where they grew up. Winters had no mother or sisters, and Jones had only brothers. They had learned about sex from the animals on their farms. If Lucretia had known this, she would have pitied them. She had learned the wonders of sex and love. At least, what she thought then was love.

The morning brought Corporal Dryer with a plate of food. By now, Lucretia was dressed once again like a lady. She asked him to place it on the mattress as she had the day before. She ate everything, as her last meal had been breakfast the morning before.

When the first shot rang out, she sighed deeply and took cover in her little cocoon, as she thought of it. It was another long day, another long, cold day. She played her counting game for a while, but when the in-fort screams outnumbered the outside-fort yells, she became stressed and then frightened.

At dark, she opened the door and looked out for the first time in two days. There were bodies everywhere. The gate was open and the men carried out the dead Indians who had managed to get inside before dying. That they were so close was incredible to her. Was the army too inadequate to protect even themselves?

She watched the bodies of her own people taken out to the cemetery. She realized that a kind of truce gave both sides time to deal with those who had perished. She stood by the gate, watching the digging from yards away by lantern light. There were no markers this time. She figured that there was simply no time to make them. She hoped that someone would remember who went into what grave later.

She smelled food and located Corporal Dryer in the old kitchen area. "Where did Greta and Frank go?" she asked him as she approached.

"They left while we were on our way to the depot, apparently. No one knows where they went. They were just gone the next morning."

"Can I help you, Corporal? I do know how to cook."

"Thank you, Mrs. Sawyer, but you will get that lovely dress mussed in here."

"Do not be silly, Jed. Dresses can wash, but stomachs need food. Now, let me clean those potatoes. Are you putting them in the fire to cook?" He nodded, flustered by her presence. "The meat on the spit smells good. What is it?"

"Best, ma'am, you do not know."

"Nonsense. What is it?"

He mumbled as he spoke. "Horse. One of the ones wounded in the fighting yesterday."

Lucretia felt herself gag, but she fought it down. It was a horse. *So what?* she thought. *Is it much different from a cow or a rabbit?* Yes, it was. She was ravenous, but doubted she could eat any of it. Thinking so, she found another potato to wash for the fire. She would have a second potato. That would do just fine.

The men from outside the gate wandered in singly and in pairs. She pointed to a bucket of water warming by the fire pit. They looked at her, uncomprehending. Jed spoke. "The lady warmed you some water to wash up before you eat."

Once they understood, they practically tripped over one another to get to the water first. She was horrified that they skipped the towels she had laid on the table, preferring to wipe their clean hands on their filthy, blood-covered trousers.

She walked away a few yards, closed her eyes, and bent her head forward. To herself she said, "Dear God, this is a place fit for no one. I am so afraid I will die a lonely death like so many have done in the past few days. I am the only woman here and the looks from some of these men leave no doubt in my mind what they want to do to me. I think the only thing that stops them is Captain Grant. They are afraid of him, and so am I now. He is not the same man who Jeffrey brought to our bed."

# Chapter 47

"Are you praying, Mrs. Sawyer? I hope so. Pray for all of us, because our time is short." She had not heard him approach until he spoke. He touched her shoulder and she jumped away. "Are you so frightened of me? I am sorry. I will not hurt you, I promise. You do not have to like me, but I would appreciate your respect." Eagle's gaze was unblinking but not unkind.

"Is there any reason, Captain, that I should respect you? I know you feel nothing like that toward me."

"You are wrong, Mrs. Sawyer. I do respect you. When I saw you cooking and trying to civilize the men with a bucket of water, you earned my respect. Now, will you join us for supper?" He left her no choice, as he took her arm and led her to the table. Several men were already eating when they arrived, but when a couple stood like gentlemen, so did the others.

They had started to reseat themselves when she spoke. "Please remain standing. Those of you with hats, please remove them. Now, let us bow our heads." Only Black Eagle Grant stood staring ahead. "Dear Heavenly Father," she said softly, but loud enough for all to hear her. "Please bless our food that it may strengthen our bodies for the ordeal ahead. Please bless those who sacrificed their lives to protect us. Welcome them to your side and everlasting life. Forgive us of our sins. Our Father who art in Heaven…" Only Lucretia spoke the words. Slowly, other voices joined hers, hesitant at first, and then louder until most of the men were praying with her. "Amen. Now enjoy this meal, prepared by Jed Dryer."

She carefully put two potatoes on her plate and one lonely biscuit, which was hard as a rock. She sat beside the corporal and slowly ate. Now and then, she contributed a little to the conversations, but otherwise lost herself in her memories.

Lucretia returned to her cabin to find her mattress already on her bed and water warming on the stove. A pile of wood was stacked neatly within easy reach from her cocoon for tomorrow. A lantern burned dimly on the table, giving the cabin a glow that welcomed her home. She sat at the table with her head on her arms, feeling the loneliness that only a widow or widower can feel. She missed Jeffrey, if only for his presence.

"Come in," she replied to the soft rapping on the door. Once again, his presence filled the doorway. "Hello, Captain. What can I do for you?"

"Mrs. Sawyer, I want to personally thank you for your presence tonight. It boosted morale more than anything I have seen in weeks. The prayer helped a lot, too, for those who believe in it."

"Captain, do you not believe in prayer?"

"Yes, I do, but my beliefs are different from yours. My Indian people pray to many gods for individual needs. For a successful hunt or a healthy child."

"I do not think that is too much different, really. We pray to only the Lord, but we ask for the same things. Tonight again, I will pray for our rescue. What will you pray for?"

Eagle thought a moment. "I will pray for that, too, but I will pray hardest for our messenger to have reached the depot and telegraph office."

"A messenger? You sent a messenger? When? Should he be there by now?"

"Not so fast, Lucretia." He used her first name. She noticed it, but somehow did not mind. "Actually, a messenger has gone out every night since the ambush of your party. We have no way of knowing if they reached the depot or fell into the hands of our enemies. All we can do is wait."

"Do you think, Captain, that any of them made it? If they were captured, would they be killed?"

"Probably not and yes. Probably not made it and yes, killed, in most horrible ways. It is the Indian way to punish enemies. There is much dancing and singing to the gods before the sacrifice begins. Do not ask me more, because you do not need to know more. It sickens the heart of non-Indians who have seen what is left of the prisoners."

"Dear God, Captain, that is barbaric. How can you talk so calmly about such things?"

"Calm down, Lucretia, and listen for a minute. Some die at the stake, burned alive, just as your Bible tells of such things. Some will have water dripped into their nostrils until they drown. Is that no different from the witch hunts in Salem? We could compare such things all night, but it will change nothing."

She dropped her gaze and her anger slipped away. "Captain, are we going to die?"

# Chapter 48

"I hope not, but in all likelihood, yes, we will all die. If we are to die, then let us live one last night. Let me stay with you tonight. No, do not mention your husband. He would want you to live and love one last time, and this will probably be it."

Lucretia looked at Eagle a long time without speaking. Inside, she felt a loneliness that went beyond her body and plumbed the depth of her soul. For her sins to her husband and her selfishness to others, she knew she belonged to the devil. And she saw the face of the devil in the man who stood before her.

She stepped around him and latched the door. He moved to her and lifted her face. He put one hand on each side of it and pressed his lips to her forehead, then her eyelids, her nose, and finally, her mouth. The kisses were soft and sweet.

Eagle moved his lips down her neck and kissed the hollow in her throat. He heard her intake of breath.

She felt shivers run all over her body as he unpinned her hair, letting it fall in golden curls. He buried his face in it and moved his hands to her breasts.

He felt her nipples begin to harden, just as his cock had hardened.

He kissed her again, but with more force. His tongue took control of her mouth. His penis jumped when she touched her tongue to his. He was losing control, he could feel it. He pushed away from her and pulled off his shirt. She looked at his dark, muscular chest and felt the need to kiss it. She pulled him to the bed and pushed him down, dropping beside him. Her lips and tongue explored his upper torso completely before returning to his mouth.

He reached behind her to loosen the ties holding her dress. The bodice dropped to her waist, baring her full tits. They were white with large pink rosettes and saucy, upturned nipples. “Now my turn.” He pushed her back and covered her breasts with kisses, bites, and squeezes. Her breasts dimpled as he sucked the now-rock hard nipples.

“More, please more,” she breathed into his ear. She touched inside his ear with her tongue and he knew he was doomed. He dropped his trousers, pulled up her skirt, and ripped her littles off in one quick movement.

“I am sorry, Lucretia, I cannot wait.” He spread her legs and lowered himself down and into her pussy. “You are wet. Wet and wonderful. You feel even more wonderful than I remembered. Or as I used to dream. I dreamed of you, night after night, wanting you just as you are now…naked and under me. Oh no, not yet, please not yet. I am coming. Too soon. I promise to make it up to you.”

“Never mind later. Now, do it now. I want you, too.” She wrapped her legs around his hips and moved to his rhythm. It was exquisite, better than she had ever felt before. His cock seemed to fill her entire being as she took it and rocked up to meet his every stroke. He could feel her vagina sucking him in, deeper each time. It was more than he could take and he emptied his seed into her. He heard her cries of passion under him as she reached her climax, too.

They lay together, spent. He slid his arm under her and pulled her head up on his shoulder. When their breathing slowed, he said, “That was wonderful. I hope I did not hurt you. I could not wait. You felt too good to stop.”

“No, you did not hurt me. I was as ready as you were. It was good for me, too.”

She turned her face and kissed his neck. He moved his face to nuzzle her head. They both knew it was not over, but he was surprised that her little kisses were making his cock jump.

"Do you know what you are doing?" he asked. "If not, look down." His dick was half hard again.

"Mmm, I see." She ran her fingertips around his nipples. She moved her mouth over one and then the other. He was surprised and found it stimulated him even more, but when her hand continued down across his stomach to take his penis and squeeze it, he groaned. "Do you like that, Eagle?" Somehow now was totally different from their night shared with Jeffrey. She forced Jeffrey out of her mind. Tonight she would love for the last time.

Lucretia sat up and moved to kiss her way down his rock-hard stomach, letting her tongue make a trail from his neck to the hair below. She ran her fingers through the density of his curls, surprised at how soft and fine they were. She blew softly into the hair and enjoyed his response of a quick intake of breath. She blew on his ramrod, too, and touched the end of it with her tongue. He moaned then and even more so when she slid her mouth over the tip.

"I dreamed of this too, but never thought it could happen." He held her head, entangling his fingers in her hair. He did not force her head down on his cock, as she had expected, but instead let her control everything she did. Her lips opened to take his length inside her mouth, but he was too big for her to take it all, so she wrapped her fist around the lower part and moved the skin up and down on his shaft.

"Stop!" His voice was urgent, but stern. "Wait a minute." He reached for her torso, which he turned so that her hips were near his head. He turned toward her, opening her legs. He touched her inside, making her jump. "I think this will be better, because I want to taste you, too." He pressed his mouth into her. She understood, now, and began to suck his cock again.

When his tongue found her clit, she lifted her hips…not intentionally, but in reflex to push against him. Having his dick in her mouth while he worked her button was so sensual that she had trouble keeping her mouth in the rhythm she had set. He took her head by the back of her neck and pressed her down on him. She could feel the tremors building in him even as she felt her own.

She climaxed a second before she felt his eruption in her mouth. He held her head in place, forcing her to swallow his come. At first, she felt she would choke, it was so much. She took it all into her mouth until she sucked him dry. He licked inside her pussy, taking every drop of her wetness into his mouth, using his tongue to delve deeply into her vagina.

Lucretia was exhausted. Eagle turned on the bed, dragging pillows with him. Again, he lifted her head to his shoulder. "Here, sweet Lulu. Sleep." She sighed, kissed his neck again, and was asleep before he even relaxed. He looked down at her face, almost angelic in slumber, knowing that she was the devil he needed.

# Chapter 49

Black Eagle Grant dozed too, only to wake two hours later by some internal clock he had learned to use after spending time in the white man's world. The way of Indians had no clocks, just the dark and light to guide them. Now he slipped quietly out of bed and dressed in the dim light of the lantern they had left on so they could see each other while making love. He pulled the blanket up and covered his woman. He stopped short, realizing he thought of her as *his* woman. She was not his. She was no one's and maybe everyone's. He did not know her at all, except in the biblical sense. She fucked better than any woman he had ever met. She could not have learned all the movements and muscle control from her dead husband. A dozen men on her might—just might—have taught her all those things. He shook his head, trying to banish those thoughts from his mind.

He would not have appreciated knowing he harbored the same thoughts that Jeffrey had…that the woman was no innocent. He shrugged, but bent down to kiss her forehead before leaving the cabin.

This night he would send no more messengers. He knew they were all dead. Perhaps he would be no luckier, but his Indian blood would give him an advantage they did not have. He felt no remorse about their deaths. They were soldiers, just as he was, and it was their job to follow orders. If they did not reach Cottonwood Creek, then in his mind, they had not followed orders.

The fort was quiet. He walked soundlessly to the enlisted men's quarters, where another dim lantern cast its soft glow, making it easy for him to find Jed Dryer. He touched the man's shoulder, bringing him upright and awake instantly.

"Quiet! It is Eagle, Jed. I am leaving you in charge as of this minute. Shake my hand and wish me luck. I am going to try to get to the depot tonight. Now, come and close the gate behind me."

"Damn it, Captain. You will die just like the rest of them."

"No, I think I will make it. First, I will not take a horse. It will be better to just steal one of theirs. If I am not back in two days' time, then you will know I am gone. Our enemy will just keep coming until everyone in the fort is dead. Now, listen, and listen well. Under no circumstances are they to take any prisoners. Make sure that Mrs. Sawyer dies before it is too late to stop them. I recommend that you and whoever is left by then meet your makers the same way. You know how you will die if they get to you first. Good-bye, now."

Before Jed could say anything in return, the captain was gone, armed only with his sidearm and knives. Jed crossed himself and said a prayer to Mary, asking her to protect Eagle Grant, as he followed to close the gate.

Moving like the Indian he was, quiet with no sounds to give him away, Eagle crept in a large circle to the right of the far campfires of his brothers…his enemies. There would be guards around the horses, but by now, he suspected they were probably asleep. Aside from that, he knew they might think it unlikely that anyone would come to the back of their camp, so the number of sentries they posted would be small.

The night was cold and very dark with no moon or even stars, as it had been the past few nights. That was a good thing, making it harder for anyone to see him. On the other hand, it also made it hard for him to see. He stopped every few minutes to listen until finally, he heard the sounds of horses not too distant. He moved cautiously in that direction until he saw the watchman on the ground, leaning against a tree.

Eagle had no trouble eliminating the guard with one swift slice of his knife. He hoped it was no one he knew, but war was war. Within seconds, he cut the rope of the nearest horse and led it farther away from the encampment. He mounted the Indian way—bareback—and urged the horse into a walk at first, until they were far enough to prevent hoof sounds. He pressed his knees to urge the horse into a full run, praying to his gods to let them get to the depot before his mount gave out.

# Chapter 50

The first shots woke Lucretia, just as they had for the last several days. She looked beside her, remembering the incredible night she had spent in Eagle's arms. He must have already been outside for quite some time because his side of the bed was cold. She grabbed a garment from the floor, wrapped it around her body, and ran to put wood in the stove. She was surprised that Eagle had not stoked the fire before leaving, but he probably was in such a hurry he forgot.

From her trunk, she found some fresh clothing that she laid on the bed. She washed with the lukewarm water and then dressed. She had to go outside to tell them she needed more firewood. Again, she wondered why Eagle had not done that himself. She pulled on her heavy coat and carefully opened the door a crack. There were already two bodies on the ground and the number of shots coming into the fort seemed to have increased while the number going out had lessened.

She looked around and counted only seven men firing. None of them was Eagle. She ran as fast as she could to the officers' office and found it empty. On her way back to her cabin, she stopped for some wood from the pile nearby. A voice came from behind her. "Mrs. Sawyer, what are you doing out here? Give me that wood and get back inside."

Corporal Dryer grabbed the wood and ran to her cabin. She followed quickly in an attempt to talk to him before he left. He was already moving her mattress. "Get in here, ma'am. Hurry. I have to get back outside." He had never spoken to her like this before and it frightened her somehow.

"Jed, what is going on? Where is Captain Grant?"

"He is gone. Now I have to go." He did not wait for her next question. He ran out, slamming the door behind him.

*Gone? Gone where? Oh, dear God, does that mean he is dead?* Her mind filled with hundreds of thoughts and questions, none of which had answers. She huddled down in her cocoon, trying to shut off her mind and the sounds of the battle. Realization began to set in. Seven men. That was all she saw. Was that all that was left of the troops? Now she understood what Eagle had said. They would all die today, just like Jeffrey, Deke, Molly, and the others. She lowered her head to her folded arms, resting them on her pulled-up knees. She felt sadness, but no tears came this time. She began to pray.

# Chapter 51

His horse was tired. He could feel its heart beating and the sound of its lungs about to give out. Killing the horse would not accomplish anything, so Eagle slowed the pace, giving the beast time to recover. *Hell, he could run this fast,* he thought. He stopped the horse and slid off its back. He flexed his legs several times, drank deeply from his canteen, took deep breaths, and started to run. It could be no more than a few miles to go.

He knew he was out of shape when he started to feel his lungs burn and the beginning of a deep stitch in his side. The muscles in his legs screamed for rest and his feet hurt in the army boots. He desperately wanted to stop, but every minute counted. In his heart, he was afraid he was already too late. He cursed himself for not doing this ride earlier. He should have done it the first night, instead of sending an inexperienced trooper. He had sent the young man to his death as if he had shot him. At least the man and those who followed him could have died from a bullet rather than the torture he knew they suffered.

He could not let that happen to those few left at the fort. He could not let that happen to Lucretia. How had he let that white yellow-headed female get under his skin? How had he wanted her even though she was married—and married to his commander? How did his dreams always become so real every night that he woke wet with sweat? Finally, he faced the fact that he loved her more than life itself.

Yes, he needed to think about her body and ignore the pain. Think of her full tits pressed against his chest, her downy legs wrapped around his waist, her soft stomach as he kissed his way down to her delightful pussy. Think of her delectable smell, the taste of her mouth, the way her head fit his shoulder, the feel of her arms around his neck, the scratching of his back in her wild climaxes. Just think of her and keep running.

Eagle lost track of time, but the sun was beginning to paint the eastern sky in pinks and reds as he saw his destination ahead. He tried to shout to the men he saw on the train tracks and outside the building, but his voice failed. He had no choice but to keep going. He fell to the ground, exhausted, a few yards from the station, but someone saw him, and shouted.

He awakened on a cot inside the depot. An older woman, ugly with scars he could see up under her veil, was feeding him water. It hurt even to drink, but he had to communicate, so he drank to relieve his parched throat.

"Need to telegraph St. Louis. Tell army we are under attack and most dead. Need immediate help. Hurry, no time to waste." He lay back and waited. The reply was that help was on the way. He wanted to go back to the fort immediately, but his body would not permit it. He closed his eyes and slept the sleep of the dead.

* * * *

The gunfire became spasmodic as the day ended. This evening, there was no burial of the army dead. The three dead Indians remained on the ground where they fell. Only Corporal Dryer and Private Jones were standing. Everyone else was dead.

Lucretia climbed out of her cocoon and walked outside. The two men began to pick up the bodies of their dead to take to the stables. "Ma'am, it looks like we are the only three left. Is there anything we can do for you?"

Scared to her inner being, she forced a smile. "Why, yes, there is. The horses…yes, the horses. Go get them and bring them to the officers' quarters. It is the warmest place I can think of. And blankets for them. Both for over them and under them. We can cover the windows with blankets, too, to help keep them warm. Bring them grain and buckets of water. At least when this is all over, the horses will have lives."

She left them to follow her orders, without thinking they might not. She ran back to the cabin and began to dress against the cold. She put several of her jackets on first, then added Jeffrey's heavy coat. On her head, she pulled on her warmest fur-lined bonnet, followed by one of Jeffrey's. Her skirts she wrapped around her legs before jamming them into her stockings and shoes, over which she forced a pair of her husband's boots.

She followed the two into the officers' quarters as they finished tethering the horses near the stove. They turned to look at her. Their laughter came in a roar of volume that caused the horses to start. "Mrs. Sawyer, are you in there?" Jed asked. "You are wider now than you are tall with so many clothes."

Lucretia looked down at herself, seeing what they did. Her smile turned into a grin as she joined their enjoyment. The laughter released their tension, even as they pushed their plight away, at least for a few minutes.

"We need to get serious again. Water, now, we need water. After the horses have theirs, drag one of the water troughs over by my cabin door. Every drop we find anywhere in the fort, we can put there."

"But, ma'am, it is all frozen solid. What good will that do?" Private Jones looked confused.

"We can melt it with just enough warm water from the stove to break it apart, then we can heat it. But for that we need wood. All you can find, even break up the furniture. It should be easier because it is not frozen solid yet.

"Now, what am I forgetting? Ah yes, food." She sent them in search of water and wood while she went to the cooking shack to look for something…anything she could find. There were a few potatoes and prairie turnips, together with some onions and a variety of spices she found in jars. There was no meat left and she did not want to think what had happened to the mangy pair of mutts that used to wander everywhere. But the vegetable soup would fill their hungry stomachs at least one last time.

The few sticks of wood in the old cooking stove might be enough. She struck the flint to the kindling, both of which were on the table nearby. Soon the meager soup was heating.

"All done as ordered, Major Sawyer, ma'am." Jed grinned. "Anything else?"

"Yes, there is, Corporal. If tomorrow I am going to meet my dear Lord, I would like to be clean. Would you mind dragging the tub into my cabin and putting some water on to heat? After we eat, I will scrub myself clean, although it will be a waste of time if it turns out I am going the other way."

The men laughed. "Not a chance of that, Mrs. Sawyer," said Private Jones. "An angel like you has nothing to worry about."

"I appreciate that you think I am an angel, but let me assure you I am not. I have done things I regret and wish I could forget, but God makes me remember them so I can suffer, as I should."

Corporal Dryer said, "No, I do not think so. The Lord only forces the evil to suffer."

"I think not," answered Lucretia. "If that were true, then why are you suffering from that gunshot wound? Why did it take so much time and pain before Jeffrey finally died? Why did Deke and Molly have to die, Corporal?"

"God makes His decisions to test us. The lucky ones are like Deke and Molly. He took them without pain. That is good. Why your husband suffered…well, I do not know, but the good Lord does. We must accept those things and live the best we can until He is ready for us."

"My goodness, Jed, I have never heard you speak that many words at a time ever before. I had no idea you were so God-fearing. Look, the soup is almost ready. Let us eat before we move the tub and water. I will carry the bowls if one of you will carry the soup pot. There is no reason we cannot be warm while we eat."

She hurried to her cabin and set the spoons on the table. Jones put the soup pot on the stove, along with a bucket of water Jed carried. She filled the bowls as the men moved the small table to the end of the bed so that, with the two chairs, there were three places to sit.

She motioned Jed, with his long legs, to sit on the bed, but he shook his head no. "It is not proper for me to sit on a lady's bed."

Lucretia's laughter erupted like a merry volcano. "Nonsense. Is it any more proper for a lady to sit on her bed with two men not her husband or family in the room? Do you think under the circumstances there is anything proper or improper here? Now, just sit down and eat. I am sorry it is not better, but it will warm us and fill our stomachs. In the morning, none of this will matter, now will it?"

* * * *

Eagle Grant awoke, knowing he had slept far too long. The two hours he gave himself had lengthened to four hours. He jumped up, nearly falling. He was hungry and dizzy. He asked for water. The strange lady handed him a canteen full of cool liquid. He nodded his thanks and started out the door.

"Hey, Captain, where are you going?" asked the telegraph operator.

"I have to get back to the fort. I cannot let them get her. It may be too late already, but I have to go."

"No, sir. While you were asleep, your orders came. Major General Stanley Cotton wired that you are to remain here to wait for him and the troops stopping here on the late train before it goes on to the south."

Eagle ignored him. "Where can I get a horse?"

"Over at the stable, yonder. But did you hear what I said? You are to stay here."

Eagle grabbed the sandwich the telegraph operator apparently intended for his own meal and left the building without another word. Within minutes, he rode by the window, heading east as fast as the horse could run. It would take him hours to reach the fort, but in his heart, he could not believe they were all dead.

# Chapter 52

Lucretia and the men ate in silence, devouring every drop of the soup. Jones gathered up the dirty dishes and utensils. The two soldiers left, only to return in minutes with the bathtub. They filled it with hot water, then cold until she said it felt just right. Lucretia felt the blast of cold air that rushed into the cabin as they started to leave.

"Is there someplace warm where you can stay tonight? I hate to think of you freezing under those thin military-issue blankets you have. At least you can gather up several, since there are so many not being used anymore," she said.

"No place warm, but yes, we can use the blankets," Private Jones replied. "We reckoned we would stay with the horses. Their bodies will help warm us."

"We used up all the wood the last few nights in the barracks. What you used to make the soup tonight was the last of what we brought in before the attacks started. Captain Grant would not allow anyone to look for any after dark, because he said it was not safe to go that far away from here. He said they would not attack us after dark, but that if we were out there, they would enjoy capturing and torturing us. Just for the hell of it, he said. Oh, sorry, Mrs. Sawyer," Corporal Dryer explained. "I guess we can start taking the place apart and burning the lumber and such."

"That is not a good idea. I am sure Captain Grant will be back soon with the army to rescue us. So there is no reason you cannot stay here with me until they arrive. Now, one of you go to the officers' building and bring that whiskey that my husband had in his desk. Look in the other desks, too. They will not care. Oh, and some more blankets, too. When you get back, we will divide the cabin so that you two have half of it and I have privacy for my bed."

As soon as they left and without thinking, Lucretia took off her clothing. She settled her body in the warm water. She bent forward to soap her hair and then rinsed it. She toweled it to remove the excess water before wrapping it tightly while she washed the rest of her body. She lay back as far as the tub would allow, her towel-wrapped head on the back. Her breasts floated as white and pink balloons on the water and her bent knees exposed her legs.

When the door opened, she jumped up, unthinking. The two soldiers stood inside looking at her water-sparkled naked body. No one moved. Lucretia finally recovered enough to ask, "Can you please turn around while I get out? I am sorry. I should have waited until the blankets were hung, but I was so eager…"

The men turned away but the image of her still filled their minds and fed their growing cocks until both men hurt with desire. Lucretia continued talking as she dried herself and pulled on a long flannel nightgown and robe. "It is not like you have never seen a naked woman before. After all, you are soldiers and surely you met many women in your travels. You can turn around now."

"No, Mrs. Sawyer, I ain't never seen a naked woman before," Jed replied. That was not a lie, because the women he paid for the use of their bodies simply lifted their skirts for him to slide between their legs, from either the front or back.

"Me neither, ma'am," said Private Jones. "You are just beautiful. No wonder the major could not leave you alone. We crept up outside, some nights, and listened to you."

"Jones, you shut that up. I am sorry, Mrs. Sawyer, sometimes he is dumber than a rock." Jed's face was a brilliant red. Neither man could take his eyes off her as she finished drying her hair and began to brush it.

Lucretia had no idea how fetching she looked with her face scrubbed clean and her hair curling as she brushed it, lifting her arms.

Her breasts moved upward with her arms and strained against the cloth, showing her nipples like little flower buds.

One of them moaned. Lucretia did not know who, because all she heard now was the sound of the door opening. Standing there, dripping sweat and panting for breath, was Black Eagle Grant. He took in the scene with one look and began to shake his head.

Lucretia jumped out of bed and ran to him, trying to put her arms around his neck, but he grabbed her wrists and held them away. "Did I interrupt something here? Apparently, I did. Well, men, carry on." He closed the door behind him and let himself drop to the ground, exhausted. Even in his anguish, he asked himself why he had ridden the horse to death and ran himself nearly that hard, only to find that she already had replacements in her bed. He was nothing to her, he knew now.

Lucretia followed him, only to have him push her away again. "Go away. I do not want you near me. I thought we had something between us, but it seems as if all I was to you was a hard cock. Go back inside and let those two service you. How many men does it take, Mrs. Sawyer, to satisfy you? Your husband was right about you. Apparently, I was not enough last night to scratch your itches. Go away, just go away."

His words tore through her like knives and were as painful as stab wounds. She stood and backed away slowly, not believing his cruel words. Was this the same man who had loved her so tenderly such a short time ago? Was this the man she dreamed of all night and cried for when she found out he was gone? No, this could not be the same man.

She ran back inside and flew to the bed, sobbing. Dryer and Jones stood like rock statues, not knowing what to do. Jones moved over to the bed and sat down beside her. He patted her back as he had done to his sisters when they cried. She was not his sister, for sure, but she was hurting nevertheless.

Corporal Dryer went outside and stooped beside the Captain. "Sir, it is not what you think. Mrs. Sawyer never—"

"I do not want to hear your excuses for her. She, Corporal, is a slut, no different from the ones who fuck in rooms above taverns. She is just better-looking, better-smelling, and younger. No, get back inside and finish what you were starting to do when I interrupted you."

"Sir, please, no. Let me explain."

Eagle pulled his knife so quickly that Jed did not see it coming. "Corporal, I am telling you this only one more time. You will go back inside and fuck her. Both of you will fuck her. She will like that. Hell, I will just sit by and watch. Maybe I can learn something about how to please a woman."

"Sir, you can use that knife on me, but I will not force myself on her or any woman."

Eagle lowered the knife and turned away from the corporal, ashamed of what he had said. His was an emotion of pure jealousy as he thought of her giving herself to anyone else, even as he remembered how she had given herself to him both before with her husband and after his death as well.

# Chapter 53

Both men returned to the room. Eagle took a chair and leaned it back against the wall on two legs. "Lucretia, turn over and look at me." She did not reply. "Very well, then, we will do it another way. "Jones, stand her on her feet and turn her so I can see her face. Very good. Now remove her clothes."

Lucretia looked calmly at Eagle, eyes now tearless. "Is this what you want, Captain? Do you hate me so much you will have these young men rape me while you watch?"

"Since when do you have to be raped? I have seen no sign of that before. I am tired, but if that is what you want, I can do it myself."

"No, Captain Grant, that will not be necessary." Lucretia's voice was cold. Her eyes narrowed into slits of sparkling midnight as she looked at him. Her hate was evident and he basked in it. "What you are doing to your soldiers is wrong, but since it is an order, I think it only fair that they enjoy themselves."

"The water is still warm, Corporal Dryer. I suggest you take a quick dip, as the lady likes her men clean. Then you also, Private. Would you like her to wash you? She does it very well, as I recall." Eagle's voice filled with loathing as he looked at her, standing brazenly naked in front of them all. The men stripped and stood, trying to cover their genitals with their hands. Jed stepped into the water and sat down, legs over the end. "Just clean your faces and your cocks. Never mind the feet and legs. She will probably not suck you there. At least, I do not think so."

Lucretia never took her eyes from his as she sank to the floor and began to wash Jed, first his face, and then down his body. He moaned as her hand touched his penis and even more when she soaped him. In his life, never before had he felt anything to compare to her ministrations. He cried out, ashamed, as his semen exploded outside the tub, hitting the wall with force.

"Good, Dryer, now you will have more lasting power for the next bout. Out now, and Jones in." Eagle met her gaze from a face as unmoving as a mountain.

Jones fared no better than his friend, but his explosion dropped his cum onto the floor at the end of the tub. Lucretia stood. "Now what?" she asked Eagle in a soft voice.

"I think I will let you direct them in the ways of pleasing the beautiful Mrs. Sawyer. Maybe if you do it well, I just might fuck you again myself. Would you like that? Yes, of course you would. Never too many cocks for Miss Lulu."

Her nickname was reserved for only those who loved her and she reacted. She ran toward him and dug her nails into his face, drawing blood. "You can call me every filthy name in the world, but do not call me Lulu."

He caught her wrists as he had done before, squeezing them so hard she bit her lip to keep from crying out. "As you wish, Mrs. Sawyer." He stood, holding her with one arm while he stripped away his clothes with the other. He bent his head to press his lips to hers, forcing his tongue inside. She struggled, but could not break away from him.

As suddenly as she had attacked him, she stopped fighting and pressed her tits against his chest. His intake of breath told her what she wanted to know. She felt his cock push against her. "Wait," she said. "I want to do this right. Come here, both of you." She took one of the young men's penises in each hand before dropping to her knees to take Eagle's hard cock into her mouth.

The young men both hardened the minute she started moving her hands on them. They watched as her mouth slid up and down on Eagle's dick, each man praying she would do that to him. She looked up at the captain's face. "I think, sir, that since these two young men are virgins and we are all to die tomorrow, it seems like they deserve one real fuck before that. Can you wait for your turn a bit later, Captain Grant? You have more staying power at your age, I think."

She stood. He knew the age comment was an insult. He smiled and nodded. She turned to face Jed. She slipped her arms around his neck and pressed her body to his. She moved her tits against his chest until his moan and hard cock announced his desire to come. Jones did not need instructions as he moved to return her embrace, rubbing his cock against her.

She led the young men to the bed by their cocks. "Lie down on your backs. We will have some fun now." She knelt between them, taking one cock into her mouth, teasing it before moving to the other. "Do you like that?" Groans were her only answer. She moved upward, kissing one mouth while pressing the other's hands to her tits. When she switched to the other mouth, the other hands replaced the first set. She let them kiss and rub her for several minutes.

She moved again. This time she sat astride a pair of hips and lowered her pussy down on the throbbing cock below. She pressed her tits against his chest and teased his mouth with hers. She rocked back and forth until the man exploded into her before she moved to the other one. When they were both empty, she stood looking down on them as their cum ran down her legs. "If you want to do it again later, we will have to get permission from your commandant."

She moved back to Eagle and bent to take him into her mouth. As he hardened, she reached up to gently scratch his chest and pinch his nipples. She stood to straddle his hips and let his cock find its way inside her, still wet with the semen from the other two. She sat down when he started moving and pressed against his chest, sliding her arms around his neck. She kissed him deeply and moved with him. This time, it was not a boy inside her; instead, it was a man. All man and the man she wanted. Her passion began to build as she rocked.

His hands on her waist moved down, one to under her ass and the other between her legs.

She moaned and tossed her head back and forth, tossing her hair into a mass of wild curls when she reached her first climax, crying out the "more, more, more," they had heard outside the walls of the first cabin. Watching and listening to the major and this woman had been exciting, but actually seeing her ride the captain's giant hard-on was beyond their wildest dreams and their dicks responded, too.

Eagle Grant hated the woman he fucked, hated her with his entire being, but he could not get enough of her. He watched her face as she came and smiled to himself. At least he could say he gave her what she wanted. However, he knew she gave him what he wanted, too. He buried his face between her breasts as his hips pushed up into her once last time, bursting with cum. She sagged against his chest and he held her tight. He was sated physically, but he did not want to let her go.

Still in his arms, she lifted her eyes to his. "You do not understand, do you, Captain? You just do not get it. I am so sorry for you."

# Chapter 54

The sound of horses told them their rescuers had arrived. The enlisted men quickly donned their clothes, both wishing it might have arrived much later. Eagle lifted her off his lap, stood her up, and reached for his pants. None of them wanted the night to end, because it would never happen again. They ran out, leaving the door open behind them.

Lucretia climbed quickly into her bed and drew the blankets up to her neck. She was physically sated from the almost combat-like coupling with Eagle, but her mind ran wild. Slowly, she realized that Captain Grant knew reinforcements were coming, but he did nothing to distill her fear that they would die tomorrow. He manipulated her into sex with him, and even worse, with the naïve young men.

The joining she did with Jones and Dryer was nothing more to her than an exercise in physical contact. She felt nothing beyond a selfish satisfaction that she gave them a gift of her body rather than have them die without knowing the pleasures of a woman, and forcing Eagle to take her again, this time in anger and hate. She tried to convince herself that it was rape, but deep down, she knew she could have stopped it if she had wanted to. Instead, she wanted her life to end with the juices of her lovemaking with Eagle drying inside her.

Her anger built, knowing he had used her again, but she could not deny that fucking him was not without pleasure. Dear God, what was wrong with her? Her husband was dead and she had betrayed him within hours with a man she did not even like—not once, but twice.

Outside the door, she heard voices. She recognized that of Eagle, who called out, "Mrs. Sawyer, may we come in?" He never asked before, so why now?

"No, go away. I never want to see you again."

"Please, may I come in? I am Major General Stanley Cotton from St. Louis." He did not wait for her reply, but stepped inside. "My condolences, Mrs. Sawyer. Your husband was a great soldier and a good man. When we finish with these renegades, I will personally escort you back to St. Louis."

The general saw nothing but a riot of blond curls and a pair of wide eyes peering at his from the face of an angel. If he had seen her just a short time ago, he would not have believed his eyes at the things she did to and took from the three men. She had been anything but the angel he saw…she was the devil who took control of a man and drained his soul, leaving him to want for more.

In a small, timid voice, Lucretia said, "Oh, thank you, General Cotton. I will be so grateful to turn myself over to your competent hands. The captain here said we would die today, but you will not let that happen, will you?"

"Indeed not, Mrs. Sawyer. It is as I telegraphed the captain yesterday, my troops and those from three other forts will be an army so large that we will rout them tomorrow and that should end the conflict once and for all." He tipped his hat and left the cabin.

"Look at you," growled Captain Grant. "You lie there, looking so damn innocent with the general ready to eat out of your hand, or eat you instead. If he could feel the dried semen all over your body, he might think again. Or smell the leavings of three men you fucked."

"Stop right there! You were one of those three men. You lied to me, you used me, and now you condemn me. You let me think we had no hope for rescue, when you knew help was on the way. What kind of man are you? You are not fit to wear the same uniform as the general and Jeffrey."

"Oh, so now you want to talk about your dead husband?" His voice was so cold she felt a chill. "That is a subject you best leave alone, like he is in his grave. You used him and he loved you. What did you give him in return except your body, and obviously, you give that to whoever wants it." He spun around and left the cabin, shutting the door softly behind him.

Lucretia's anger and self-loathing kept the tears at bay. Instead of crying, she jumped up, locked the door, and wrestled the bathtub to its side, dumping the water on the floor. It spread, but quickly ran down through the cracks, disappearing below. She put the last bucket of water on the stove to heat while she stripped the blankets off the bed, piling them in a corner. She had used the blankets the men brought earlier to warm them the long last night they were to live, to cover her bed.

When she finished her bath, she dumped the smelly, soiled blankets into the water. That would wash away the evidence of what they had done. She put her nightgown back on and laid out a warm outfit for morning. She crawled into bed again, but this night was not for sleeping. It was for tossing and turning, for listening to the arrival of more soldiers, for sweet dreams, and for painful nightmares. She was awake again long before reveille, thankful the night was over.

The Indians did not attack the fort that day. Their scouts relayed the information that they were now far outnumbered, so instead, they retreated, even before daylight. Eagle and two other scouts followed them for three days until they camped far away from the fort. Eagle and one other man stayed near the camp, while the third one reported back to General Cotton. While they waited, the general and a large contingent escorted Mrs. Sawyer and her trunks back to the depot. He would miss her company, as he found her most charming as well as beautiful. He felt protective of her, much the same way he felt for his own daughters.

The Kansas City-bound train arrived that afternoon with only a few minutes to spare, barely time to thank the general for his assistance. Lucretia bought her ticket and waited as the train slowed to a stop. As she stepped toward the coach, having seen that her trunks were properly stored aboard, she heard a soft voice behind her. "Lucretia, is that you?"

# *PART II*

## Chapter 55

Lulu turned to face the veiled woman with the soft voice. She knew who it was, but did not reply. Instead, she opened her arms and welcomed her dear Ruby, whom she thought was long gone, or dead even. They hugged and kissed and cried and laughed.

"Where have you been, Ruby? I looked for you. I went to your place and it was empty. Why did you leave without a word? I missed you so much."

"Let us sit down and we can talk. First, I am here because I was trying to find you. I heard you had left the city to join your husband, so I decided to see for myself. I had no idea how dismal and forsaken it is out here. I arrived in this place…wherever it is…and tried to get to the fort, but they told me about the attack and all the deaths and that no one was alive. I decided to go south to New Orleans, as there is nothing left for me in St. Louis.

I was waiting for the train when an incredibly handsome man ran into this place. Ran, and I mean that literally, Lulu. He was practically dead with exhaustion, but managed to get his telegraph sent to the army before he dropped. He collapsed on the cruddy cot over there and slept for a few hours. He awoke and mumbled about sleeping too long. He wanted a horse to return to the fort. The telegraph man told him his orders were to wait for reinforcements, but he just ignored him. It was not five minutes before he raced that poor horse at full speed back out of town."

"Whoa, slow down, Ruby. We have all the time in the world to talk later about that. I want to know now about you."

"Later, Lulu. Here comes the train. Please come with me. Let us go to New Orleans together and start our lives over." Ruby stopped talking. Her eyes reflected her unseen face, still veiled. "I saw your aunt Liz carried onto a northbound train, accompanied by an army sergeant, but I did not talk to them. She appeared to be ill, but well enough to sit up and smile at the man."

"That is wonderful. Then she is recovering. She had to have her appendix removed, but it became infected. It was doubtful she would make it this far, let alone be well enough to travel to St. Louis. That man wants to marry her and I suspect she will say yes. I must send her a telegraph right now, telling her I am alive and going south for a while."

They sent the wire and waited for the train.

"Now, Jeffrey. Tell me about him."

Lucretia shook her head. "He is dead. He and some of his men were escorting me and another woman to the train when the Indians attacked. Jeffrey was the first military man shot, but he did not die right away. He suffered many hours in a lot of pain. He never did know I was not the wife he thought he had married. He deserved a loving wife, but instead he got me."

Ruby stood and walked to the ticket window. "I need another ticket to New Orleans. Make sure Mrs. Sawyer's trunks are removed from the northern-bound train and moved to the southern one." She returned to Lucretia. "Yes, we will start new lives. Why, we can even change our names if we want, and no one will know. Come now, little darling, stop thinking about the past and think of the future."

They boarded the train and found their seats in a car with no other passengers. They had a private sleeping room, but that was for later. The conductor brought them coffee and Ruby ordered two shots of whiskey, too. "It will relax us and make it easier to talk. Actually, Mr. Conductor, make them doubles."

"Ruby, I thought we were friends."

"Why, honey, do you say such a thing?" She giggled. "It is not just anyone I allow to hide in my closet and watch me do…well, all those things. But seriously, of course we are friends. Why would you doubt it?"

"Quite simply, because you disappeared without more than a small note. No explanation, really, or information. I wanted to find you, but you were gone. I went to your room. There was nothing there. Your landlord said only that you had moved on and would tell me nothing, either. Why, Ruby? Nothing could be so bad you could not share it with me."

Ruby hesitated before lifting her veil. The scars were still fresh enough to be brilliant red. Her cuts crisscrossed her face. Lucretia counted nine. "If you think these are bad, Lulu, wait until you see the rest of my body."

Lucretia kept her eyes on her friend's face before moving to make direct eye contact. "Did you think I would not take care of you? That I would abandon you? Oh, my God, Ruby, how did you stand the pain? Who did this? Tell me what happened."

Ruby dropped the veil back in place. "It was just another john, but a new one. I was having a drink at the Cattle Club when he approached me. We talked for a while and he was quite gentlemanly. He agreed to my price, even promising a little more for something special he wanted. This was not the first time someone wanted 'something special' and always before it was something like licking cream off my tits or sucking my toes. You know, that kind of thing.

"This guy wanted to tie me up. That was all right too, a lot of men want that. Makes them feel dominant or such. Anyway, he tied me, naked, naturally, to my bed, and stuffed my mouth with my underwear. By that time, I began to worry, but it was too late. He pulled a knife from his jacket and slowly, without a word, began to cut me. One of my neighbors saw him leave and noticed the blood on his clothes, so she peeked inside. That is all I will say about that part of it.

"When I woke up, I was in a hospital bed, in unbearable pain. They gave me drugs and treated me like a baby, but it still hurt. I wanted to die and begged them to give me something, but they refused. Later, I found out I had been there for two weeks. That is when I sent you the note. I knew you would wonder. However, that was not the worst of it. The drug they gave me was laudanum, so when they stopped treating me with it…well, getting over it was worse than the cuts. It took several really bad weeks more to get past that. Again, there is nothing more I will say about that."

Lucretia listened to her friend, never taking her eyes away from Ruby's veil. Tears slid down her pink cheeks and soaked her dress bodice. Finally, Lulu stood up and bent to embrace her wounded friend. She held her so tightly that Ruby nearly cried out from the pressure on her scars.

"Ruby, I love you. Please let me take care of you. You are all I have in the world."

"No, Lulu, let us take care of each other. Now, drink your whiskey so I can order us another and we will talk of better things." She laughed. "If we can think of any."

They rode in silence for a time, watching the barren land rush by. Now and then, they crossed a river with trees and houses nearby. Horses, cattle, and buffalo ran freely and an occasional cowboy raised his hat in a salute as the train passed. Maybe it was not a salute, exactly, but a wave of indignation, as many ranchers disliked the railroad and tolerated it only because it helped move their cattle to market.

Lucretia's money made the trip bearable because they had their own sleeping room with benches that made into beds, with storage for their luggage above and room service for their meals, if they chose. Even then, they felt the cold until the conductor came with a small woodstove that slowly warmed the room.

Ruby finally spoke. "After I recovered enough to leave the hospital, I had no money left and no way to earn any. I tried to get jobs…bartending, hotel maid, washing dishes, scrubbing chamber pots, anything, but my scars and the veil always got me only a 'not hiring.'

"A scarred whore attracts no customers. Once in a while I might be lucky and some man got excited about having a mysterious veiled female, but that would end immediately once he saw my body. Even in the dark, they could feel my scars. I only had one customer who actually liked it and he came to me several times a week. He paid me well enough to cover what little I ate and the tiny room I found. I could have subsisted on that until the night he wanted to add to my scars.

"I had no choice but to run. I had no friends anymore. The only place I could think of was to run to you. I was waiting at the depot for the wagon that was supposed to run daily from there to the fort. I planned to send you a note. If you did not answer, well, truthfully, I had decided to just walk in front of the next train."

Once again, Lucretia hugged her friend. "How could you think I would not want you? That is so silly."

"It was not just you involved. What would your husband think of an old, scarred whore as your friend? What about Aunt Liz?"

"None of that matters a whit now, Ruby."

"Yes, it matters to me. Tell me."

"I honestly do not know. It would not have made any difference, anyway. You are my friend and that is all that counts. Truthfully, I think Liz would have no problem with it, other than that I watched the things you did. Jeffrey, on the other hand, already knew about it. I told him during one of our frequent fights. He was so jealous he even dreamed of me with other men, so I wanted to hurt him when he tried to rape me. I did hurt him, more than even I could have imagined. I do not think he ever recovered from his disappointment in me, even to the day he died. We never made up after that. I think he wished for the wife he thought he wed, not the real one.

"Honestly, I realized only a few weeks after I got to the fort that I did not love him. Oh, I did love the sex part of it, but that was really all we had in common. He was handsome, charming…everything a young girl could ask for in a husband. There was no conversation about books, music, and such. Instead of talking about things that interested me, he talked only about the army, weapons, enemies, and those kinds of things. My interests were nothing to him or his to me. No couple was more ill-suited than we were. If it had not been for Aunt Liz's presence, I might have just walked out into the prairie and let the land take me."

*What did you and Eagle have in common, Lulu?* she asked herself. She pushed the question away and resumed her story.

"It was a cold and miserable place and I complained constantly, making it sound like everything was his fault. Actually, it was my own fault, for expecting a man I knew a few short days to be a perfect life companion. I cannot tell you how sorry I am for his death or how guilty I feel for the time we spent together. I know that he was distraught and let his guard down on our trip to the depot, or we would not have been ambushed and no one would have died. So, Ruby, you see, my guilt is for more than just my betrayal to my husband."

Ruby looked deeply into her friend's eyes. "There is more, I think, Lulu. Do you want to tell me the rest?"

"Later. We have been talking for hours and I am hungry. How about you? Shall I ring for the conductor, or do you want to go to the dining car?"

# Chapter 56

They opted for the dining car. It was only one car away from theirs, but Lucretia felt out of place as they walked through it. On either side of the aisle were seats, most of them holding rough-looking men and women who either ignored the two women or shot them unfriendly looks. The railroad company had made a mistake placing this car between the ones with berths and the dining room. It was obvious to Lucretia that these riders had no money for food and that they knew she and Ruby did. For the first time in her life, she felt resentment from others for her affluence, and it was not a good feeling.

Their meal was better than expected and actually included a small bowl of vegetables, a rarity outside big cities and farms. "You are so quiet, Lulu. Is something wrong?"

"Actually, I am feeling bad. Those people have nothing to eat and we are sitting here gorging ourselves. Wait, I have an idea." She rang for the waiter. "Go to that coach and count the number of people there, then go to the kitchen and make sandwiches—two for each—and pass them out back there. Add the cost to my bill."

"Madam Sawyer," said the waiter, his hand trembling. "I do not think we have that much bread, and the others will be expecting it with their meal tonight. This is quite unheard of."

"Well, you have heard of it now. I couldn't care less if the other diners will miss their bread tonight. There are plenty of other things for them to eat, as you listed when we sat down. Besides, there will be bread available at the next stop, I am sure. That should be soon, as it seems to me this train stops at every place there is a building. Now, enough of your argument. The sandwiches, one with nice sliced beef and one with ham for each person. Oh, yes, and cake, a piece of cake for each. Did not Marie Antoinette say something about giving them cake? So, give them cake, my man, and do it now. I will wait to see that it is done as I instructed."

The frightened man raced to the kitchen. The chef started to come through the door, but when he saw Lucretia's determined expression, he returned inside. In a remarkably short time, the waiter returned with a heaping tray of sandwiches. He stopped beside Lucretia and waited for her nod to continue.

He returned with an empty tray and a huge smile on his face. "Madam, I have been instructed to thank you."

"You can express to them that they are welcome when you return with their cake. I will add my appreciation to you when I pay my bill."

She and Ruby received shouts of thanks and appreciation as they walked down the aisle to their car. They pressed hands to those who offered until, thankfully, they reached the other door.

A large woman with an incredible amount of makeup stood just inside in the aisle so they could not pass. "Well, what have we here? Are you passing yourself off as a saint or something? If you have extra money, why not share it with your own kind, rather than this riffraff? How about a game of five-card stud?"

Ruby pushed past Lucretia to confront the woman. "Well, hello, Mrs. Kraft." She turned a bit to those watching. "She calls herself Mrs. Kraft, but be reassured there was never a Mr. Kraft. Mrs. Kraft left St. Louis with the law on her ample ass and a purse of other folk's money. You have all heard of the harlot with a big heart, I am sure. Well, now you have met a whore with no heart at all. Ladies and gentlemen, meet Mrs. Kraft."

With a flourish, Ruby pushed by the dazed woman, pulling Lucretia behind. A roar of laughter and derisive shouts followed them as the door closed behind them. They were still laughing when they closed the door of their cabin and slipped the lock for the night.

# Chapter 57

It was easy to sleep, at least for Ruby. The clickity-clack of the wheels on the tracks and the swaying of the car put her to sleep within minutes. For Lucretia, they were reminders of the life she was leaving. She pictured her sweet Jeffrey as he had been on their honeymoon, but the picture would change into the demonic depiction of Black Eagle Grant. Instead of Jeffrey's straw-colored hair, there was the dark brown from a blond mother and an Indian father. Instead of light skin, there was a sun-baked color. When the picture slid to the groin, she sat up abruptly. She forced her eyes open and cursed herself that she could even consider comparing them there. *Each in his own way was far superior to the other,* she thought.

Stop it, she told herself. Only Jeffrey mattered. Forget Eagle. Forget the night you spent loving them both and how wonderful it had been. Forgot those penises, just as you forgot the two men you fucked in front of the devil. Actually, Lucretia had no memory of even doing them, beyond the fact that she knew she had. It was like a bad dream, all of it. She got up, relieved herself in the chamber pot, and slid back the curtain a bit so as to allow her to look out at the moonlit night of the ever-changing landscape.

Even in the relative darkness she could see that the land was no longer so flat and that there were taller trees and thicker forests. Once in a while, she saw a light in the distance. Their stops along the way came more often and for longer periods, as the towns seemed to get bigger.

She now questioned her decision to go to New Orleans with Ruby. She should have gone back to St. Louis to care for Auntie Liz. Not that Michael would not care for her, but once again, she let her own selfishness make her justify what she did. Aunt Liz would forgive her, no questions asked, and Lucretia knew it. Obviously, Aunt Liz loved her far more than Lucretia loved her aunt. In her entire life, she realized that it had always been that way. Even Ruby gave her friendship and helped the selfish young bride and asked nothing in return. Others gave and Lucretia Lucinda took, never thinking of anyone but herself.

With Jeffrey, it had been the same. He gave, she took, and blamed him for her failure. Eagle's face suddenly appeared in the reflection in the window where her own face had been. It was the face beside her on the pillow. It was the face softened by sweet sex. It was the face that kissed her so softly and nuzzled her hair. It was the face of the man whose name she cried out for in the night. As she watched, the face changed into the hard mask she saw the evening he gave her away as if she were no more than a pair of old boots.

*No, not this time,* she thought. *I am not at blame this time. He refused to listen to me. He used me. He hurt me. No, this time, I gave to him and he treated me like...like...like I have treated others. Oh, dear God, please forgive me.* She cried softly until there were no more tears and fell asleep with her face pressed against the window.

Ruby was awake and heard Lulu crying, but she did or said nothing. The wise woman that she was, she let Lulu handle her pain in her own way. The trip would be over soon and with it, the opportunity to find out who or what had caused her sweet Lucretia such misery.

After breakfast in their car, they took turns in the bath down the corridor. "Ah, Ruby, it is so nice to have water again, at least for a bath every other day. I swear the minute we get our own place, we will never have to scrimp on water consumption, even if it means dipping in one of those swampy places…what did the conductor call them? Bayou, yes, that is it. Even if we have to dip in bayous."

Ruby laughed. "I guarantee you will change your mind when you see one. Let us go to the smoking car, where the windows are bigger. Perhaps we are far enough south now to see them."

This was their first visit to the comfortable car reserved for those who had accommodations in the berths, not the regular seats. The chairs were red velvet with gold trim that matched the heavy window coverings, now tied back for viewing the land that was foreign to Lulu.

Ruby once lived in the city for a few years with her then-husband, a suave gambler who had died at a casino table when his sleight of hand met with a small handgun from under that same table. She decided she had worn out her welcome, too, when she was fortunate enough to be arrested rather than shot for the same thing. The judge agreed to release her if she promised to ply her trade elsewhere. She felt it was safe after all these years to return. Once they were settled, she would show everything and everywhere to Lulu.

In the meantime, Ruby pointed out special places and answered as many of Lucretia's questions as she could. When she failed to know the answer, a kindly gentleman, more Ruby's age than Lulu's, offered to help. Soon the three of them were conversing like old friends. Ruby detected almost immediately that the gentleman, who introduced himself as Devereaux Benoit LaClaire the Third, a titled gentleman who offered nothing further about himself than his name, was far more interested in Lucretia than the scenery.

"Ah, Mr. LaClaire, we are so fortunate to have you here to teach us things about our new—or soon-to-be home. My ward, Mrs. Mills, recently lost her husband of a few short weeks and thought a change of location might help her get over her loss. Is that not right, darling?" She looked pointedly at Lucretia, who shook her head slowly as a look of misery crossed her face. She dropped her eyes to her hands, forcing a tear down her cheek.

"Yes, Mrs.—" She had no name to call Ruby on such short notice, but her inventive mind kicked in gear. She coughed, as if that was what had stopped her from speaking. "Yes, Mrs. Redstone, you are right. However, I am not going to let my loss cloud our future. I will never again let my pain ruin our plans." With that, Lucretia lifted her head and smiled, wiping away the tear.

"Well, Mrs. Mills, if you ever need a shoulder, mine are wide." Mr. LaClaire sat up straighter, as if to display them, his robust chest, and his patrician face.

"Oh, yes, sir, they are. I will remember your offer. Oh, look, what is that in the water? Oh, there is another one on the riverbank. They look ferocious. Do they eat people?"

Before Ruby could answer, the gentleman spoke. "Oh, yes, my dear, they have eaten people, but not often. They are called alligators and these two are not particularly large. Why, I have seen them up to twenty-five feet long."

Ruby shot him a look that said, "After how many glasses of rotgut?"

"That is more of a bayou than a river, but I suppose you could call it that. Most of the bayous have their own names, as do the rivers or streams that feed them. Look carefully, ladies, in that tree…do you see the snake? It is poisonous, whereas the alligator has teeth to protect himself. The snakes often hide in the Spanish moss you see hanging from the trees and drop onto unsuspecting passersby."

"Really, Mr. LaClaire. I think you have frightened my ward half to death. Dear Lucretia, would you like to return to our car? I have some laudanum there to calm your nerves."

Lulu nodded, hoping her face reflected the fear she was supposed to have. "Good afternoon, sir, perhaps we will meet again."

"I am sure we will, madam. I will make it a point to see that it happens again."

# Chapter 58

Back in their cabin, Ruby sat beside Lucretia and took her hand. "I think it is time for you to tell me what kept you awake half the night. You cried enough tears to fill the Mississippi River."

"Oh, Ruby, I'm sorry I woke you—"

"Are you trying to avoid my question? If it bothers you to talk about it, then I will understand. Nevertheless, I know from experience that it helps to unburden oneself and share whatever it is that is hurting. Maybe together we can work it out."

Lucretia remained quiet for a few minutes while she put her thoughts together. If it had been anyone but Ruby, she would never have considered telling her horrible secrets, but she knew Ruby would never condemn, nor stop loving her for the things she had done.

"The man you saw at the station was Captain Black Eagle Grant. He was Jeffrey's second in command. We were headed to the station from the fort when we were attacked. He disobeyed Jeffrey's orders and caught up with us just after the Indians attacked. Without him, surely we all would have died. Somehow, I hardly remember any of it, only that my husband was wounded. Anyway, we got back to the fort.

"Eagle took command and ordered the troops to get water and wood to get us through a few days when reinforcements were to arrive. Well, they did not arrive and our supplies were low. Every night a soldier left the fort, hopefully to make it to Cottonwood Creek, but apparently none did. The day you saw him, he rode or ran or walked, however he got there, but he did. He left while only the guards were awake. It took him that entire day to get back to the fort. Reinforcements arrived shortly after he did."

Ruby watched Lucretia's face as the young woman talked. "Lulu, while he slept at the station, he mumbled over and over about having to get back to her. He disobeyed orders in returning. Are you the 'her' he wanted to get back to?"

"Well, since I was the only woman left, I guess it would have to be me. But, it makes no sense, because he did not even like me. Actually, he seemed to detest all white women. I remember telling Auntie that the captain looked at me the same way he viewed a dung beetle."

"Do you love him, Lulu?"

Lucretia looked aghast at her friend. "Love him? For God's sake, no! Actually, I hate him. Where did you get such an idea?" Her face drained of color and she clenched her fists at her sides. Every muscle in her body was rigid and she radiated fury.

"Call it insight or just knowing you so well. Or perhaps it was the way you said his name…Eagle. Or the way your eyes softened when you told me how he rescued you and got you back to the fort. I suspect, my sweet friend, that you do not even admit it to yourself, but yes, I think you love him."

For the first time Ruby could remember, Lucretia seemed without words. She sat quietly, head bent. When the tears started, she lifted her head and stared through them, as if seeing something Ruby could not.

When she finally spoke, it was barely above a whisper. "The things he made us do…the two young soldiers and I…how could any woman love him? He smiled and watched like the devil he is while… We thought we were going to die, but he knew better. He knew the general was on his way, but he let us—no, encouraged and actually ordered his men to enjoy themselves on me on their last night alive. I did all those things with the two of them…like you showed me how. They would have gone to their maker happy, Ruby.

"But I felt nothing for them, but that they enjoyed sex for the first time. What I did next was the unforgivable thing. I taunted him, forced my body down on his, and fucked him. I wanted him like I had the other time. Only more. Jeffrey was barely buried when I took Eagle to my bed.

"And it was not the first time. One night, Jeffrey brought Eagle to our cabin and we had a night of unbelievable sex. Oh, Ruby, I am exhausted. No more tonight, please. I promise to tell you the rest some other time."

"Yes, precious, you rest." Ruby helped her remove her clothing and slid a soft nightgown over her head. She sat beside Lucretia, bathing her swollen face with wet clothes until the girl slid into a deep sleep. *How much pain this child has endured*, thought Ruby. *How much guilt she bears.* Ruby would have bet the man called Black Eagle Grant loved this woman, but how could he have done such things to her if he did? Still, she suspected there was much more to Lulu's story.

# Chapter 59

Devereaux Benoit LaClaire the Third was true to his word. He was waiting in the dining car the next morning when they arrived for breakfast. He rose to meet them, bowing over their hands and seating them at the table he held. "I took the liberty of ordering the pathetic concoction the chef calls 'chocolate' for us, although the only resemblance to the real thing is the color. Certainly not the taste. Ah, here it comes now."

The waiter poured the steaming beverage and then set the pot down before Ruby. Devereaux looked up, surprised, as he expected to serve refills himself, as was his family custom. Surely, society did not dictate that the eldest female serve it. Well, if so, so be it. He did not want anything, even the slightest nuance of poor deportment, to interfere with his plans for the lovely Mrs. Mills. First, he would have to find a way to separate her from the formidable chaperone he detected in Mrs. Redstone.

"Tell me, lovely ladies, did you sleep well last night? My chair was most uncomfortable, but no berths were available when I made my reservation."

Ruby lifted her eyes to his and said, "We slept well, sir. I am sorry about your accommodations. Strange, but when we came onboard in Cottonwood Creek, I can distinctively remember the conductor asking if we wanted one or two cabins. Seems strange he would have offered us two if none were available."

Lucretia covered her friend's hand with hers. "It matters little now, as we will be arriving in New Orleans in a few hours. I am looking forward to seeing the city that I have heard so much about my whole life."

Devereaux smiled back at the women, adoring one and detesting the other…to possess one, he would have to eliminate the other. "Then, I will be more than happy to be your guide. Having lived here for going on twenty-five years, there is little I do not know about it, from the good to the bad. First, we will get you situated in my home…you can have the entire second floor…and when you are rested, we will start looking at the beauty that is New Orleans. My servants will be delighted to have something to do but cater to the whims of this fidgety old man."

"Surely, you do not think of yourself as an old man, Mister LaClaire." Lucretia smiled at him as she spoke, but before she could continue, Ruby interrupted.

"I think you are presuming far more than is the case, Mr. LaClaire. We have a suite at the Orleans Royale and would not dream of staying with you. For your information, Mrs. Mills is in mourning, but circumstances have not allowed us the opportunity of purchasing the proper attire for her."

Devereaux forced a smile when he really wanted to hit the pompous woman. How could he ever get to the juicy morsel of her ward with her around? Yes, she would have to go, and soon. "Of course, I meant no disrespect. That is the last thing I would ever do to either of you lovely ladies. It is just that I have such a large old home, it seems a shame for you to spend the incredible amount those hustlers demand for their rooms."

Inside he smiled to himself. This had worked out perfectly. He knew Mrs. Redstone would refuse his offer, or so he hoped. His home was dilapidated inside and his servants consisted of an old black couple who had been with him since he was a child. Sam was arthritic and did the best he could maintaining the outside of the house and the carriage. He drove Devereaux, while Peg, his wife, did the cooking and as much cleaning as her elderly body allowed. He paid them practically nothing, but they had a roof over their heads and food in their bellies. He considered himself a good employer…he seldom yelled at them anymore and had not hit either one in years. Besides, he knew they had nowhere else to go.

Maintaining his image was of utmost importance to Devereaux. In a town so deep in bloodlines and proprieties, it was a façade he had to maintain in order to be received in the best homes and restaurants. To be penniless was a crime worse than murder in the eyes of those patricians who ruled society.

He forced the negative thoughts away and focused on the bright face of Mrs. Mills, who broke his revelry. "Really, Mr. LaClaire, it is nice of you to offer, but Mrs. Redstone is right. How would it look for us to reside in your home, where no lady is present? In St. Louis society, such would never do. We want to start our lives here with propriety. I hope you understand. Moreover, you need not worry about the expense. Thank you anyway."

Devereaux learned that she had money, which he suspected. Widow, be damned. One way or another, he would get his hands on her delightful body, her pretty face, and the funds to bring his home back up to its prime.

"You are welcome, both of you. I do understand, but do not forget my offer if ever you need anything." *And you will, that is a promise*, he said to himself.

# Chapter 60

After breakfast, the ladies returned to their cabin to finish packing. The conductor arrived and took their luggage to the baggage car for unloading as soon as the train stopped. They departed and were met by a driver from the Orleans Royale, who escorted them to their carriage to wait while he gathered their bags. *The joys of telegraph lines have made travel so much easier than in the past,* thought Ruby, remembering long waits for transportation and searching for suitable lodging. Not that she ever needed much in the way of lodging. A room with a bed was enough for one in her line of work.

"Oh my, Ruby, I had not expected it to be so hot and wet feeling. Is it this way all the time? Why, my shirt is sticking to me already. However does one get used to it?"

"I hate to tell you this, but this is winter and it gets worse in the summer. You will adjust, at least a bit. And there are a few tricks females use, but that are never admitted. For one, you will get rid of all those petticoats but one. Your pantaloons can go, too. And those heavy long stockings. A thin pair to cover your ankles will do. After all, a lady should never show an ankle. Heaven forbid that a patch of leg be exposed.

"But exposing your upper chest, shoulders, and a bit of cleavage is encouraged for daytime in the warmer months. The ladies know the gentlemen like that. Moreover, at night, for balls and such, even more cleavage is acceptable. The more modest women add a thin layer of fabric called lawn to cover themselves, but in my opinion, it makes them even more interesting to men to want to see what is under it. Oh, damn. Here comes that LaClaire."

Devereaux maneuvered the carriage to stop beside them. "I intended to take you to the Royale myself, but I see you already have transportation. Again, feel free to send for Sam anytime you need to go anywhere. We are at your disposal." With that he bowed, tipped his hat, and the carriage moved away.

"That is so nice of him, don't you think, Ruby?"

Ruby sighed. Lulu was so naïve. "Honey, let me warn you about that man. He is a gold digger after your money. And your body, I suspect. I have seen countless men like him and take my word for it, he is not to be trusted."

Their driver returned and asked if they wanted the quickest route to the hotel or a more roundabout way to see more of the city. Before Lucretia could answer, Ruby said, "Straight to the hotel. We have all the time in the world to see the city." To Lucretia she whispered, "After we get a bath, some fewer clothes, and pampering, we will enjoy another ride."

"Not quite yet. I am sorry, but I have one stop to make. Take me to the closet bank. I have a couple of things to deal with first." When the driver stopped, Lucretia told him to wait under a tree so that Ruby was out of the sun while she went inside. Her business with the banker was quick and easily done. She signed documents giving him the right to telegraph her St. Louis bank and at the same time, changed her account name to Mrs. Mills, not wanting any trace of Mrs. Sawyer being in New Orleans. The banker was confused, at best, but did as instructed. He was still shaking his head when Lucretia smiled at him and returned to the waiting carriage for their continuing trip to the hotel.

Their suite was as luxurious as could be had in the modern city of New Orleans. Even before they had time to do little more than give their names at the counter, a porter whisked them to a remarkable closet that moved up and down between floors so that a person no longer had to walk the endless stairs. Inside was the operator, dressed in a red uniform. He smiled as he accepted Lucretia's coin, slid a gate in front of them, and moved a lever until the closet stopped on the highest floor.

It was a massive residence that opened before them, so beautiful it took away Ruby's breath. She had never seen such luxury in her life, let alone stayed in such a place. Embossed gold wallpaper covered the wall. Floor-to-ceiling windows of cut glass had heavy draperies to cut out the sun and heat. Outside was a balcony that ran from one side of their apartment to the other. The huge building had three other units of this size, so that only four suites took up the entire floor. White marble tiles with Oriental rugs of gold and red marked the placement of the seating areas, which consisted of velvet furnishing and shiny dark wood tables. Accents were pieces of art the likes of which neither woman had ever seen. Oriental vases and statues sat in alcoves around the room.

"Lucretia, we cannot afford this. There has to be a mistake." Lulu looked as mystified as she was as she pulled the call rope. It was answered in less than a minute. "I think this is not the right room. Not that it is not perfect, but it is not what we asked for."

"The gentleman warned us you would say that, but I assure you that it is the proper room. He asked us to give you this note, should you object to your accommodations."

He handed the folded paper to Ruby and quietly closed the door behind him. She offered it to Lulu, who said, "You read it."

Ruby opened it and stared at the page. Tears began to fall behind her heavy veil until they dropped to her shirt. When she did not utter a word, Lucretia turned to her and saw the wet spot on the dark blue fabric. "What is it, Ruby? Is it terrible news?" Still Ruby did not reply. Lucretia lifted the veil to see her friend's face and knew something was wrong. She took her in her arms and together they sat on one of the red velvet settees scattered around the room.

Lulu took the paper from the trembling hands and read aloud. "Dear ladies. I took the liberty of stopping here before returning home to make sure all was as it should be for such a gracious, beautiful pair of travelers ever to set foot in our fair city. The room they had set aside for you was inferior, so I suggested a suite more in keeping with your sensibilities. Sincerely, Devereaux Benoit LaClaire the Third. Post Script: Please do not refuse my hospitality for the second time today. I will be devastated should you do so."

Lucretia looked askance at her friend. "Surely, Ruby, while the man is definitely overstepping himself, it is nothing to cry about. Why…" Slowly, realization began to dawn. "Ruby, is it that you cannot read?"

Ruby's head slowly rose from its bowed position so she could meet the eyes of her only true friend. "No, I cannot read. I am so sorry."

"Why are you apologizing? If you do not read, it is of little real importance. I am here to read what is necessary and I will teach you in no time. It is easier than you think. But I do not understand…those books you showed me. Surely, you read them?"

"No, I did not, Lucretia. You remember, they were all full of pictures and few words. There is a saying about a picture being worth a thousand words, and those pictures certainly told it all."

She took a deep breath before continuing. "I never told you before, but perhaps now is the time. It is an ugly story and now I am as ugly as my beginnings were. After you hear it, I shall leave, as you do not need the sort of person I am. What I am is really far worse than a whore."

# Chapter 61

A knock on the door came at the most inopportune time, and Lucretia moved to answer it. A uniformed hotel employee handed her another note and waited while she read it. She took a coin from her pocket and handed it to the man. "Please tell the gentleman we are having our supper in our suite and have plans for most of the week. We will contact him at his home in a few days. Thank you." She shut the door firmly behind her and slipped the lock.

"It was our Mr. LaClaire here to take us out for the evening. He is becoming a bit of a pest and—" She spoke as she turned and saw that Ruby was no longer on the settee, but was closing the door to her room. Lucretia's first thought was to follow her, but prudence brought her to a stop. She would let Ruby have her privacy, as she herself often needed. She moved to the bathroom off her bedroom and drew a full tub of water, adding the oils and perfumes provided to well-heeled customers, like the hotel personnel thought she was.

"I might as well take advantage of what is offered while I can," she thought aloud, as she slid out of her heavy linen dress and multiple petticoats. When she was fully undressed, she looked at herself in the full-length mirrors that surrounded the room. An open window, shaded for privacy, allowed the steam to escape. A pile of white towels sat on a counter behind the tub. The faucets of the lavatory and bath were gold colored, probably even gold plated. Nothing was too good for those who could afford it. She giggled as she slid into the perfect water.

On the side of the deep porcelain bath was a bank of windows, also shaded. She lifted the edge of one shade to see only blue sky beyond. She pulled the drawstrings and let out an exclamation of disbelief. Below her was a panorama of the city, from its slow-moving river full of ships on her left, to the streets and avenues as far as she could see to her right. She settled back into the water, never taking her eyes off the hustle and bustle of life in New Orleans.

After a while, the warm water and her tired body won out and she sank into a soft sleep. In her sleep, images of Jeffrey and Eagle slipped and slid around her mind like ghosts, laughing and taunting her. She was tied to a tree on a hill with both soldiers and Indians riding around her, chanting and laughing at her nakedness. The wind blew cold while the clouds moved to dump showers of frigid water down on her. Both the major and the captain sat on horses and stared down at her before turning to ride away, leaving her to her fate.

When she awoke with a start, it was to a dark sky and cold water. She pulled the plug and wrapped one of the huge towels around herself. She picked up her clothing and put it in a basket with a tiny label saying “laundry.”

As she stepped into the sitting room, the corridor door closed. Just inside was a cart with two place settings, two bottles of wine, and several covered bowls. “Ah, you are awake.” Ruby was smiling at her. Her veil was gone and she wore a soft, silky dressing gown with matching slippers. “I peeked in at you when you were so long quiet. You looked like an angel asleep in that massive tub. It is big enough for two, easily, as I decided when I used mine. Have you ever seen the likes of this place?”

Lucretia grinned. “Never. I could have never even imagined such things. Our little house in St. Louis was a hut compared to this, and I always thought it was rich and beautiful. Did you look out the windows?”

"Yes, and it took my breath away. Now come and sit down. I ordered our supper when my stomach reminded me that breakfast was hours ago. Since we are about as far south as we can get, I ordered southern cooking, leaving it up to the chef to select for us. If we do not like it, well…we will just order something else. Mr. LaClaire will be amazed at what two women can eat, will he not?"

# Chapter 62

Unfortunately for Mr. LaClaire and his purse strings, the two ladies "oooed" and "ahhed" as they consumed nearly everything. There was shrimp Creole, sherry crawfish, dirty rice with chicken livers, chicken croquettes, grits, fried okra, fried green tomatoes, gumbo, and peach cobbler with thick, sweet cream. It was a meal fit for a king—or, in this case—two queens. They ate until their stomachs said "no more." They decided to save the dessert for later…and some of the other things as well.

They poured their wine and moved to the balcony overlooking the city below. Although they did not know many of the names at the time, they could see Jackson Square, miles of canals, the Ursuline Convent and the Archbishop's Palace, the Claiborne Market, the French Opera building, and the Parish Prison. The sun had set, but a light breeze kept the mosquitoes at bay for the time being.

They talked of inconsequential things. When the conversation lagged, Ruby said, "I suppose this is as good a time as any for me to bare my soul. If you want me to leave when I have told you my worst, I will understand and go immediately."

Lulu reached for her friend's hand and held it tight. "There is nothing you can say that would make me want you to leave. You are my friend and I love you."

Ruby squeezed back and took a deep breath. "I have never told a soul what I did. Even the children never knew. Well, not my children. Yes, they *became* my children, although I have borne no baby alive. They were my brothers and sisters and cousins and orphans from the hills and valleys of the mountains of Appalachia.

"I was the oldest child, nine when my mother died in childbirth with my youngest brother. He was the third brother and I had two sisters. She was a frail woman, as I remember her. Not the kind to bear a child every year, especially when she felt my father's fists and boots when he had too much hooch, which was nightly."

She stopped talking and rose to fill their wineglasses. She laughed bitterly. "Here I am drinking and at the same time berating my father."

Lucretia smiled and said, "This is hardly the same thing. I cannot believe you would ever hurt a fly, drunk or sober."

"How little you know of me, sweet Lulu. Soon you will know the difference. Anyway, without a woman to fall on every time his pecker got hard, he decided I would have to do. He swore at me, hit me, and raped me whenever the mood struck. There was no one to care for the babies, so I did it. Sometimes he would bring home food, but mostly it was deer or rabbits and such. He loved to hunt. Guess he liked playing God. So I planted a pathetic little garden, milked our pathetic cow, fed our pathetic chicken, and all else to fill our bellies.

"I was just a child, but I grew up real quick. I am not complaining, just telling you what happened. By the time I was twelve, he was bringing home other men who paid him to use me. He liked to do things with my brothers, too, then the small girls, but he kept them all for his own use. At least until they were older.

About that time, he started bringing home girls he found in orphanages. He did make more of an effort to see that we had food, but that was all. The girls were just another way to make money, and he liked money. He brought fancy laces, feathers, and such for us all to wear. He said it was to make us sexy and the men would be willing to pay more.

"I guess he was right because he had another building put up. It had several 'rooms,' as he called them. 'Some men want privacy,' he said. Each room had nothing but a mattress on a wooden frame, but that is where he sent us with whichever man wanted us.

"It was more than I could take when he started selling my babies—both the boys and girls—to the one with the most money. Their crying and yelps of pain pushed me into some hell on earth and I ended it."

By now, tears ran in full rivers down her scarred face. Lucretia moved her chair beside Ruby and held the older woman to her chest as she would a child. "Ruby, stop talking. It does not matter. Truly, it does not. Let me help you to bed. You are exhausted."

Ruby shook her head and took another deep breath. "I waited until he snored in his chair, waiting for more customers. I walked to the building with rooms and took off my dress. By now I had actual breasts and body hair, so the men really liked me. I went from room to room, suggesting that I join the pair there, holding the knife behind my thigh. Naturally, the men were delighted with the idea, so it was easy to entice them to face away from me while I rubbed against them. I cut the throats of a couple, stabbed another couple between the ribs, and saved the best for the last one.

"I returned with the children to the main house, where my father lay asleep. I awakened him, letting him see me naked. His penis hardened and he grabbed me, probing me as I reached down and quickly cut it off. Then I cut his throat as he bellowed in pain at the loss of his manhood, if you could call it that. Blood went everywhere and the children all gathered at the door to watch him in pain. It was sick, so sick. They applauded while my father slowly bled to death.

"I told the children to gather up everything they had and take what we could use. Then I set fire to first the house, then the newer building. We all stood and watched them burn. I directed them to the creek, where we washed ourselves clean. I knew there was no way I could feed them all or find them a place to live. I had no choice but to take them all—including my brothers and sisters—to the orphanage. It took us two days to get there, because those who had traveled from it were vague as to its location. But arrive we did, and every child knew it might be their home until they were sixteen, but it was better than where they had been.

"I was mature for my age. I had no talents, no intelligence, no nothing. So I did the only thing I knew how to do. I whored then and have never stopped." She stood and walked to her bedroom. Lucretia followed and saw Ruby take a suitcase from her closet.

"Where do you think you are going?" She took the bag from her friend and returned it to the closet. "The only place you are going tonight is to bed. And right now, unless you wish a bath first." Ruby shook her head and stood still while Lulu undressed her and dropped a nightie over her head. She turned back to the bed and waited for Ruby to get comfortable before sitting down next to her.

"No matter what you think you did that was so horrible, I can see nothing wrong with anything you told me. Those men deserved what they got and even worse. I think they will suffer for eternity in hell. You did what had to be done and I am so damn proud of you. I could never have done what you did. I would have taken the coward's way and killed myself." She bent forward and kissed the wet face on the pillow. "I love you, Ruby. I love you!"

# Chapter 63

"No, Captain Grant, I will not accept your resignation. You are too valuable to the army for me to let you go. Let us make a compromise. I will give you an open-end furlough and you can return here or to any other base when, and if, you decide you want to return."

Black Eagle nodded and shook hands with his commandant. He returned his saber and his army-issued guns, but the general insisted he keep his coat, horse, and personal belongings. As a parting gesture, he handed the rifle back to him. "You will need this, no doubt. Where will you go now? What will you do?"

"Sir, I have no plans. I think I will visit my father's people and perhaps go to Mexico or California. Who knows, maybe I will strike gold or become a bounty hunter. Yes, I would be good at that. Thank you, sir. I appreciate your understanding." He saluted crisply, turned smartly, and left the officers' area for the last time. Outside, by his horse, he let his mind wander through the days he had spent there. When an image of Lucretia Lucinda Sawyer reared its golden head, he shook it away and mounted.

He rode away from the fort with nary a look backward. That part of his life was done. As he had told the general, he had no plans other than visiting his former home with the Indians, primarily to visit the death platforms of his grandparents. He need to pray to his gods and to ask Summer Swan for help. Help with what, he did not know, but somehow it was important to visit her.

He did so that same afternoon. The ladders were long gone and the platforms were too deteriorated for him to consider climbing upon them. Nevertheless, he dismounted and sat on the ground, where he could see what little remained of their bones.

He closed his eyes and pictured them together in his mind's eye from his childhood. "Grandparents, it is I, your son's son. I am Black Eagle, the half-white boy you named after yourself. My life is half over and still, I am not contented. The ways of our world are gone and now we are taking on the ways of the white man. Worse yet, we are taking to us white women. None is as strong or loving as you, Grandmother. Oh, yes, they warm my feet, but so do dogs. I am here to ask you to help me drive out the memories of one of them. Somehow, she will not leave my mind and I think she is in my soul now, as well.

"Give me a sign or omen from the gods on how to rid her from me. Please! I feel as if I will never have a life until she is gone." He waited and watched the sky, but there was nothing. He pulled his bedroll from his horse and lay on the ground on it, beside the platforms that sometimes frightened unknowing visitors on nights such as this. He felt no need for a fire. H watched the fog as it formed and rolled across the plains while coyotes howled to the moon-slice, which slid in and out of the clouds. He watched the sky until sleep overtook him and he sank into the world of dreams.

They came to him then. His grandparents walked in the sky above him, holding hands as they had in life. He knew they were dead, but he was comfortable with them as they stood finally at his feet. His grandmother waved her hand at the sky; the clouds blackened, thunder broke the silence, and lightning tore across the sky. A wave of intense cold seemed to envelop him.

He turned his eyes skyward, as did his grandparents. A bolt of energy rolled into a white ball and moved toward him. Its brightness forced him to shield his eyes. He heard his grandmother's voice in his head. "My son, you must decide if you fear what you see or desire it. Only then will you have a path to follow."

The light ball moved closer until he could feel its heat replace the cold. As suddenly as it came, it disappeared, and the prairie returned to its former calm and fog. When he turned to his grandparents, they were gone.

He sat on his bedroll for hours, thinking of what he had seen and what his grandmother's words meant. When dawn came, he was no closer to understanding than he had been the night before.

Black Eagle did not wait for sunrise. He mounted his horse, letting it pick the direction they would go, but was not surprised to find himself on the hill beneath the branches of the old tree. He looked down at the plains below. Nothing moved as far as he could see, but for the wind and the things it touched. He had felt loneliness most of his life, but for the first time, he seemed to be absolutely alone in the entire world. His soul felt hollow, completely devoid of emotions. Not even sadness penetrated that hollow. Nothing, nothing at all.

# Chapter 64

Lucretia opened the door just a crack. Ruby was asleep on her side, snoring lightly. It appeared the older woman would sleep the night through, she was so exhausted. Her rumbling stomach reminded Lucretia that she had not eaten for quite a while Her first thought was room service, but then she decided it would be nice to see some smiling faces and hear inane chatter, so she took the elevator down to the dining room.

Immediately, the maître d' appeared at her side and escorted her to a table near his post. He wanted to insure no one would bother the lady. It was seldom that a lady dined by herself, and he planned to make sure it was a pleasant meal for her. After all, was she not in the most expensive suite in the hotel? He suggested thick shrimp consommé, a salad of assorted greens, and an assortment of fresh seafood, followed by a chocolate concoction the chef would create just for her, along with a bottle of the cellar's finest wine. Lucretia laughed. "I will need a seamstress to alter my clothes if I eat like this very often, but it sounds wonderful and I bow to your splendid choices."

The dining room was resplendent, with gleaming lanterns along the wall covered with ornate, flocked blue paper, and gilded statues of Greek gods and goddesses in alcoves every few feet. The floor felt to Lucretia like she was walking on air with the matching blue carpets. The table linen was white damask so bright it seemed to shimmer in the light. The tall candles stood in silver holders, and a bowl of gardenias floated on each table, permeating the air with their perfume. Lucretia was sure heaven was scented with gardenias. She closed her eyes for a moment and savored the light wine the steward poured for her.

"Hello, and can it be? Mrs. Mills, is that truly you? I have left message after message for you and was about to call the militia to see if you were truly in the hotel or if you had been abducted and spirited away to hide in the sky among the stars, as surely they would welcome another such as you."

Lucretia did not need to look to know the voice belonged to Devereaux Benoit LaClaire the Third. She smiled up at his face as he took her hand. "Hello again, monsieur. I believe that is the correct term here in the city with roots to the lovely French. Would you like to join me? I have already ordered, but no matter."

"Ah, lovely lady, I am delighted to see you have not forgotten me. How could I turn down such an offer? I would be delighted to join you." He waved to the maître d', indicating a chair should be brought.

Innocent Lucretia had no way of knowing that the man in charge did not like Mr. LaClaire, never had, and was sure he never would. He motioned a waiter to bring a chair and see to the needs of the man who joined the lovely lady. He wished he could somehow warn her about the man trying to charm her, but he knew there was nothing he could do. If he said anything to her and word ever got out, he would lose his job. It mattered not that what he said was true. LaClaire was considered one of the aristocrats of New Orleans and, as such, enjoyed the protection of society and even the law—no matter what his true character might be.

However, Lucretia knew none of those things. She found the gentleman at her table to be charming and witty. Her conscience bothered her for thinking that it was much more pleasant dining with him without Ruby, as for some reason she seemed to actively dislike Mr. LaClaire. Tomorrow, after Ruby recovered from her trying tale, they would take a drive through the city and she would ask her about her dislike for the man she now called Devereaux.

"Tell me, my dear Mrs. Mills, how do you like our fair city so far?"

"Please, call me Lucretia, as I call you by your given name. To be honest, I have seen so little of it that I cannot say anything about it. Well, except for what we can see from our rooms. The view there is incredible. In addition, we thank you so much for the chance to see it all and for your generosity. Tomorrow we shall seek less costly quarters. Actually, I wish to purchase a small house close to where we are now."

"Perfect. I shall pick you up at…say, eleven. We will have a true New Orleans breakfast, then see some of the homes available. Before I come for you, I will contact several brokers I know, who will be delighted to show you the properties. However"—he took her hand and looked her in the eye—"it will be necessary for them to have a figure of money from which to work. Say, the top amount you wish to spend.

"Oh, perhaps you wish that to remain confidential. I understand. I shall have the waiter bring several envelopes and paper and you can write the amount for me to hand deliver to them when I arrange viewing times."

Lucretia laughed. "Sir, I hardly think that necessary. One should be sufficient. I will write a note to the bank, telling them to disclose to you my discretionary funds. You have been so kind to us, I see no reason to doubt your honesty and confidentiality. I feel, Devereaux, as if I have known you for years. You so remind me of my uncle, God bless his soul. He was my protectorate from the time I was a wee child until he passed and I still miss him so.

"But enough of maudlin things, sir. Thank you for joining me. A solitary meal is just a time to be less hungry. Company makes it a pleasure." She stood, offering her hand. He raised it to his lips for what she considered an overlong amount of time. But, perhaps the French had different ideas of politeness.

# Chapter 65

It was all Devereaux could do not to turn handstands. Everything had gone far better than he could have hoped for, but for one thing. She had forgotten to give him the note for the banker and he was unsure of how to ask for it without seeming overzealous. His smile faded as he walked her across the expansive lobby to the elevator, his hand possessively around her upper arm.

"Oh, wait, Devereaux." She pulled away from him and moved to the desk, where she spoke to the bell captain. The man handed her a sheet of paper and an envelope on which she wrote a few lines. She asked for the hotel seal to fasten it shut. She thanked the man and returned to Devereaux, handing the envelope to him. He took it, sliding it into his jacket pocket as he punched the button for the elevator.

"Let me escort you to your door, Lucretia."

"No, that is not necessary. So until forenoon, good evening." The doors closed behind her.

Damn her. If she had not sealed it, he would know what she had written. Now, he would have to wait until he got to the bank and that was something he would rather not do, but he saw no choice now. She seemed to make everything so much harder for him than necessary. Well, that would change later.

A carriage rounded the corner, nearly striking his horses. Sam, his age and health aside, was quick to pull their team up quick enough to avoid a real accident. Devereaux was furious as he jumped to the ground. The other driver jumped down also, but nearly fell before catching himself. "Devereaux, my friend, is that you?"

LaClaire recognized the man as Thomas Bozeman Winthrop, son of one of the most wealthy and influential men in the city. "Yes, Thom, old man, it is I. Here, let me help you. Your cups seem to have caught up with you."

"Appreciated, LaClaire, but I am fine. My friends and I are heading to Bourbon Street for a night of music, imbibing, and perhaps a lovely lady or two. Why not join us? Evening will be on me, for my reckless driving. Say yes, my man, and we will be off."

Devereaux quickly accepted the invitation, which he knew he would not have received had Winthrop been sober. Sam shook his head, but followed the other coach as instructed. "Now, Sam. None of that head-shaking. I am a grown man, not a child anymore, and I can take care of myself. Just park the buggy behind the other one and take a nap until I rouse you to take us home." Again, Sam shook his head and did as told.

Winthrop and his three friends waited, swaying to the music pouring out of the club. *Or, just swaying, perhaps,* thought Devereaux, *from too much to drink.* He shook hands with all four and with Winthrop's arm around his shoulder, he followed his host's drunken escort. They found an empty table near the band, but it was not to Winthrop's liking. He demanded one close to the stage where the ladies would perform at the hour, as they did every hour.

No table was available there, so he and his friends staggered over to the one closest to the stage and physically dumped the men seated there onto the floor, laughing all the while. A fight ensued, but the management quickly stopped it. After all, Mr. Winthrop was too important to go to jail for a barroom brawl. The men on the floor were helped to their feet and led to a different table, appeased by the free drinks the manager sent their way.

Alcohol flowed freely. At no time was there ever an empty glass on the Winthrop table. The ladies danced, removing items of clothing as they did so, accepting bills stuck into whatever articles they still wore. By the end of their dance, the six men were falling-down drunk.

Several employees helped them into their waiting carriages. Sam drove to the front door and helped get the passed-out LaClaire into the buggy.

At home, he just drove the vehicle into the carriage house and let his employer sleep it off there. As he tucked a blanket around the comatose man, he felt an envelope on the seat. He could not read, but decided it must be important, so he slid it into his own pocket.

Devereaux awoke in the carriage, wrinkled and unshaven. He hurried to the house and his room on the second floor. He quickly washed, shaved, and changed his clothes. He left the dirty laundry on the floor for Peg to find and launder. It was late and the banks would be open already. Rather than find Sam, he decided to drive himself to see Lucretia's banker and then pick her and that damned Ruby up for touring homes.

He was forced to wait, growing more irate with each passing minute. Finally, his name was called and he followed the secretary to the office of Melvin Charles Duval, Esq., who did not rise to shake his hand. "Hello, Mr. Duval. Mrs. Lucretia Mills is a dear friend of mine and suggested I speak to you regarding the limit and/or dollar amounts you would suggest she spend on a suitable residence here in our fair city. She gave me this letter of introduction…" He felt in his jacket pocket before realizing he had changed clothes and not removed the letter from the soiled one.

"I am so embarrassed, sir, but it is in my suit at home. I will bring it by for you later. If you would be so good as to give me the figures, it will help me limit the brokers when showing her the houses."

Mr. Duval stood. "You really cannot expect me to discuss my client's finances with you on simply your word that you have such a letter, which, frankly, I doubt. Please do not return to waste my time further until—and if—you actually do have a document. Good day, sir." The banker walked to his office door, opened it, and motioned for Devereaux to exit.

Devereaux was furious beyond belief. He was irate at the banker, at Sam, who should have taken him to his room, and even at himself for failing to transfer the envelope. He raced the carriage through the streets like a man possessed. He ran up the stairs to his bedroom, only to find the dirty clothes gone. He started screaming, "Peg, Peg, where are my clothes?"

When she did not answer, he continued to scream her name as he ran through the house. He found her singing a soft gospel song as she hung his laundry out to dry. He pushed her rudely out of the way and jerked his wet coat from the line. Feeling in the pocket where it should have been, he found nothing. He checked every pocket in the coat, then in the pants and vest. Nothing.

"Where is it, Peg? What did you do with my letter?" His face was red and his voice was hard.

Peg was not intimidated, having served his family since he was a child. "Now, Mr. Devereaux, you better calm youself afore you bust you heart in half and bust a blood vessel. Ain't no letter in any of you pockets, sir. Jist a few coins and you comb. I left 'em on you dresser. I dona find ena letter."

# Chapter 66

"I cannot believe it. How could you have given that man permission to know *anything* about your finances? What were you thinking? Or were you thinking at all? Lucretia Lucinda Sawyer, he is a crook—a scoundrel. I know you are naïve and innocent, but I never thought you were without common sense. He wants your money, and your body, mark my words. He will try his damndest to wed you and if that fails, only God knows what he will try."

Ruby had never yelled at Lucretia before. Actually, Lucretia doubted that Ruby had ever yelled at anyone. She hung her head, knowing that Ruby was probably right. She did not even try to make excuses for her actions. Devereaux Benoit LaClaire the Third had wined and dined her and charmed her into doing exactly as he wanted.

They were enjoying their breakfast on the balcony when she casually mentioned that Devereaux would be calling for them in a couple of hours to show them houses in their price range, when Ruby asked how he could possibly know what Lulu's price range was.

"Well, I gave him a letter for Mr. Duval at our bank."

Ruby had looked at her for a long time before she jumped up and paced up and down the balcony, ranting and raving at cowed Lucretia. Lucretia realized the older woman was correct that she should not have given Devereaux permission to know their money situation, but she did doubt the man would ask her to wed, or any such thing. It was apparent to Lucretia that Devereaux was a man of society and surely had money of his own.

Finally, Ruby's tirade died down. She knelt before the chastised girl and took her hand. "Honey, I am sorry I yelled at you. Actually, I was yelling at that devious man and at myself for not taking better care of you. And honey, what kind of money you have or do not have is no one's business but your own and your banker's. Not even *I* need to know and I do not want you to ever tell me. Do you understand?"

Lucretia put her head on Ruby's shoulder and hugged her. "Yes. Oh, Ruby, I love you. What would I do without you?"

"You will probably have to find out, Lulu, if that blackguard LaClaire has his way. Mark my words—he will do his best to have me gone so he can get to you without any obstacles. But I will not let that happen. I promise. No, let us dry our tears and get on with searching for a home for you." They hugged again and took the elevator to the ground floor, where they ordered a carriage.

As they waited in front of the hotel, Devereaux arrived with his carriage. He looked distressed and angry. When he saw them, he forced his face into a smile and jumped to the ground beside them. "I am sorry I am late, lovely ladies. I did not forget our promised meeting time, Lucretia. I ran into some small problems that I had to take care of first. So, are you ready? Shall we go to the bank first?"

Ruby stepped forward as he tried to take Lucretia's hand. "It will not be necessary for you to drive *Mrs. Mills* and me anywhere." She emphasized the *Mrs. Mills*, pointing out to him that he should not have called her by her given name. "We have our own carriage…here it is now. Good day, sir."

"Oh, Ruby, you were so stern and rough on him. He only wants to help."

"Help, oh, yes, he certainly does. He wants to help himself to your money and your body. We will ask Mr. Duval about him so that any doubts you might have about my protectiveness are well founded."

They were escorted immediately to the banker's office and offered refreshments that awaited them on his desk. Ruby demanded she be excused while Lucretia and the most astute gentleman discussed

Lulu's finances—even over the younger woman's pleas that she remain.

Mr. Duval gave Lucretia an envelope to show the property brokers in search of what he called an "estate" for Mrs. Mills (whom he knew as the former Mrs. Sawyer). When Ruby returned to the room and asked for background on Mr. LaClaire, the banker's face changed.

"It is not my place to pass judgment on my fellow man, but in his case, I think a mild warning might be in order. I do know he is a gambler and lives far beyond his means. His parents left him well off, but demon rum and the casinos took most of it. He has made no secret of the fact that he is seeking a wealthy wife. You are free to make your own decisions, but as a fatherly figure, I would suggest he might not be what a dainty young lady should look for in a husband."

# Chapter 67

The women left Devereaux standing alone, boiling with hate for that Redstone bitch, as he thought of her. She had to go. No doubt. It should be easy to have her run over by a team of horses or struck by a falling flowerpot from a Bourbon Street balcony, or to disappear into the bayous. And the sooner, the better.

He turned his carriage toward the bank, positive that was the destination of the women. They were just climbing into a carriage, this time with a tall, well-dressed man whose name he did not know, although he recognized him. Well, he would find out who he was.

He did so by blocking that vehicle with his own. He jumped down from his and walked casually to the blocked one. He put out his hand to the man seated across from the ladies. "Hello, sir, I am Devereaux Benoit LaClaire, at your service. I plead guilty to the charge of tardiness, as I was supposed to drive the ladies today."

The man looked at him with distaste evident on his face. Only good manners forced him to accept the outstretched hand. He shook it without removing his glove, a slight not missed by Devereaux. "I am an associate of Melvin Charles Duval, Esquire, owner of this banking establishment." He tipped his head to indicate the building beside them. "If you would please move your carriage, we would appreciate it. We are on a tight schedule and do not wish to be delayed further."

Devereaux seethed. He had been slighted with the glove, and now the man did not identify himself. Another social insult. He had no choice but to move his carriage when he would rather have pulled the pompous man out and hit him or, better yet, challenged him to a duel. Instead, he removed his hat and bowed to Lucretia and Ruby. "It is nice to see you both and, again, I apologize for my lack of punctuality." He turned without waiting for a reply. Instead, he smiled as he climbed into his vehicle to take the reins. He drove away, turning left at the next corner, where he circled around to the right and hid his carriage behind an overgrown bougainvillea with crimson flowers. He could see through it, but they could not see him. He planned to continue following them until he determined who the man was and where they were going.

It did not take long for him to realize that they were looking at houses. The man was a broker and he dimly recalled having seen him around town on several occasions, but they did not travel in the same circles. Damn! With Lucretia's money, he could travel in any circle he chose. Oh, how great it would be to get even with the snobs who had looked down their patrician noses at him for so long.

After the death of his parents, he had a noble house and an upstanding position in society. His bachelor status had made him a target for unmarried females and their matchmaking mothers. What he had failed to acknowledge was that he, himself, was to blame for the circumstances. He had gambled and whored it all away until he was a seedy shell of the man he had been.

The afternoon was long for him, following the two women and the real estate agent, who appeared to be having a gay old time together. Some places they stayed only a short time, some a bit longer. The last one was in the French Quarter, a four-story mansion with carriage buildings, wrought-iron fencing, and a massive porch that seemed to wrap itself completely around the house. The white clapboard had cheerful yellow shutters and endless decorative gingerbread. Begrudgingly, Devereaux had to admit, it seemed the perfect place for Lucretia.

Still nursing his hangover, he was slow to realize that the dwelling was incredibly expensive. "Hell, if she has that kind of money, I am not letting her get away. Besides, a body like that…well, no sane man would want to lose the opportunity to have it as well. Yes, I will have her and her money." He looked around, realizing that he had spoken aloud. Fortunately, no one paid him the least attention, even as he smiled broadly and turned his carriage toward home.

# Chapter 68

"The house is perfect," bubbled Lucretia. "And empty is even better. I am sorry the owner decided that New Orleans weather was not to her liking anymore, but on the other hand, I am delighted. Mr. Duval said he would take care of everything if we found the place we liked. Tell him, please, to do his magic and let me know how soon we can move in."

The broker could practically feel the dollar bills in his hands, but he kept his smile businesslike. "I am sure it will be only a matter of days before you can take possession, as the lady is very motivated to sell. Now, about the furnishings—"

"Yes, we want everything just as it is. Even down to the servants, if possible. I can think of nothing right now that is not perfect for us. What do you think, Ruby?"

Ruby hugged her little friend. It was wonderful to see her smile again and laugh with pleasure. "Well, I think perhaps the hunting wallpaper in the formal dining room is a bit much. Deer being shot and dogs chasing them would give me an upset stomach if I had to look at it while eating."

They all laughed. "We can have that taken care of immediately. I will send a decorator to your suite this afternoon for you to select your new paper. Something a bit…well, you will surely make the right decision. Now, I will return you to your hotel before I go to my office. The decorator will be there within the hour." The agent knew that ordinarily it would take weeks to get an appointment with a decorator, but with her kind of money, all things were possible.

The ladies went straight to the hotel desk and requested another room. One on a lower floor for just a few days. No view necessary, no amenities, and no daily laundry or maid service. Just the bare necessities. Ruby explained their needs to the man behind the desk. "We feel that we have taken advantage of Mr. LaClaire's kindness enough."

"But madam, he has paid in advance through the end of the month and we have a no-refund policy for long-term visits."

"Sir," said Lucretia. "Here is what we will do. From this day forward, you will keep a running total of our expenses and we will stay in the suite. At the end of the month, we will give you a bank draft for that amount in the name of Mr. LaClaire, and you will see that he gets it. You will have your money and so shall he. Moreover, we will continue to enjoy the suite. How about that?"

The man nodded, pleased that the situation was resolved. "Also," she continued, "please send up a bottle of your wine cellar's best champagne. We are celebrating the purchase of our house here in the French Quarters. We will practically be neighbors. And be sure it is on our account, not Mr. LaClaire's."

"Sometimes, Lulu, I think you are just too kind. That man is a dismal excuse for a human being and deserves what he gets."

"Oh, Ruby, he is a sad, lonely individual. And it costs us so little to give him a bit of respect."

"Not that he deserves any," Ruby mumbled as she turned and nearly ran into the approaching LaClaire.

"I say, what good luck seeing you here. I came to invite you to have dinner with me. Antoine's is one of my personal favorites and I—"

"No, Devereaux, I am afraid we must pass. We are meeting a decorator in a few minutes and will be involved all evening," said Lucretia as she smiled sweetly. "Perhaps another time."

He once again had no choice but to nod and smile as he moved away. “Yes, perhaps another time.” Rage built inside him again. He had overheard most of their conversation and knew that he *must* get rid of the older woman. Without her, he was sure he could handle Lucretia.

By the time the elevator arrived at their floor, they had forgotten Devereaux. They shared the ride with the wine steward, who poured for them and left them to enjoy the perfectly chilled champagne and the incredible views from the balcony.

“To us, Ruby, and our beautiful new home. We will be so happy there. We can begin our lives anew, just as we talked about on the train.”

“Listen to me, Lucretia. Yes, it is a beautiful home and we can begin our lives, as you said. But, remember, always remember, that it is *your* house, not mine. I have nothing to contribute to it but my love for you. I am penniless and would probably be whoring in the worst places in the city without your kindness. Do not think I am not appreciative, because I am forever in your debt. But I am a relic from your past, nothing more.”

Lucretia started to cry silently. Tears ran down her cheeks onto the silk of her dress, turning the soft yellow into dark, ugly spots. She did not say a word, just arose and went to her bedroom, where she sat at the desk and wrote a letter to Mr. Duval. She sealed the envelope and returned to the living area, where she pulled the call cord before returning to her seat beside Ruby.

When she returned to the balcony, she stopped behind Ruby and bent to encircle the woman’s neck and to pull her head back against her chest. “Ruby, now you listen to me and listen carefully. I never again want to hear the drivel you said a few minutes ago. We are partners…no, we are mother and daughter. I love you and, as of this moment, adopt you as my mother.”

Which is exactly what she did. The letter to Mr. Duval at the bank instructed him to locate a judge who would make Ruby her mother. Yes, she would adopt Ruby, with or without the older woman's involvement, until she was legally Ruby Clanton Sawyer, mother of Lucretia Lucinda Sawyer.

Mr. Duval read the letter twice, not quite believing what he was in it. He called for his carriage and drove to the courthouse, where his friend Judge Franklyn Carter Mountebank was between trials. He gave the letter to Mountebank, who laughed aloud as he read. "This is the first such request like this I have ever seen, but there are precedents. I see no reason to deny this request. Consider it done. I will have the paper delivered to the young woman today. She should have them within the hour."

Mr. Granger, the decorator, was definitely not a ladies' man. He seemed averse to even shaking hands with them. Ruby smiled through her veil, which she wore at all times, except in their suite and when only Lucretia was present. Mr. Granger, no first name offered, asked a few questions about the house, including its past owner. When he heard the name, his manner changed from irritated and put-upon to subservient and gushingly pleasant.

"Oh, yes, lovely ladies. I do remember that hideous paper. The matron's husband insisted on it, as I recall. Definitely not suitable for ladies of your breeding and status." He chattered on as he showed them page after page from his sample portfolio.

"Here, Mr. Granger, this is the one. Do you like it?" Lucretia handed the sheet to Ruby, who nodded. It was in pastels, showing couples in formal dress walking through gardens. "Then, we want this. How soon can it be done? Within the week, I hope."

"The perfect choice, Mrs. Mills. A week? Hardly. It must come from Boston and that will take at least a month via ship."

Ruby spoke for the first time. "It seems to me, Mr. Granger, that for what you will charge, you can arrange its arrival sooner than that.

Have it sent by train instead. It must be complete before we move into the house. If this is not acceptable, perhaps we should find another decorator."

Mr. Granger could not see her face, but prudence told him not to disagree. "Of course, madam, but that will be more costly. I always try to save my clients as much money as possible. However, if that is your desire, most definitely, by rail it shall be. I will telegraph the factory immediately."

When he was gone, the women began laughing. Soon they were in the throes of near hysteria. Finally, Lucretia said, "I have never met anyone like him before. Why, you would have thought I had leprosy, or some other dire disease. What was the matter with him?"

"He is part of a group of males who like other men instead of women. I had no customers like them, so you never saw them in action. I know you found women who like women distasteful, and the same can be said of these men. I can tell you more about them, if you like."

Lucretia shuddered. "I think my imagination is enough, thank you very much." They laughed again. A knock interrupted their merriment. The bellman handed a letter to Ruby, who answered the door. Although she could read little, her lessons from Lucretia were improving that ability, but not enough to decipher the words scrawled on the paper. The envelope was addressed to "Mrs. Lucretia Sawyer and Mrs. Ruby Clanton Sawyer." She looked askance at Lulu, who nodded and told her to open it

She did so, but it might as well have been Greek to her. "All these fancy words. I cannot read it at all." She handed it to Lucretia, who skimmed it and grinned from ear to ear.

"It says, simply, that from this day forward, you are Ruby Clanton Sawyer, my adopted mother. It is all legal and signed by Judge Franklyn Carter Mountebank. See the signature."

Ruby said nothing. Lucretia suddenly realized that perhaps she had overstepped herself. Perhaps Ruby did not want her for a daughter. She should have never done this without asking. "I am sorry, Ruby. I love you so much that I wanted you in my life forever. I think of you as the mother I never had. I did not think you might not want to be my mother. Oh, dear God, I am sorry."

She turned toward her bedroom, but the arms that stopped her wrapped themselves around her. Through her tears, Ruby said, "I cannot say what I feel, Lulu. No one has ever wanted me before, except for what they could take from me. No one has ever loved me before…really loved me. I love you, too, and if I had a daughter, she would be you."

Lucretia turned and lifted the veil. She showered the scarred face with kisses as she held the older woman tight. They stood and cried together for a long time, until there were no tears left. Only smiles…smiles of happiness. They moved to the balcony, where they stood arm in arm and watched the sun sink over the bayous to the west.

# Chapter 69

Devereaux returned home with two bottles of rotgut rum that he intended to consume entirely by himself while he formulated a plan for the disappearance and demise of one Ruby the Bitch. Halfway through the first bottle, his plan was clear enough in his besotted head to take it to the worst barrooms in the city. He would walk so that no one could identify his carriage, and the trek would help rinse some of the rum from his head.

He passed several waterfront bars, but none would do. Too many customers who might remember him, since his recent life had forced him to seek companionship at places like these. Finally, at the furthest point before the river turned away from the bayous, he found what he was looking for. Inside the smoke-filled shanty were a dozen rickety tables, a slanted bar, and hungry-looking men of many colors who watched him stagger inside to the nearest chair by the door.

A slovenly barmaid waddled over and stood with one hand on her incredibly large hip. She bent down to expose her ample bosom and rubbed a pudgy hand against his cheek. "Anythin' I cane git you, darlin'? Anythin' at all?"

In the time it took to grab her hand from his face, his plan changed. He pulled the obese woman closer. "There sure is, my beauty. What would you do for a ten-dollar gold piece?"

"Hell, anathin'. Wan' me ta strip right here or up the stairs?"

"No, that is, no stripping. Something much more exciting than sex, and I think you are the perfect one for the job. Get us a couple of drinks and sit down here so I can tell you all about it."

She returned with two glasses of rum. "Lemme see da ten dollars first."

He motioned her to sit and moved his chair as close to hers as he could, considering the odors that emanated from her body. A fleeting thought ran through his mind, and he wondered when, or if, she had bathed in her lifetime. He slid his hand inside his vest pocket and removed a five-dollar gold coin. "The other half of the money when the job is done."

"Ya got youself a partner. Whata we goina do?"

"What if I told you we are going to kill someone? Would that bother you?"

"No, but I shoulda asted for more. But a deal is a deal. Ten dollars is a fair price for a killin', as long as I dona git hirt."

"Oh, you won't. I promise you won't." He smiled at her while he thought, *No, not hurt. Just dead!*

She complained the entire walk back to his home. No one paid any mind to a drunken man and the obese whore wandering the streets in the wee hours of the morning. He led her up the back steps to a storage shed where the yard equipment was stored. It had started raining and Sam would not be using any of it in the rain. Things were working perfectly for Devereaux. He found some rags and cleaning solvent in the little building and handed them to her. He did not know her name, and did not want to.

"Now, shuck off your clothes—all of them—and stand out in the rain until you are wet. Use this rag and scrub your body until it sparkles in the rain. You stink and I cannot fuck a stinking woman. That is, if you want to fuck."

"Fuck? Hell, yes." She dropped her skirt and pulled the filthy blouse over her head. She wore nothing else. He had expected to be disgusted by how she looked, but he found her so different from other women that he felt a first stirring of arousal.

Devereaux reached out to one saggy tit and lifted it. She was grinning her toothless smile when she lifted the other one to lick its nipple. He felt his cock jump as her tongue worked the end of her breast.

He slid out of his jacket and pants. His penis was at full alert and his balls pulled up inside him. He moaned as she took his dick in her hand and bent forward to take it in her mouth. She felt his penis tighten and stab into her mouth, signaling his impending explosion. "Not so fast. Fuck, you said."

She stood and continued scrubbing. Now she was rubbing between her legs. He watched until his cock grew painful. "Turn around and bend over." She did so, leaning her shoulders on the steps while her enormous ass and hips opened for him. At first, he was afraid he would not make it inside her, but she spread even wider until he felt her pussy hairs. He pounded into her as she bounced back to meet him. It was over in seconds, but she was panting as hard as he was, so he guessed she got what she wanted.

She turned to sit on the stairs. She pulled him to her and took his limp cock in her mouth. She squeezed his balls and mouthed his entire length until he was ready again. This time, she lay back on the stairs, spreading her thighs open wider than he thought possible. He looked through the darkness and rain to see a patch of hair larger than any he had ever seen. It excited him. He dropped between her legs and pushed himself as deep into her as he could. This time took much longer for consummation, but both cried out their satisfaction before he withdrew. Together they stood in the rain, cleansing their bodies.

"Follow me and do not make a sound. We will go up to the second floor and sleep until morning. I will find you some clothes then and we will get to work on our little project."

# Chapter 70

"Peg, there are some clothes on the ground in front of the yard shed. Do your best to clean them up and bring the skirt and blouse to my room. My things can wait for later."

Devereaux knew neither Peg nor Sam would ever question his orders, so he was beyond surprised when Peg returned to the kitchen immediately, carrying the dripping clothing held between two fingers.

"Mr. Devereaux, there ain't a thing Peg can do with these things. They stink worse than chicken bones set outside in the sun for a week. If these came on a woman…well, I hope you are well medicated, sir."

Devereaux grinned, and then laughed. "You are so right, Peg. But if these cannot be salvaged, what can we do about dressing the large—all right, huge—woman upstairs? She must look presentable for a task I have for her. Is there anything in the attic that might work? As I recall, my Aunt Eugenia was huge, too. Knock the moths out and shake out the mold if you can find anything. Also a shawl and parasol. Whatever you think we can make do with for a day or so. And shoes. She must have shoes, even if they are men's shoes."

"Lordy, Mr. Devereaux. I will look, but I ain't no miracle maker."

Devereaux poured himself a cup of Peg's wonderful chocolate and, as an afterthought, poured a second for the woman upstairs. She was still asleep, lying on her side. Mountains of fat rolled from her stomach and met her sagging tits above gigantic thighs. At first, he felt repulsed, but as he looked at her black thatch between those thighs, he felt the desire to empty himself in her again.

"Hey, woman. Wake up. We got things to do." She opened her eyes and watched him disrobe. He set the cups of chocolate on a bureau and advanced, cock at the ready, to mount her. She sighed with pleasure as her ass lifted her twat up to meet him. He squeezed her big tits, pulling the nipples hard. She giggled and wiggled as they bounced on the old bed. Their combined weight, along with the activities they were doing, was too much and the mattress crashed through the ropes holding it to the frame, bringing it to the floor with a crash that shook the entire house.

"Man, dat be da noisiest fuck I ever done and you were de best too. Next time, we jist skip the bed and do it on de floor. Are you ready again yet?"

Devereaux shook his head, but continued to squeeze her tits, listening to her sharp breath intakes. "You like it hard, do you? Do you like a little hurting, too?" She nodded and closed her eyes. He bit her nipples until they beaded with tiny drops of blood. He turned her on her side and slapped her ass as hard as he could. She moaned in pleasure. He had never done these things before and he found himself hard again, aching and wanting to hurt her more. Oh, what a toy she might be.

When Peg knocked, the woman rolled off the bed and opened the door, displaying her assets for all to see. Peg stepped back and shook her head. "Come on in, honey, I ain't modest. Whata got there?" She did not wait for any answer, but jerked the garments out of Peg's hands.

Peg looked past her at the exhausted man on the bed. He did not even try to cover himself. "Mr. Devereaux, I found some things that might work to…cover this." She nodded in the direction of the whore, who was pushing her body into a dress obviously three sizes too small.

"Hey, looka me? Perfect fit." She pirouetted in front of the mirror. "Now, I look jist like da ladies I see on Bourbon Street with their beaus and husbands. Who do I haft ta kill for my money?"

Devereaux flew out of the bed and gently shoved Peg through the door, locking it behind her. "You stupid bitch." He kept his voice as low as he could, not wanting Peg to hear, but in his anger, the pitch kept rising. "I ought to kill you myself. If anyone finds out what we are going to do, we will both go to meet the devil. Do you understand?" The woman just looked at him. "God, you are the most useless creature God ever put on this earth."

"Ya didna think I be useless awhile ago, when you was shoving it ta me. Ya had plenty of use fer me den." She lifted her skirt, exposing her nakedness. "If'n I be bad, ya can spank me first. I be a bad girl and need a beatin." She bent over, exposing her ass. Devereaux grabbed his belt off the floor and hit her as hard as he could. She moaned and cried out, "More, again. Yes, more."

Outside, Peg had heard more than she wanted to hear. She crept downstairs, away from the hideous noises above, and went in search of Sam. He would not want to believe what she would tell him, but in the end, he would.

"The trick"—he told the sated woman after their third mating—"is to find the two separated. It really does not matter which, as long as we have time for you to convince her to go with you. I will deal with the old one, either way. Now, get dressed and cover your head with that shawl there. We must not be seen together. Do you understand what you need to do?"

"Yessir. I git her ta go with me into da alley and ya give her sumptin ta make er sleep. Easy. Den I get my ten dollars. And de new clothes. Fer sure."

Devereaux hoped it was "fer sure." They separated behind his house. He took the carriage and she walked in shoes that hurt her feet, she told him. "For that ten-dollar gold piece, you can put up with it for a while. Throw them in the river later, for all I care, but now you wear them."

Ruby and Lucretia came outside and mounted a carriage waiting for them. They stayed together in shop after shop, until Lucretia went to her bank, leaving Ruby to browse the millinery store alone. Devereaux drove by the wandering fat woman, who pointed to the window, where he could see Ruby trying on hats.

"I gonna earn my money right now. Yessir, I am." She went inside and approached the surprised woman in the veil. "Madam, is that your girl jist left here?"

"Yes, why do you ask?"

"She done twisted her ankle round da corner and needs help. I show ya."

Ruby did not think, but followed the woman around the corner into the alley littered with trash. Halfway in, she felt an arm slip around her neck and a cloth cover her nose. Her last thought was of her most recent visit to a dentist and the smell of the ether he had used.

They lifted the woman into the back of the carriage and dropped a blanket over her to look like it was dropped casually by the last person who sat in the back.

"Good job. Now go back to my house and wait in the yard shed until dark. I will come for you then."

"Sure like 'nother round on da yard shack steps."

"Maybe, if you do as I tell you. Now, damn it, go."

"Kin I take off dees shoes now? De sure does hurt ma feet."

"I don't care. Just go." He watched as she waddled away, singing to herself. He shook his head in disgust, both with her and himself for the things he did to and with her.

He drove the carriage out of town to the east, over bumpy roads pitted with holes from traffic. Having lived in the area his entire life and grown accustomed to the swamps where he fished and speared frogs and killed gators as a young man, he knew all the back roads and abandoned shacks deep in the bayou.

He stopped in front of a dilapidated old house missing half its roof. The mosquitoes were dining on him in droves, as usual. He hated them and never understood why he was a target when his companions were ignored. Some of the boys had covered themselves with chicken grease, but Devereaux was too finicky to do that. So, they smiled and laughed as he slapped and batted the biting insects away.

Ruby was making small noises in the back of the carriage, so he quickly pulled the blanket away and tied her hands together before pulling her into an upright position.

"Hey, bitch, can you hear me?" He shook her shoulders. She only groaned. He lifted her veil to slap her face, but pulled back and stared at the hideous scars. "Looking like you do, you should thank me for what I am going to do to you. Do you hear me?"

This time Ruby mumbled, "Yes. What are you doing? Where am I?"

"Look around you, bitch, and enjoy the outdoors. It is the last time you will see it because I am going to kill you. And enjoy doing it. It will be a death worthy of the way you have treated me. Fun part of it is that I am going to keep you alive for a while, just to keep you aware of my progress in wedding and bedding lovely little Lucretia. I will pass along every detail, including how she tastes and wiggles under me."

"You bastard. When I get my hands on you, I will tear you limb from limb and hurt you in ways you never dreamed possible." She twisted her arms, trying to shrug off the ropes, but they were too tight. She kicked out at him, but missed.

He laughed and wound his hand into her hair, pulling it so hard she screamed in pain. "Now start walking. If you do not do exactly as I tell you, I will pull every hair out of your pathetic head."

The shack was moldy and smelled like the rotten creatures half-eaten inside. Once inside, he released her hair and hit her on the back of her neck. She fell forward, unconscious. He rolled her over, untied her hands, rolled her again, and tied her hands behind her back, then tied her ankles together. Just for the fun of it, he kicked her in the side and spit on her face.

He sang to himself as he drove back to the city and home.

# Chapter 71

Lucretia left the bank and returned to the millinery shop where she had left Ruby. When she did not see her, she asked the clerk if she had seen Ruby leave. "Yes, I did, mistress. A large, strangely dressed woman came inside and they left together. I wondered about the unlikely twosome, but they seemed to be in a hurry. I forgot about them until you asked. Sorry I cannot be of more help."

Lucretia went back outside and looked up and down the street and into the alleys on either side of the block. *Perhaps she felt ill and returned to the hotel*, she thought. However, the carriage was still waiting. She climbed inside without waiting for the driver to assist her and ordered him to drive slowly to the hotel. She did not see Ruby anywhere, so she explained to the driver, who agreed to search other streets for her. At the desk, she saw both their keys in the room slot.

"Hello, I am Lucretia Sawyer and I seem to have misplaced my mother. No, not a joke. Sorry I sound flippant, but I am most concerned. No, my name really is Sawyer. We used Mills to guard our privacy from certain individuals who might be overly interested in two ladies traveling alone.

"My mother was in a store, waiting for me to return. The clerk told me she left in a hurry with another woman, but that is strange because we know no other ladies in the city. My driver today is out looking for her…I hope you do not mind. I will pay for his time. Could you send out other drivers we have used? The ones who would recognize her?"

The desk clerk agreed immediately and soon, several drivers were combing the city in search of the missing woman. Lucretia sat in the lobby watching everyone outside when Devereaux LaClaire drove up. She ran outside to him with tears on her cheeks.

"What is it, dear sweet girl? Why are you crying? Can I help in some way?" He enveloped her in his arms, smiling as he rested his chin on her soft hair. *This is the way I want you,* he thought. *Soon I will have you.* Inwardly, he felt a rush of power and desire for her and her money…mostly her money, he finally admitted to himself.

She explained Ruby's disappearance again. "My God, Lucretia. That is horrible. Have you notified the police yet?" She shook her head. "Well, come, we will do so immediately. They will find your…guardian."

"Oh, Devereaux, she is more than my guardian. She is my mother." She could not know that her words hit him like a knife in his stomach. He forced himself to remain still, while he wanted to shake her and her words away. "Mother. I did not realize she was your mother."

"Do not say *was*. Say *is*. She is only missing and the police will find her. You are right. Hurry, please take me to them."

After their visit to the police, Lucretia asked him to drive her back to her hotel. "Perhaps we should stop for supper. I would wager you have not eaten at all today. How about Antoine's for a bowl of gumbo or chowder? Nothing heavy. Just a light meal while you wait. I am sure the police will have news within the hour."

"No, thank you. I wish to wait for them at the hotel. I appreciate your help. You are always there when I need something, it seems."

"Yes, that would be best. As for always being there, I will *always* be there for you, no matter what." He decided a bit of attention now would go unnoticed in her fear, so he took her hand and raised it to his lips, where this kiss was real, not a gesture. He was right…she did not notice. "Shall I come in and sit with you?" He hoped not, because he had to get the whore into the bayou before dark.

"No, thank you again. Just let me out here and I will go up to our suite to wait. It would not do for me to have a man there without my mother." He nodded, lifted her down, and using his thumb, wiped away her tears. He kissed her forehead softly before she moved away and she did not seem to notice. He smiled, knowing he was already ahead of the game. However, the mother thing was an obstacle he had never imagined. Well, he would simply eliminate the mother and things would go as he planned.

At his home, he found the whore sitting on the yard shed steps. As he approached, she lifted her skirt to expose her naked thighs. He felt his cock stir. "Take off your shirt. I want to cum on your breasts." She did so and he buried his face between the udder-like bags. She giggled as he licked her nipples. "Spread your legs. I am going to fuck you first, then shoot my seed all over you." That is what he did.

"Now get dressed. I do not care if you wash or not. We have to hurry." She slipped into her clothes and climbed in the back of the carriage. "Now cover yourself up. I don't want anyone to see you with me." She did as told and began to snore within minutes.

She awoke as the carriage bounced along the sandy road. "Kin I sit up now?"

"Yes. We are here anyway. Get down."

"Kint ya help me? I be a big lady."

"Big, yes. Lady, no. Get down yourself." He left her standing in the carriage. She finally got down and followed him into the shack.

"Hello, Bitch. I brought you some company. This here is Whore. Whore, meet Bitch. You two are going to be spending some time together, so you might as well get acquainted. She is here to make sure you do not get away.

"Whore, there is a box of food in the carriage bonnet. Go outside and bring it in. If you want to share it with Bitch, that is fine with me. Whatever you want to do with it, I couldn't care less. But remember it has to last you until I bring you more. It might be fun to watch Bitch starve to death. You probably should eat it all yourself. I would not like for you to get skinny on me. Anyway, Whore, lift your skirt and bend over. I want one more poke in you before I go."

Ruby was amazed to see Devereaux had a huge hard-on. She knew some men liked fat women, but this one was beyond fat. Nevertheless, he slid his cock into the woman and started pumping. The fat woman met his every stroke and cried out even before he shot into her. He pulled out, patted the ass in front of him, and said, "Fond adieus, my lovelies. I will be back in a few days. Now, Whore, if she tries to get away, just lay her down and sit on her face until she stops breathing, and then roll her into the bayou. The gators do not care how ugly she is. But you might want to watch out…you would make a dozen big ones happy with all your lard."

# Chapter 72

The two women in the shanty eyed each other. Finally, the one known as Whore flopped down on the filthy floor across the small area from where Ruby was tied. "I have been here hours," Ruby spoke, "and I really need to pee. If you will help me stand and pull up my skirt, I promise not to try to escape."

Whore looked at her for a long time and then heaved herself up. "Guess it cain't hurt nuttin' ta let ya pee." She pulled Ruby to her feet and lifted the once fashionable skirt. "How da hell ya goina pee with all dem other thins on? Guess ya think I can pullum down fer ya too."

"Actually, it would probably be easier if you just tore them off of me, or cut them off. I do not care. I just want to pee."

"I hate ta run such beautfil thins. If'n I cut you legs free, promise not ta run?"

"Whatever you want. I will not run. But hurry, before it is too late."

Whore took the knife from inside her thigh, where she always had one taped to her. She quickly cut the ropes and slid the underwear down Ruby's legs. Ruby balanced herself carefully and bent to relieve her overfull body.

When she stood, she said, "I cannot thank you enough. I have no money to pay you, but I would if I did." She laughed thinly. "Did you understand any of that? And what is your name? If we are going to be here together, I guess I should call you by your name."

Whore looked at her and nodded. "Kin I have ya thins…da thins round yer feet?" She never took her eyes off the silken garments on the floor around Ruby's ankles.

"Of course you can." Ruby carefully stepped out of them and watched in amazement as the other woman grabbed them and tried to pull them on under her skirt. They were far too small, but she did not care, even as they ripped and tore.

She smiled at Ruby. "Names Claralee Holcomb. Ain't nobody call me dat fer so long, I might not know it was me they be callin'."

"Claralee, that is a beautiful name. My name is not so grand as yours. I am Ruby Clanton…er, Sawyer. My friend just adopted me yesterday and I am not used to the name, so if some called me by that name, I might not answer either. Say, we have a lot in common, Claralee."

The fat woman's face clouded. "Me, I be a whore."

"Well, so was I."

Claralee laughed. "A lady like ya are cain't be no whore."

Ruby replied, "Oh, you are wrong, I was a whore for most my life until a john did this to me." She stepped toward Claralee. "Lift my veil and see, then let us sit down again and get acquainted."

Claralee lifted the veil and drew in a sharp breath. "Da sum mean critter dun dat to ya. I heared of men like dat, but never fucked one. My good luck!"

Ruby backed up to the wall and slid down so she could sit. Claralee flopped her big body on the side wall, so they were closer together. They talked of men, pain, and lives of misery and children they lost and loves never returned. It was no different from the way other females conversed, except for language that was never heard in a parlor or polite company.

Claralee was silent for a time before asking, "Why da gentleman do dis ta ya?"

"First, let me tell you he is no gentleman. He is a scoundrel who wants my daughter and her money. I stand between him and that, so it was necessary for him to get rid of me. I am not sure why he did not just kill me in the first place, but as he said, maybe it is just that he wants to share his success and let me suffer as my Lucretia will suffer once he gets his hands on her. As I said, he is a very bad man. Very bad."

"Well, he fuck purty good. An' he give me dis purty dress, too. But, I dunna like him call me Whore all de time."

Claralee opened the food basket and found fried chicken, shrimp salad, and a dozen sandwiches. "How ya going eat? I know…I hol up a samwich and ya bite inta it." Ruby ate a small bite at a time, relishing every bite of ham and relish. She wanted something to drink, but did not ask. Claralee sat back, holding a fork in one hand and a drumstick in the other. She consumed all the salad and most of the chicken before she was done. "Betta stop now. No tellin' when he brin' us more."

They talked for hours like old friends until sleep overtook them. At least, overtook Claralee. Ruby heard every animal cry, the snorts of the gators, hoots of owls, and a myriad of unnamed creatures.

She was ready for daylight, but not for the return of Devereaux LaClaire, who arrived even before the mosquitoes. Ruby was glad her dress was long and covered her free ankles. He checked her wrists and gave her hair a hard pull before he dropped his pants. "Bend over, Whore, I want a little cunt before I go back to town, I would do the Bitch, but she is too ugly to look at." Without another word, he pulled up Claralee's dress and grabbed for her ass. "What the hell is this? Where did you get these things?"

"Ruby dun give em ta me."

"Ruby, is it? You two on a first-name basis now? How did she take them off?" He reached over and lifted Ruby's dress. "You stupid whore. I told you not to even get near her." He swung and slapped her across the face with the back of his hand. He tore the under things from her body. He pulled up her skirt and pummeled her body with his fists, hitting her breasts, stomach, and face as she cowed and tried to pull away from him. When she fell, he turned her on her stomach and, lifting her hips, pushed his throbbing penis into her. This time she did not respond. He did not notice nor care. Claralee was unconscious. "Thanks, Whore, I like it better and better after beating you."

He tied Ruby's ankles again, this time so tight they hurt. "Listen, Bitch, your little Lucretia is so devastated by your disappearance that she has already let me kiss her. I will have her in my bed within a week. I wonder if she will like a few slaps on the ass or bites on her tits. I will let you know; then I will kill you and give your ugly face to the gators." He laughed as he climbed into his buggy and bounced off in the direction of town.

# Chapter 73

Devereaux was sexually drained, but mentally consumed by plots and plans. Intellectually, he knew he should kill both women in the bayou shack, but he wanted Ruby alive to hear of his conquest of Lucretia. The whore he wanted because he could beat her and fuck her with no reprisals. When he tired of her, she would become gator food, too. In the meantime, he needed to focus strictly on Lucretia.

He arrived at her hotel to find her in the lobby talking to two policemen. He put on his most concerned face and walked briskly to the threesome, slipping his arm protectively around the distraught young woman. He knew she was distraught because she wore the same dress she had on the day before…the yellow satin that was so shiny and beautiful was wrinkled and soiled today. Her face was haggard and her eyes red from crying. Oh, yes, she needed him. He would make sure.

"Tell me, officers, have you found any sign of the lady's…mother?" He hesitated using the term, but was glad he did when Lucretia gave him a wan smile.

"Not a clue, Mr. LaClaire, I am afraid. We are checking the riverbanks and have boats in the nearby bayous. Oh, sorry, madam, I know even thinking of such a thing is painful, but it is part of our missing person's search."

Lucretia felt faint, picturing the creatures in the bayous. The menacing monsters she had seen from the train. She shivered and did not object as Devereaux drew her close. He turned her slightly to rest her head on his shoulder, making it easy to kiss her head and forehead.

"Come, Lucretia. When was the last time you ate? Probably not since Ruby… Well, let us have some light breakfast here in the dining room."

"No, thank you, Devereaux. I am a mess. I just want to go to my room now."

"Of course. I understand." He led her to the elevator and stepped inside, thinking that this was perfect. Better even than he could have hoped.

Once in her room, he rang for a bellman and ordered orange juice, beignet donuts, soft-cooked eggs, and milk—for two, delivered in one hour. "Now, my dear, while we wait for breakfast, why don't you take a long soak in that magnificent tub. I will draw your water while you find something to wear." He steered her into her room, closing the door behind her as he rushed to the bathroom and started the water. He added a generous amount of perfumed salts and laid out a huge white towel, then as an afterthought, a second towel.

He took a third towel and rapped on her bedroom door. "Here, wrap yourself in this. I promise to turn my back." He opened the door a crack and stuck his arm into the room, holding it out until she finally took it. He closed the door softly. "I will wait in the sitting area. Call me if you need anything." He stood so that the room reflected in the windows and watched as she moved gracefully from her bedroom to the bathroom, closing the door behind her.

He closed his eyes, picturing her dropping the towel and stepping naked into the bubbly water, where she lay back, eyes closed, breasts floating, one trim leg bent above the water, knee showing. Dear God, that he could kiss that knee and all the way up to her forbidden womanhood. That was not something he particularly liked to do, but for Lucretia, if she wanted, he would do anything.

He had the drug he bought from the illegally and wanted to use it immediately. But common sense told him to wait until she trusted him. She must feel secure with him before he used the liquid that would guarantee her compliance with whatever he wanted. He would have to wait for that until they were married. The man warned him that too much might kill her, so if that happened after they exchanged vows, then he would be a very wealthy man. With or without the lovely lady.

He waited by the door until he was sure she was asleep, probably for the first time since Ruby the bitch had disappeared. He carefully opened the door and crept to the side of the tub. She was so beautiful he had to restrain himself from touching her as she lay like an angel in the cooling water.

He opened one of the towels and spread it wide, holding it so he could not see her.

"Lucretia, darling, wake up. The water must be cold by now and it will not do Ruby any good to return to find you down with pneumonia."

He heard her moving in the water. "Devereaux, what are you doing in here? Get out!"

"Darling, you are freezing. Here, I cannot see you, so it is safe to stand and let me wrap the towel around you."

"I will not move an inch until you leave. Get away from me."

"If that is what you wish, I will do so." He turned and took two steps before dropping the towel. She stood, stepped out of the cold water, and reached for the towel. He quickly grabbed the third towel and wrapped it around her as she stood from retrieving the other one.

"There, now you are covered. Let me dry you."

"Devereaux, that was a rotten trick, unbecoming a gentleman. I am disappointed in you. I thought you were different from other men, but you are all alike." She struggled to get away from him, losing the towel as she did so.

"Oh, my dear. I am so sorry. Here …" He scooped her up in his arms and carried her to her bedroom. He had already turned down the bed, so it was easy to lay her down on the crisp white sheets.

"If you touch me, Devereaux, I promise I will kill you."

Quickly, he covered her delectable body with a blanket. "I would never touch you against your wishes, Lucretia. I will do nothing until we are wed and go to your marriage bed as husband and wife."

She looked at him as if seeing him for the first time. Pictures flashed through her mind. On the train, where Ruby had warned her not to trust him. In his carriage, in the dining room, and here in the suite. Ruby was right. The idea of being in bed with him made her slightly nauseated. "Thank you, Devereaux. I am feeling a bit unwell now, and would like to sleep. Please go and I will meet you for supper at seven in the dining room." She had to get rid of him before she did get sick.

"But, my darling, I want to stay with you. To help you, to nurse you."

She cut him off. "No, Devereaux. I must insist you leave. How will it look for us to be alone together? My reputation in this town will be ruined even before I have been here long enough to have one."

Devereaux frowned, but agreed to leave to appease her and her anger. Her anger was the last thing he needed. He knelt to kiss her forehead and tucked the blanket tightly around her soft form. "Breakfast is waiting for you in the dining area and I will lock the door behind me. I plan to spend the day searching for Ruby. I am so looking forward to dining with you tonight."

# Chapter 74

"Claralee, can you hear me? Claralee, wake up. Honey, listen to me. It's Ruby. Oh, may God strike that cretin dead. Claralee, oh please wake up." She could hear the labored breathing of the unconscious woman, and suspected that she was badly injured. Ruby scooted on her butt toward Claralee. She turned herself again until her hands tied behind her felt the fabric of the skirt. She used her fingers to pull it up and up until Claralee's legs and hips were exposed. She looked over her shoulder and down until she spotted the knife taped to the inside of the huge thigh. It was so far down that her fingers could not reach it.

Her only chance was to sit on the woman's legs above the knees and lie back on her prone body until her fingers and hands finally found the hilt of the knife, which she pulled away from the tape. Careful not to cut her own fingers, she rolled off of Claralee. She lay on her side with the mucky floor against the side of her head. She tilted the knife until it made contact with the rope.

It seemed like an eternity until one strand gave way. Then another, then another. She pulled her swollen hands free and quickly cut the ropes binding her ankles. She tried to stand, but her feet would not support her. She ignored her own misery and with much difficulty rolled Claralee onto her back. She cleaned the filth off her face and forced her mouth open.

"Oh, Claralee, I think you have breathed in so much of that stuff, you are drowning in it." She forced Claralee's mouth open and pressed her own against it. She began to suck and spit. The taste of what came up into her mouth was beyond imaginable. She sucked, spit, sucked, and spit for what seemed like hours. When exhaustion began to take over, she heard a small sound from the comatose female.

"Claralee, can you hear me? Listen carefully. I am going to try to sit you up on your side. I want you to help me if you can. Then you need to cough out the shit in your lungs. Here is my hand. Squeeze me if you can hear me."

She felt a tiny movement, but it was enough. She was crying as she rolled Claralee over on her side. "Come on, girl. Cough, even if it is a little." Her reward was a small barking sound. "Hooray, you did it! Now, again. Yes and again. Oh, Claralee." She hugged the filthy woman and kissed her cheeks. "You are going to be all right. Now, let me help you sit up. Good, now cough some more."

Claralee lifted her head and tears spilled down her cheeks. Her throat hurt when she tried to speak. "Tank ya."

"Do not even try to talk. Just rest. We both are going to be fine." They sat together with Ruby's arms around the large woman. "I have a plan. I will talk and you nod yes or no. We might end up dead if the plan does not work, but we are going to end up dead anyway when he gets back.

"Can you read or write?" Claralee shook her head. "Well, neither can I, except a few words Lucretia taught me. So you will have to remember the words. Can you do that?" Claralee nodded. "'Lulu needs help.' That is what you have to learn. Can you remember that? 'Lulu needs help.'"

The large woman smiled and nodded. Ruby continued. "Now, more to learn. You need to know the names I will say to you, just so you can tell the man at the telegraph office."

Claralee shook her head. "Dunna know telergraph." Her voice was raspy, but she could at least be understood.

"Do you know where to find a telegraph office?" Claralee shook her head again. "Then ask a policeman or go into a bank and ask or even hotel lobbies. Or a train station. Yes, that is the best place. You will need some money. We can steal it if we have to, but we will get some someplace."

"I git money." She smiled her confidence.

"Then let us get back to the words you need to learn. They are the words you must say to the man in the telegraph office. You want to send telegraphs to Cottonwood Creek, General Stanley Cotton in Saint Louis, Mrs. Elizabeth Harold, and Sergeant Michael O'Brien in Saint Louis. I know that is a lot to remember, but they are the only people I can think of who can find the man we need."

Claralee practiced until she could recite all the names in a singsong rhythm, much like children used to remember the alphabet. Ruby hugged her again to show her delight. "Now I am going to tell you a story that will explain why we must find this man. His name is Black Eagle Grant…like Mr. Grant, the president. He was a soldier at the fort where…"

The story was long, but Claralee listened with excited eyes. "Da love themselves? Like a storybook?"

"Yes, they do, even if they won't admit it. He is the only one who can stop LaClaire if I do not make it out of here alive, and that is likely. So we must get him to New Orleans. Now, when you go to the telegraph office, tell the man to say in the telegraph that the Eagle must go to New Orleans to help Lulu."

Claralee giggled. "Eagle! Dat's a funny name fer a man. Eagle!"

Ruby was careful to keep impatience out of her voice. Claralee was like child in so many ways. "Yes, it is. He is half Indian and that is an Indian name."

"Ain't never fuck an Indian. Da like reg'lar men?"

"Yes, like regular men with all the same equipment. Now, Claralee, what are you going to tell the telegraph man?"

Claralee became serious. "Dat Eagle need go ta New Orleans to help Lulu. Dat right?"

Ruby hugged her again. "Just perfect. Now, let's work on you remembering who to send the telegraphs to." It seemed to Ruby that it took forever before Claralee finally got them all right.

"Now, as long as the monster can fuck you, he will keep you alive. He hates me, so he will kill me. Unless…unless we can trick him into believing I am already dead." It was such a simple plan that they decided it would work. Claralee would babble and cry about the alligator—biggest in the entire swamp—crawling into the shack and dragging Ruby with it into the water. Claralee would run down the road toward town and act like she was in a daze, totally frightened.

Ruby took off her dress, which left her naked but for her chemise and underskirts. She dragged her dress back and forth from the water to the shack and back several times, making it look like something heavy had scraped the mud. She then tore her dress into pieces and tossed them to float away on the slight bayou current. They stood arm in arm, watching the sun rising low between the trees as the sound of a carriage carried toward them, warning them to start their final part of the plan. They kissed good-bye before Claralee ran toward the noise and Ruby disappeared into the muddy, dark swamp forest behind the shanty.

# *PART III*

## Chapter 75

Another pair of eyes watched the sun as it sent its first rays of the day across the barren landscape of the high desert of Mexico. The bright light hurt his eyes, which were bloodshot and burning from lack of sleep and too much tequila. He was lying on the ground in the dust behind a cantina in some sleepy town just outside of nowhere. His last memory was stepping outside the back door to take a leak. His pants were still down and his shriveled penis was exposed. He quickly looked around, but no one was in sight. He stood, pulling his filthy army pants up, and tightened his belt.

*To all the gods, what have I become?* he thought. He knew what he had become: a drunken man with an Indian father and a white mother. A man wanted by neither and no one, except the army. He never should have resigned. He had been good at his job. Now his hands shook so much, he could not hold his gun enough to shoot a moving turtle.

He rubbed his eyes, trying to make the blurring go away. He was still drunk enough that he staggered as he walked to the stable across the street. It took him two tries to get his horse saddled. He tried to remember if he had paid in advance, but could not, so he left a couple of pesos on a saddle on the ground beside the stable doors.

He filled his canteen and a couple of water bags from the questionable water of the horse trough in the shade of the stable and then mounted. He turned his horse north and let the beast set its own pace in the blazing heat.

Whether or not it was sleep or he had passed out again was unimportant, but when he awoke, he felt some better. He realized they had traveled some distance because the terrain had changed. Ahead he saw a line of small trees, indicating water. He urged the horse forward.

He and the horse both drank from the small creek. He emptied his canteen and water bags, rinsed them several times, and refilled them with fresh water. He walked into the water and sat down, letting its coolness penetrate his clothes, which he stood to remove. He pounded them on rocks first to get out as much of the dirt and grime as he could before rinsing them again and laying them on the riverbank to dry in the sun. He returned to the water, where he scrubbed his body with gritty sand and then lay on his back in the stream to wash it all away.

The sun above warmed his body, while the water cooled him. He closed his eyes and soon dozed. He dreamed of his grandmother, Summer Swan, who sometimes spoke to him with messages from his gods. This time she was silent, but mouthed one word over and over. Finally, he realized the word was *Lulu*. An image of the woman floated through a black sky where Summer Swan had been. The image changed as it settled down in front of him. Her face moved to his and he awoke. A school of tiny fishes was nibbling at his hair.

This time he did not curse his dream. He closed his eyes, hoping it would return, but as most dreams, it would not. Finally, he climbed out of the creek to retrieve his clothing. He stopped short. His clothes were gone and so was his horse. He ran to the bank, looking in all directions when he heard a noise in the shrubs. He moved nonchalantly that way until he was close to where the noise had originated. He suddenly dove into the bushes and grabbed a head of hair so hard it produced a scream.

"Let go of me, you shit."

If the language had not surprised him, the small woman did. She kicked him in the groin so hard he let go of her and groped his manhood, moaning as he bent. When the pain subsided somewhat, he looked up. "Why did you do that? Christ, all you had to do was ask."

"You were hurting me, asshole." She had the blackest hair he had ever seen outside his own tribe. It was braided and fell nearly to her full hips. The size of her tits made it clear that she was no child, even though hardly taller than one.

"I am sorry I hurt you. Now, where are my clothes and horse? I want to get moving."

"You are not going anywhere until we say you can."

"We? Who is we?"

"My friend and I. Her name is Concha. She has your horse and clothes. If you hurt me, you will never see that animal again."

"Why did you take them? I have no money."

"It is not for money. We saw you in the water and decided you look enough like her husband that you could be brothers. He is cruel to her and beats her because she has not given him a child. If you mount her and she gets your seed, her husband will think it is his and will be happy."

"What do you think I am? A horse ready for stud service? I have never heard of anything so loco as that. Forget it. Now give me my horse and clothes."

She laughed. "You are not in any position to order me to do anything." She walked casually toward him, sliding her dress over her head as she walked. He felt her tits against his chest and a prick of a knifepoint just above his penis. "I think you might want to give in to my demand." She continued to rub her breasts against him.

He watched her face, seeing a change in her eyes. Without conscious effort, he lifted a hand to cover her hardening breast. Her intake of breath told him what every man wants to hear. She wanted him. Just as he slid his hand down her taut stomach, she stepped away. "Concha, come. He is ready for you."

A few seconds later, another young woman stepped out of the shrubs. She was taller than her friend, but just as endowed. Concha was already naked as she moved to him to press her body against his. "I have been watching you and Mayte. Your cock likes Mayte. Will it like me, too?" She bent her head to his chest and licked one of his nipples and then the other.

Eagle felt his penis harden even more. His hands had minds of their own as they roamed her sleek body until they found her tits and the bush between her legs. He rubbed her, feeling the wetness as he used his thumb to work her clit until she moved and began to moan. He moved her body to the ground and, without further preliminaries, gave her what she wanted. His cock slid into her easily. His hips moved in a rhythm she immediately matched.

Mayte dropped down beside them to reach between their bucking hips. Her fingers found Concha's swollen button and rubbed it, adding to her friend's pleasure. Eagle felt her fingers moving against his dick, too, exciting him further. When they exploded, she lay beside them smiling. "How was that, my Concha? Did you feel his seed?"

"Yes," Concha answered weakly. "It was good and his seed went deep. Next time, he can put it in me from behind so it goes to the opening where babies are made."

Eagle rolled off and looked at them in amazement. "Next time? What next time? By all the gods, there will be no next time."

Mayte laughed. "Oh, stud man, there will be a next time. Maybe several next times. If you are a good boy, you might be on your way by dark. Now just rest and watch. The next time will be your idea, I promise."

# Chapter 76

He was on his way by dark. He did not remember ever being so drained, physically and mentally. The two women had used him in every way he had ever known a man could be used. In addition, he had enjoyed it until he could barely move. They gave him water and some pemmican to eat and let him sleep for an hour at a time, but that was all.

Mayte had promised the next time would be his idea and he had to admit it was. He watched as the two naked females rubbed each other with some sort of oil that made their skin glisten, even in the shadows where they lay on the fragrant grass. Soon they were rubbing their breasts together and suckling on each other.

He felt himself stirring as Concha spread Mayte's legs and her hands moved up into the joining. Mayte spread her hips as wide as she could. Concha lowered her head so she could insert her tongue into Mayte's wetness, lapping at the swollen clit until Mayte was crying and moving her hips up and down.

Black Eagle could stand it no longer. He moved to drop to his knees behind the swaying ass Concha offered him. He grabbed her by the waist as she pushed herself up on her knees to give him a perfect angle to reach her innermost womanhood. She moaned, but did not stop licking Mayte's pussy. From his position, he watched his cock slide in and out and the movements of the women.

Mayte's orgasm came first, then his own. Concha did not move, but remained with her ass in the air after he pulled out. She smiled at him when he dropped on his back beside her. She lifted her head to kiss his mouth gently. Mayte rolled her head under Concha and began to suck the swollen clit as if it were a cock. Concha moved up and down as if fucking it into the other woman's mouth until her cries for more let them know she had her release, too.

Still, she did not move. Breathlessly, she explained that the seed would work its way into her hole more easily in this position, which made sense to Eagle. He was exhausted and beginning to feel like the stud horse he had mentioned earlier. Not that he had not enjoyed it, but it was sheer sex and nothing more. Not like with Lucretia…

Lucretia was the last thing he wanted to think about when he felt a mouth on his dropping penis. Behind his closed eyes, he felt and remembered. He remembered the softness of her mouth, the gentle sucking that brought desire back to him, even as his cock was still pulling away. This was much the same. His hips moved to the slow rhythm of Lucretia's mouth—no, Mayte's mouth. Soon it did not matter. She rode him hard and he called out her name as he spurted. "Lucretia, Lucretia."

Mayte did not stop until her body found its release. She collapsed atop of him, letting her cheek rub his chest. "Who is Lucretia? She must be something, as no man before you has ever mistaken me for anyone else."

Eagle did not answer, just rolled her away as he stood. "Now I want my horse and clothes. Or do I have to tear the hair out of both of your heads to get it? You got what you wanted. I got more than I wanted or expected, but now I want to be on my way."

Mayte, graceful as a deer in her nakedness, disappeared in the shrub and returned a few minutes later with the horse and clothes. He washed again in the creek and dressed in the stiff pants, but just folded the shirt and put it in his saddlebag.

Concha remained on her shoulders and knees, ass in the air. "Good-bye, Stud Man. It is best we know not your name and you cannot find us. Your seed will find its way into my belly and it will be a fine boy for my husband. Mayte is already with child, so there will be only one. Thank you."

Eagle laughed. "This is the first time any woman has thanked me for fucking her. You are most welcome, both of you. It was an enjoyable way to spend a day." He mounted his horse and nodded as he accepted the bag of food Mayte handed him. It did not enter his mind until much later that he should have told her that he was half white. He hoped her offspring did not show up with light-colored skin, or worse yet, blue eyes. Well, what was done was done and he could change nothing now.

It was dark, but he felt no need to stop. The horse was rested and they could ride all night. Morning should bring him to the Rio Grande. Again, he would let the horse determine their path. He did not know where he would go next, but he would at least be back where he belonged.

# Chapter 77

Claralee ran screaming toward the oncoming carriage. Her bellows were so loud that she sounded more like a banshee than a human being. Even the horses reared, forcing Devereaux to pull them down before he had time to look down the path.

"Whore!" he shouted at her as the carriage came to a stop. "You stop that wailing and come there. Tell me why you left the bitch alone, when I told you to stay with her at all times."

He raised his horsewhip as if to strike her when she cried, "No, sir, dunna hit me. Big gator got her." He lowered the whip, waving his hand for her to climb in the carriage.

"In the back, Whore. Not up here with me. You smell like a swamp. Now, tell me again, calmly, exactly what happened."

"Jist as da sun come up, I wen outside ta pee. Heard a roar 'n' a scream. Bigges' gator I ever seed was adraggin' Ruby acrost the floor and den down inta da water. Were nuttin' I could do, Sir. She scream, callin' my name. Den it git quiet but for lotta splashing. Den I ran. Maybe him come back fer me. Gators like big wimens…lotta meat on big wimens."

"A lot of fat, you mean. Well, it does not matter. Actually, the gator did me a favor. Last night I decided I would kill her this morning, but I really would have liked to watch her die."

The carriage stopped at the shanty. Devereaux jumped down to inspect the floor of the shack and the trail to the water. A piece of satin floated on the surface. "Looks like you were telling the truth. Maybe I won't kill you today, like I planned."

Claralee's face seemed to collapse at his words. "No, sir, no kill me. I be a good whore fer ya. Never charge ya ever agin to fuck. Will do anythin' ya wan. Does ya want some now?" She lifted her dress as she stood in the back of the carriage.

"Yes, I think I do. Get down here and suck me hard." He stood, dropping his pants as she strained to get down. "Oh, hell, just lie down on the seat and put your fat head over the side. Ah, that is right. Keep going. Do not stop until your mouth is full of cum."

When he was done, he climbed back in the carriage. "Tell you what, Whore. I will take you back to your place. If word ever gets out about the bitch, I will know who told. It is probably not in my best interests to keep you alive, but I like fucking you. Few women are big enough to take a cock the size of mine and you are one of them."

It was all Claralee could do not to laugh. *Big cock*, she thought. *I have seen bigger ones on little boys. Well, if you want to hear about your size, old Claralee sure will tell you all about it in the future.*

Devereaux whistled as he drove off. Once the carriage was out of sight, Ruby came out of the swampy forest wearing only her shoes, chemise, and petticoat. She'd hidden a far distance from the shack on the path, secreting herself when the road came to a cross one. She had no idea which way to go from there. When the carriage turned left, she followed that direction. She had no idea where she was, but hoped that there were not any more crossroads. The carriage was so far ahead that she could no longer see, nor hear it. From here on, she was literally alone and on her own. If you did not count the gators watching her as she walked or the snakes that dangled from the trees overhead.

Ruby looked at the wheel marks when she came to a crossroad. If the marks looked heavy and the way seemed well traveled, she chose that direction. After what seemed like hours, she started hearing sounds of civilization. A boat whistle told her the river was near. A distant train said she was nearing a railroad, perhaps with a depot. Voices floated in the air, too far away to make out, but at least within hearing distance. For the first time, Ruby actually felt a glimmer of hope.

Then it started raining. No, not just rain, but a lightning and thunderstorm seldom seen. The winds alone could knock a person over. Thunder rocked the world. Lightning struck all around. She sought refuge under a large live oak, huddled against its massive trunk, just as a bolt from above struck the center of the hundred-year-old tree, splitting it down the middle. The power of the lightning tossed the woman like a doll, away from the tumbling trunk. Ruby was pinned to the ground under a mountain of branches and limbs. Her last conscious though was of Lulu. Now she could not protect Lulu from Devereaux. She had failed her daughter as she failed herself.

Had Ruby known, she would have been delighted that she was just a mile from the outskirts of New Orleans. A passerby, as old as his ancient wagon, saw the lightning hit the tree and a woman's body tossed in the air. He pulled his team close to where he thought she had fallen and began to pull branches apart as he searched. He was afraid to use his ax because he might hit her. Dead or alive, he did not know, but either way he could not pretend he did not know she was there.

Twice he encountered angry snakes, but they were of no consequence to him. He knew the good ones from the bad, and these were just rat snakes. He would never harm one of them, knowing how many rodents they ate. He heard a rattle as another snake raised itself in front of him. It was a pygmy rattler—poisonous, but small enough for him to pick up with his cane and toss away. Life in the South teaches things only a Southerner knows, particularly a poor black one.

The storm moved away as quickly as it had arrived. Water dripped from the trees in gigantic drops. The air smelled of swamp and wet moss. Dead leaves and downed branches stuck to everything. Suddenly, he heard a moan. He listened until he could pinpoint the location, and then pulled away the branches until he could see the woman. She was face down and blood flowed from a wound on the back of her head.

Now that he knew where she was, he retrieved his ax and hacked away the limbs until he could reach her. The wound looked bad. Taking off his shirt, he wrapped it around her head, hoping to stop the bleeding.

She was heavy for such a skinny old man to carry, but he managed. Lifting her in the back of the wagon was more than he could do, and luckily, another wagon came his direction. Between the two old men, they got her up into it. The second man climbed up beside the first, and together they took the unconscious woman to their small town. They knew nothing of hospitals. The women in their town took care of the ill and injured, so it was to one of them that they took her.

"What ya two old bucks got in ya wagon to make you hurry dem horses like dat?"

She was crinkled and wrinkled from a lifetime in the sun. No one knew how old Old Betty was, including Old Betty. She had picked cotton until her arthritic fingers gnarled and she could no longer grasped the boll and her back refused to stand straight ever again.

Old Betty looked at the white woman in the wagon. She yelled for a couple of young men to come and carry the unconscious body into her small cabin. If Ruby had been able to smell it, she would have loved the smell of eucalyptus, pine needles, and bunches of garlic and peppers. She would not have appreciated the rattlesnake skins, buzzard feathers, Spanish moss, eel skins, or the jar of woodlice. These were just a few of the medicines Old Betty kept handy.

Betty carefully rinsed the wound with fresh water before packing the bleeding puncture with cayenne pepper. The pepper clung to the skin and gradually, the blood flow stopped. When she turned the woman over on her side, she pulled away the sodden, torn veil. Old Betty had seen knife scars before, but nothing like this. Her heart filled with pity for the poor woman who had suffered so much.

Old Betty cut the filthy clothing from the woman, once again sighing over the scars. She washed every inch of her, pulling off leeches from Ruby's time in the swamp. These she put in a special jar, delighted to have some she did not need to find herself. She bathed the other cuts and treated them with cayenne as well. When she was satisfied the woman was clean, she covered her with a blanket and returned to the outside so she could watch the village folk. She was the matriarch and her word was law.

# Chapter 78

Lucretia awoke with a start. She heard movement outside her bedroom door. She pulled a thin wrapper from the end of the bed and slipped her arms into it. She did not remember putting it there, but everything from the past two days was sketchy. At first, she thought it was Ruby she heard, but memories flew into her mind. Ruby was missing. She opened the door a crack, thinking a maid might be cleaning, but instead she saw Devereaux LaClaire and a bellboy rolling a food cart to the dining table.

Anger built inside her. How dare he presume to come into her suite while she was sleeping? Even more, how dare he act as if he belonged here? She closed the door quietly and turned to her closet, where she pulled out a blue morning dress and slid it over her head. Only then did she realize she was completely naked under the thin robe. Well, she could re-dress once she got rid of her unwanted visitor.

She flung open her bedroom door and, without a word, walked to the suite entrance, where she opened that door, too. She stood, looking at the bellboy and Devereaux until the bellboy got the hint and quickly exited.

"You too, Mr. LaClaire. You are welcome to leave this minute as well." Devereaux smiled at her and stepped forward to take her hand. She shrugged him away. "I mean it. Get out and do not come back."

He continued smiling as he stepped around her, giving her the impression that he was actually leaving, but instead he grabbed the door and pulled the knob from her hand. He shut it firmly and quietly. "Now, Lucretia, that is no way to greet your fiancé, who got up so early to arrange our first breakfast as an engaged couple. And, may I say, you look lovely this morning. But then again, you always do."

Lucretia stood, confused. "Engaged? Where did you get that idea? We are not engaged and never will be."

"Look at your hand, my darling. I almost had to mortgage my home to buy that size of diamond, but nothing is too good for the woman who will share my life forever. Come now, let us have a morning hug and sit down for our breakfast. I have scheduled several appointments for us today, so we will need our energy."

Still confused, Lucretia let him lead her to the table, where he pulled out a chair for her. Before she could sit, he wrapped his arms around her and held her tight. He planted a chaste kiss on her forehead, but what she felt in his pants was anything but chaste. It brought her back to reality.

She pushed him away. "I have no idea where all this is coming from, but I assure you we are *not* getting married."

Devereaux frowned as if in dismay. "Surely, darling, you remember last night. How I bathed you and tucked you into bed. How we talked until nearly morning, making plans for our life together. Oh, Lucretia, you have made me the happiest man in the world." He moved toward her again, but found himself reaching for air. She ran to the suite door again, pulling it open. She pulled the ring from her finger and threw it at him.

"Devereaux, get out! I do not want to ever see you again. Now, I mean it. Go!"

He grinned. "I know what it is—a case of bridal jitters. Nevertheless, come now, darling. You are not a shy virgin unless that man you married was an idiot. Never would I let something as delectable as you out of my bed, ever. But as I promised you last night, I will not force myself on you and am willing to wait until we are married today before we make love. It will be a long day, my wonderful Lucretia, but I will wait for our wedding night." He stooped to pick up the ring, seething inwardly at her callous rejection.

Actually, he had purchased the bauble in a second-hand store, knowing it was just glass, but that was unimportant. What was important was how she was acting toward him.

"However, if you are so anxious, I promise to leave just as soon as we have our breakfast. I know women think it is bad luck to see their intended on their wedding day, but we will have nothing but good luck from now on. Come now, let us eat and I will go."

Lucretia said nothing, just slipped into her chair and lifted her glass of orange juice to her lips. *Oh, those lips,* he thought. *The things those lips will do with me and on me.* Aloud he spoke as if to himself, "Since I will be alone today, I shall have a haircut and purchase a new suit suitable for a happy groom. Oh, yes, I have a dozen things to do today."

Lucretia took a couple of small bites from her eggs Benedict, usually one of her favorites. However, today it tasted like straw and her throat seemed to close when she swallowed. She drank the rest of her juice and sipped her coffee, waiting for him to finish his meal. He chattered on, but she ceased listening. She excused herself and went to the bathroom, feeling weak.

She was surprised to find Devereaux standing in the bathroom doorway. "Here, my dear, let me help you. You look faint. Perhaps you should lie down for a few minutes." He lifted her in his arms and moved to the bedroom. Gently laying her on her bed, he sat her up and removed her dress.

"God, you are so beautiful. You are like a sunbeam, all yellow and creamy. Do you taste like cream?" She watched in a haze as his head dropped to her breast, taking her nipple into his mouth while his tongue licked around it. She felt herself drifting away. What was happening to her body was something happening to someone else. She felt the lips, but they were not on her. She was detached as she watched and felt his hands on her body. "Yes, my wife to be. You are mine from now on." He knelt between her open legs, holding his limp cock. He stroked himself, but did not harden. Frustrated, he pinched her nipples, causing her to cry out. Ah, yes, his penis hardened. Yes, cause her pain and his dick would grow. Beating Fat Whore had taught him that. As his wife, she had no rights, no legal means to stop him. A wife was no more than a whore, but more easily accessible. What happened in the bedroom was between the husband and wife and no one else.

He squeezed her breast and felt his hardness increase. Suddenly, there was a knock on the corridor door. He tried to ignore it, but his penis would not. Swearing under his breath, he yelled, "Who is it?" while pulling on his pants.

"The police, sir. We need to talk to Mrs. Mills."

# Chapter 79

Somewhere in the southwest, Black Eagle Grant camped under a row of cottonwood trees. It was much cooler here than it had been in Mexico, but a lot warmer than at Fort Mason, where the ground was only now starting to thaw. As always when he thought of the army, his thoughts found their way to Fort Mason and the hated white vixen who had taken his heart and soul and left him a betrayed and hollow man.

He knew in his mind that if she had betrayed him, well, it was because of him. Nevertheless, that did not matter. Seeing her fucked by the nearly beardless recruits was like watching a fire race across the prairie. It consumed his all, leaving him full of hatred. He tried again, as he did repeatedly, to erase her from his memory and dreams, but she was always there.

Sometimes in the clouds, he could see her face or the shape of her body. What he needed, he decided, was another woman. One he could drown himself in and blot out the other. Mayte and Concha had been wonderful for sex, but he wanted—no, needed—something more than that. Perhaps where there were many women, he might find one—just one he could take as his own. He remembered his grandfather and his complete love for Summer Swan, his grandmother. Yes, that was the kind of love he wanted. Deep, intense, and forever.

In his dream, Summer Swan came again. This time her face was sad and she did not smile her love for him. She simply said, over and over, *Help Lulu. Help Lulu.* He did not know what it meant, but he felt compelled to do so, though his hatred for the white woman overshadowed even his grandmother's plea.

He awoke in a cold sweat, even in the warm climate. He shook his head to clear it. Yes, he would find a woman who was his only, not one who belonged to everyone. He saddled his horse and mounted, heading toward the northeast.

The prairie was much warmer than when he left a few weeks ago, or was it months? He did not know or care. He saw smoke from village fires in all directions from his stand on a small mountain. He knew which was his tribe, instinctively, but remained unsure if he even wanted to see any of them again. “Let the horse decide,” he thought. “Horse has not been wrong so far.” He gave it its head and as surely as if he had directed it, the animal moved straight to Eagle’s tribe. The decision was made for him.

He knew he had been seen hours before he reached the horse’s destination. He rode slowly and even waved a hand at a “hidden” watcher. Whoever was chief now needed to know how poorly his guards did their job.

As he rode into the village, dogs barked and children ran willy-nilly, some laughing and some crying. No one seemed to fear him, and a few even acknowledged his presence. It was as if he had left the morning before and returned today. *As it should be*, he thought. He dismounted and walked to the fire circle, where several elderly men sat smoking their pipes.

“Hello, Black Eagle,” welcomed one, indicating he should sit. He nodded as he dropped to the ground, cross-legged. It had been so long since he sat in that fashion that his thigh muscles let him know it.

The old man handed him his pipe, but did not turn to look at the newcomer. Who they were was for the younger man to figure out on his own. Black Eagle drew on the pipe and handed it back. “Thank you, Uncle.” He knew it was Land Hunter from the sound of the old man’s voice. “I do not see my father, Iron Eyes.”

“Your father’s body is on his platform and his soul is with the gods. He died during the last snows. He could no longer breathe and asked Little Crane for one of her Life Enders. She did not want to give it to him, but the elders voted and ordered her to do so. He died in his sleep, peacefully—not in battle—as he wished.

"We have had no great battles since your army came. We sometimes fight among ourselves, but it is more for practice than anything else. Soon that will stop too, as they move us to reservations. Few of us will survive the long march north when it comes, and fewer still will survive the endless cold of the Canada territory.

"Our young men, as all young men do, want to fight, but it is hopeless. There are more white men now than all the buffalo that have roamed our prairies. Why are you here?"

Black Eagle had forgotten the abrupt way his people had of changing their conversations from one thing to another. "I came to see my family. My father and you, Uncle. I look around and see no faces I recognize. Where are Little Crane, and the others?"

"Are we your people, Black Eagle? I think we are no longer your people, but I think you have no people from either world. Little Crane and many others died from one of the white man's diseases, which we could not cure. Perhaps your grandmother might have, but I doubt even she could have stopped the useless deaths."

Black Eagle understood all too clearly that he was not welcome to remain here. He did not fit in the white man's world, nor did he fit in here. Once again, he damned his father for creating his life on the white female who had been his mother. He stood without further conversation, mounted his horse, and rode away.

# Chapter 80

Claralee heaved her body out of the carriage and moved as quickly as she could into her little house next to the squalid bar. She carefully watched the businesses along the route that led to her home, but saw nothing that might have a telegraph in it. She gathered up all her money, stuffing it in a small purse that she shoved between her more than ample breasts.

She poked her head in next door, yelling out, "Ana buddy know a telegraphy place?"

"Yeah," someone answered. "Up at da ol' 'otel on Bank Street."

Claralee was delighted. One so close when she had feared she would have to walk all the way into the real city. The hotel on Bank Street, called amazingly enough, "The Bank Street Hotel," was a rundown place now used occasionally by sailors, men hiding from the law, and hookers who lived on the streets. As the hierarchy of life as a whore, Claralee was above those whores, as she had a place of her own. It was not much, but it gave her a feeling of importance, which she demonstrated as she walked through the moldy lobby to the man behind the desk.

"I wanna send some telegraphs."

"Those cost money, sister."

"Well, jist tell me how much. I got money. Now, write this down. One do go to General Stanley Cotton, army fort in Saint Louis. One go to Mrs. Elizabeth Harold, Saint Louis. To Sergeant Michael O'Brian, Saint Louis. To everone at Cottonwood Creek, Missouri." She reeled off the names just as Ruby had taught her. "Now, telegraphy say, 'Find Eagle. Help Lulu. New Orleans Merchant Bank.'"

The little man at the desk wrote and then gave Ruby a total that was more than she had stashed away. She thought a minute. "Send da one to Sergeant 'n' Lizabeth together. Both names together. Now how much?"

This time it left her with a few cents, but she had done what Ruby wanted. She had a friend and she would never let her friend down. Now, she had to find that friend. When she was sure the telegraphs were sent, she returned to her house. She was uneducated, but far from stupid, and had taken mental notes of landmarks at each turn. It was too far for one day's walk, so she had water and food. She started walking, carefully backtracking the route Devereaux had taken from the shack in the bayou.

She got as far as the place on the road where lightning had split an old oak tree right down the middle. She saw the wagon tracks in the dried mud and decided to see if she could find a place to spend the night. Just down the road, off to her right, was a small community of shacks. An old woman sat on her front grass in a broken old chair, watching the world go by. "What you wan here, fat woman?" she asked.

"My name be Claralee, not Fat Woman. I lookin' fer place ta sleep ta night, old woman. Ain't got but two little coins."

"Less see um." Old Betty nodded as she took them. "Ya cain sleep down dere, ifn't ya don na mind being pestered by young bucks. If'n I was ya, I make 'em pay me a bit first though."

Claralee was delighted. A place to sleep, some men to pay her, and hard cocks, too. What more could any woman want?

In the shabby house, the woman on the bed heard a voice she thought she knew, even in her sleep. She tried to wake up, but her head hurt so much, she let herself drift away from the pain again. Sometime later, she woke again, but when she tried to remember where she was, she could recall nothing. Nor had she any memory of who she was or anything else. She screamed, bringing Old Betty inside.

"What ya screamin' for?"

The woman on the bed sat up. "Who are you? Where am I? Dear God, who am I? I cannot remember anything. Nothing since I just woke up." She stopped talking and sat staring straight ahead.

"Well, honey, ya jist relax. It all comes back ta ya in a day er two. Always does. Now, lay ya self back and sleep. Call fer Old Betty—that be me—if ya need anathing."

Three houses away, Claralee was enjoying herself. Three young men were taking turns on her and she charged each of them for each time. When they were done, she took the money and waddled over to Old Betty to safeguard for her. She went back to the young men, deciding anything more they wanted, she would give to them for her own pleasure…and her pleasures could last for hours.

# Chapter 81

In Lucretia's suite, Devereaux opened the door only a crack. "What do you officers want with Mrs. Mills? She is sleeping for the first time in days. The news of her missing friend is plaguing her endless. Unless you have some good news for her, I refuse to awaken her."

Behind him, steadying herself on the doorframe stood the small woman, wrapped in a towel that barely covered her. "Devereaux, let them in."

He was flustered. She should not be awake, let alone on her feet. "My dear, you need to rest. Let me help you back to bed." He rushed to take her arm, but she pushed him away.

"Please arrest this man. When you knocked, he was attempting to rape me. I think there was something in my orange juice."

Devereaux stood in confusion as her words penetrated his mind. He ran to the balcony, but it was too far to jump. The two officers raced after him, even as he tried to push past them to reach the corridor door. He was no match for them and found himself with his hands in irons behind his back. "She is lying. She is a trollop who invited me to her bed. She has been after me ever since we met on the train. I am even paying for her hotel room…just ask the management. She wants my money and prestige in the city and does not care what she has to do to get it."

That brought a laugh from one of the men. "The only place I know of where you have prestige is in a horse barn. No, on second thought, that is just the horses."

The second officer turned to Lucretia. "We wanted to tell you we have a lead on your companion. Someone reported seeing a veiled woman near the waterfront. We are investigating it."

"Thank you, officer. That is wonderful news. There must be something dreadfully wrong with her that she cannot return to me. Your help is…" Tears welled up in her eyes as she clutched the towel tighter around her body.

"You are welcome, Mrs. Mills. We will return later with some papers for you to sign for Judge Franklyn Mountebank, regarding this man. Be sure, the judge will see that he stays away from you for a long, long time."

Lucretia locked the door behind them. Draped only with a towel, she went to the bathroom to wash herself. She could still feel his hands on her, even in her drugged state. Oh, how she loathed that man. And to think she ever thought him charming. Ruby was right about him—he was slime. Her thoughts wandered. Was it possible that Devereaux had something to do with Ruby's disappearance? Of course, it was possible. Ruby had said the man would do anything to get his hands on Lulu and her money. Should she tell Judge Mountebank her suspicions? If only she had someone to talk to about it. Liz was so far away. And the others she trusted were dead. The only one still alive, as far as she knew, was Black Eagle, and after the things he had done to her, she knew he was not anyone to trust. Just like Devereaux, only worse in some ways.

She slid into bed and was asleep in minutes. The drugs had worked on both her mind and body and she dreamed. She dreamed of the night that Eagle had asked to stay with her. She saw herself lock the door and move into his arms. She felt his kisses on her face and mouth. She tasted the sweat on his skin. She remembered his strength and power. She kissed his chest as they talked the night away. She knew before she slept that night that she loved him. Really loved him. Then he had betrayed her in the most foul way. When she awoke, her face was wet with tears. She cried for the lost love, one that never really existed.

She dressed and called for a carriage to take her to the police station to sign arrest papers, and then to the bank. Once reassured that the new home was hers and carrying the keys in her handbag, she returned to the hotel. It was moving day.

The hotel staff was helpful finding her men and wagons to transport her trunks. As she left for the last time, those standing in the lobby expressed their best wishes and promises to keep looking for Ruby.

Standing on the boardwalk near the waiting carriage was an elderly black couple. The doorman tried to push them away, but Lucretia stopped him. "They are doing nothing. Let them be."

"Mrs. Mills, they have been here for hours. They say they want to talk to you."

"Then, talk they shall." She motioned them forward and stared into their faces. Sadness was all she saw in their eyes. "What can I help you with? Why do you want to talk to me? I do not believe we have met."

"No, ma'am, we hav na met. We are Sam an' Peg. We was Mr. LaClaire's folk. Da police made us leave, an' the judge locked us out. We hav na place ta go."

"Why do you come to me? That man has done much to me and I hate him."

"Yes, ma'am, we know. He a cruel man. We was a hopin' you could help us. Everone knows you is a great lady, kind and special."

Lucretia laughed. "Are you trying to sweeten me up for money?" She fumbled for her purse.

Sam pulled himself up as tall as his bent frame would allow. "No, ma'am. Sam an' Peg takes no charity. We was a hopin' for jobs. Peg is da best cook and I is a great one for gardens an' drivin' n' fixin' stuff. We only wants a place to live an' eat an' a few cents when you think we deserve it…fer clothes an' such."

His pride struck her deep. If this pair could keep their values working for Devereaux, well… "You are hired. Come join me in my carriage for the ride to our new home."

"No, ma'am, that ain't right. We walk. Follow wagon."

"Nonsense, you will ride with me. And that is your first order." Sam smiled and helped Lucretia into the buggy and then his wife. He sat in front with the driver and never stopped smiling the entire day.

*When I heard the stories years later, I learned that Lucretia settled in her home with Sam and Peg. She added a few more staff members to help them. Hiring the couple was the best thing she had done for a long time. Everyone was happy…as happy as they could be, that is, without Ruby. Lucretia never gave up hope, but as the days grew into weeks and the weeks into months, realization that she might never see Ruby again became a possibility she began to accept.*

*Her life was lonely. She filled her days helping at the hospital and clinics for the poor. She gave sums of money to charities and attended charity functions, but always alone. She had no man in her life and wanted none. She ceased thinking of Devereaux LaClaire, but her dreams of Black Eagle Grant plagued her nights.*

# Chapter 82

In the village of shanties where Old Betty reigned supreme, Ruby now answered to the name Scar and wore no veil to cover herself. She was not offended by the moniker and still had no memory. She moved into a shanty of her own, the only white person in the village. She helped Old Betty with the ill, tended a garden that she shared with all, and sang wordless songs.

One day she and Old Betty sat on her porch, rocking in their chairs as they did every evening, and she asked, “Old Betty, am I ever going to remember who I am? It has been months and I still am blank. I seem to remember a place with soldiers fighting and sometimes I see a face or two. I think I lived in a city, but not here. That is about it.”

Old Betty just continued to puff on her pipe. After a long while, she answered. “I dunna know. Old Betty tried everthin’ she know, even boiling da black chicken and blew black smoke in yer ears. Gave you ever kin of tea I know ’bout. Dis is jist up ta da Good Lord, Scar. But dunna give up. I heard tell of seein’ a face, hearin’ a song, hittin’ yer head…lots of thins can make ya ’member.” She did not tell Ruby that she had also fed her boiled snakeskins, bat soup, and even spiders, knowing that the woman would never have consumed them if she had known. It did not work anyway, so no reason to ever tell her.

Ruby sighed, already knowing all this. She was content as she could be, but she knew there was more to her than this life. She began to take long walks, always by herself, hoping something would trigger her memory. One day she decided to walk the bayou road, even though Old Betty told her a storm was brewing. She looked up into a clear blue sky and wandered away from the village.

A couple of miles later, the sky darkened and the wind came out of nowhere, bring with it thunder and terrible lightning. She stopped, her mind telling her she had done this before. She looked around for shelter and saw none but a split tree trunk of an old oak. She walked to it, mindless of the storm around her. She felt compelled to put her arms around the stump, standing as close to it as she could. She closed her eyes, and memories of the other storm raced around in her head.

"A shack, a fat whore…no, Claralee. A name and a place. A man…a man mounted on Claralee, hitting her." The day ceased to exist for Ruby as she fainted, lying on the ground in the downpour of rain while trees fell all around her from the intense wind and lightning. Either way, Ruby knew none of it…she was lost in a world of memories.

The storm was over when she awoke. She was soaked to the skin, but she did not care. She continued to lie where she was, trying to sort out the flashes of remembrance. A face, but no name. A name without a face. A building, a wagon ride, a train ride, a man with a knife, a beautiful house, a tumbled down shack, warm times and cold, an outline of a girl in a park, laughing and crying, happiness and disappointments. Just pieces, but pieces she did not have before. She rose and walked the muddy road back toward the village. She could smell the freshness that came from a good rain, the smoke from the cabin chimneys, and the rot from along the river. She knew she was in New Orleans, but that was all.

Old Betty scolded her for not heeding her warning of the storm, even as she helped her remove her wet clothes. "Old Betty dun worry 'bout ya, walkin' where da Lord's strikes might a hit ya."

"I remember things."

At first, Old Betty did not comprehend what Ruby said as she continued her tirade about the storm. Suddenly she stopped. "'Member thins?" She grinned as wide as her old black face could and picked up Ruby to dance her around in circles. "Come, sit in a chair an' tell me."

Ruby laughed for the first time Old Betty had ever heard. "Can I get dressed first?"

They talked for hours, but Ruby's mind refused to accept anything new, beyond what she learned during the storm. Other villagers joined them, so she told her story repeatedly. One tall, thin boy of about ten moved to stand by her. "If'n you see other thins, maybe ya 'member other thins too."

Everyone stopped talking until Old Betty jumped up. "Outta moufs of babes. Tamorra we hitch up the wagon an' take some drives. Litta ways ever day. How does dat sound?"

The next morning Old Betty sat in the front of the decrepit wagon, which looked older than Betty herself. She took the reins and the horses followed her commands with no hesitation. Ruby sat beside her and listened to the ancient one. "I learned ta drive a team when I was jist a chile. I followed the pickers an' they load der bags in da wagon. It git full, I take it ta de barn to be unloaded. I jump from one wagon ta another an' drove back. Musta did that hundred times afore boss man decide I pick cotton 'stead."

The back of the wagon was full of children and young mothers who seldom, if ever, left their shantytown. It was like a holiday for all. They even packed lunches and water for the event. Soon they were calling out, "Scar, ya see dat church? Scar, looka dem ships." Scar this and Scar that, each wanting his or her discovery to be the one that made the white woman remember things.

On the sixth day out, with only two passengers, Ruby put her hand on Old Betty's. "See that fat woman… Yes, it is. It is Claralee." She jumped off the wagon and ran with arms extended to the woman walking down the hill to a house below. "Claralee, it's me. It's me." Claralee turned, brought her hand to her chest as if seeing a ghost, and then dropped her bundle and ran up the hill as fast as her obese body could move. They stood with arms around each other.

They all returned to the village and sat on Old Betty's porch, talking, until the moon set. They decided to go to the police the next day and tell them who she was. She would tell her story, leaving out things the officials did not need to know.

Old Betty chided Claralee. “Ya shuda tell me ’bout it when ya was here bouncing wid dose young bucks down da way. Ya shuda gone ta da police soon as ya got back home.”

“Old Betty, do not be so hard on her,” said Ruby. “I know how cruel that man can be and she was right to be afraid. But not anymore. Tomorrow he will be in jail, Claralee, and you will be free of him. So will I and so will…” She stopped, unable to remember that name she knew was so important.

“Ya be meanin’ ya daughter? Ya be meanin’ Lulu?”

Without a word, Ruby dropped into a place where no one could venture. Old Betty jumped up to catch her before she fell. “How da ya know dat name? Is Scar’s girl?”

“Sure is. Ruby dun tell me when we was in dat shack in da bayou. She tell me ’bout a lotta stuff an’ we was friends.” She said it proudly, but Old Betty was not fooled.

“If’n you was friends, ya should a told police anaway. You just a no account whore, only thinkin’ ’bout ya nest cent an’ da man who give it ta ya. Now, help me. We gonna put her in my bed an’ at firs’ light we all goin’ to da police. Yes, de three of us.”

# Chapter 83

The telegraphs traveled through the wires just as they were supposed to. The first arrived at Cottonwood Creek. The man was new and had never heard of Black Eagle Grant. Had the message been addressed to Captain Grant, he would have sent it on out to the fort. He shrugged after he read it and nailed the paper to the wall next to the window, above the moldy old couch.

The second reached the home of Mr. and Mrs. Michael O'Brian, who were honeymooning in New York City. They made no attempt to hide their infatuation with each other, much to the delight of those who watched them walk hand in hand through the parks and whisper as they rode carriages around the city.

The third telegraph arrived at the desk of General Stanley Cotton, who had not returned from the frontier, as his aide considered Fort Mason. The aide read the telegram and laid it on top of a pile of others that had arrived since he had departed in the dead of winter. The aide had heard rumors that the general would be back before Easter.

At Fort Mason, Corporal Jed Dryer was now Sergeant Dryer. His new responsibilities relieved him of his wagon trips to Cottonwood Creek. Now that the trees were budded and the grass was greening, he wished he still had that duty. His opportunity came a few days later when the regular driver reported himself sick. Jed smiled as he asked General Cotton for permission to assume the duty and the general just nodded.

Jed had not noticed the now fading telegram nailed to the wall. It was unseasonably warm, so he stood in front of the open window, watching the last of the supplies loaded in the wagon. His attention was drawn to the note, but his ability to read was limited to a few words, but Black and Grant were two he recognized. He turned to the man at the desk. “Say, what is this all about?”

“Oh, somebody is looking for some Indian, Black Eagle. Called him Black Eagle Grant. Says he is needed in New Orleans. Someone named Lulu needs help.”

Jed pulled the telegram from the nail and handed it to the man. “Read it to me.” He listened. “Read it again.” He grabbed it from the man and raced out the door to the wagon. “Get this damn thing loaded now, and I mean *now*.” The laughing soldiers jumped to attention and finished the loading more quickly than they ever had, even though their sergeant continued to yell at them.

Jed did not know what to do with the telegraph, other than get it back to General Cotton at the fort. He pushed the team of horses faster than they were accustomed to traveling, forcing him to use his whip a couple of times. Suddenly, he pulled the team and wagon to a stop. He climbed down and took the reins of the nearest recruit. “I am taking your horse. Need to get this message to the general. You drive the team, regular speed, not like I was a doing.”

Without another word, he mounted and urged the horse into a full run. The men watching shook their heads. One said, “That horse ain’t going ta last to the fort, he keeps that up.”

Jed rode like a madman until his horse started to falter. He pulled it up at a little creek moving with the fast flow of melted snow. As the horse drank and rested, he leaned against a tree, surveying the plains as far as he could see. On the hill where a younger tree grew by a dead snag, he saw a figure on a horse sitting under the boughs. He would know that figure if he lived to be a hundred.

He fired his rifle three times in the air, standing, so the man on the hill could see his shots were not aimed at him. He jumped back on the horse, hoping it could make it, as he raced toward the tree. The man also mounted and moved toward him.

He felt his horse giving out again, so he slid off to wait. His heart beat faster than he could remember, but for that night with Lucretia. God, what a time to remember that. He stood wiping the drooping head of his mount with water from his canteen until the man dismounted and walked to him.

"Hello, Jed."

"Hello, Captain."

"Not Captain anymore. Just Eagle." They grinned and hugged each other in the way men do—affectionately but distantly, pounding each other on the shoulders.

Jed's face sobered as he took the folded paper from his pocket and handed it to Eagle, who unfolded it and read it. Several times he read it before looking up into the face of the younger man. "I have to go, Jed. Now."

"Wait and listen and don't go off half-cocked. The train is the fastest way. I am going with you. No, do not say a word. I love that woman. I have loved her from the first moment I ever saw her. The wagon is an hour or so behind me, so we can send word to the general, along with this telegram. And I ain't taking no argument from you. I'm going with or without you."

"Climb up behind me. Your horse cannot carry you any further. No need to ride like idiots. No train until morning anyway." Eagle waited until Jed took the reins of his horse and tied them to the saddle horn. He mounted behind Eagle and they rode without speaking except to the wagon platoon, until they reached Cottonwood Creek. Between them, they had just enough money for the fare. Food was unimportant. Only the plea for help for Lulu mattered. But always between them—but never mentioned—were the pictures each carried in his mind of the woman they both loved.

# Chapter 84

They were a strange-looking trio as their wagon pulled up in front of police headquarters near downtown New Orleans. The sergeant on duty inside did a double take as the threesome waited for him to speak and he was nearly speechless.

The fat one was a whore he recognized. The black woman was wrinkled and appeared to be at least a hundred years old. The white woman, brutally scarred, spoke.

"Officer, this lady is Claralee." He nodded as she pointed to the prostitute. "This lady is known as Old Betty. I do not know either of them any other way. And I am Ruby."

"Ruby what?" he asked, as his mind worked to remember something about a Ruby while trying to ignore her scars.

"I cannot…I do not know much about myself. I was abducted some time ago…"

Now he recalled the event. "Just a minute, madams." He jumped to his feet and ran down the hall for someone he called "Captain." He returned, asking them to follow him into a room with a large table and many chairs.

"Please sit down. May I bring you coffee? Tea? Anything?"

"Yes," said the white woman. "We would love some tea."

The man who came into the room was big. His uniform stretched across his more than ample body. He looked from one to the other before speaking. "Now, am I to understand that you three have some information on the disappearance of Ruby Redstone? I am in no mood for games and the reward is only for proof of what happened to the woman. So what have you to tell me?"

"Do you know of a man named Devereaux Benoit LaClaire?" asked the white woman. She was so ugly with scars that he wished she would cover them, as they made him uncomfortable.

"Yes, I do. He is in jail now, awaiting trial for trying to rape one of the city's lovely newcomers. To protect her, I cannot divulge her name, but she is fine and he will not harm her in the future. Now, what does he have to do with Ruby Redstone?"

"He is responsible for her kidnapping and disappearance."

The captain decided it was probably true, but needed proof. "How can we substantiate your claim?"

"He dun kidnapped me too, sir. Took us both ta shack in de bayou, 'til we got us away."

"I am expected to believe he found it necessary to kidnap you. I would assume your 'favors' were close enough to free to hardly warrant kidnapping you. Anything else? Well, thank you for stopping in." He rose to leave and was ready to close the door behind him when the scarred woman spoke.

"I am Ruby Redstone. No—I remember now! I am Ruby Clanton Sawyer. Lucretia Lucinda Sawyer is my daughter!"

From one open door to another, sound carried in the old stone building. The jailer opened the door to the cell chambers just as Ruby spoke. Her voice carried along the corridors into the cells nearby. One prisoner heard the words and they went through him like an electric shock. "The bitch is not dead. The whore lied to me. Once they testify against me, it will be certain death for me. Kidnapping on top of rape. If they can kill me more ways than one, they will do it. I have to get out of here. Come hell or high water, I will kill them all before they get me again." From that moment on, his entire life revolved around plans to escape.

In the other room, things happened so fast that it became a blur to the women and the officers as well. One raced outside, jumped on his horse, and tore through the streets. He slid off his horse before it even halted and bounded up the stairs. He did not even stop to ring the bell. He burst through the door shouting, "We found Ruby Redstone. She is at the police station waiting for you."

Sam rushed to the carriage house, but Lucretia did not have any intention of waiting. She pushed the officer out the door, demanding he take her back to the station. He would have agreed anyway in his excitement, but sitting behind her with his arms around her was like taking a ride with an angel.

She ran up the long flight of brick stairs into the dark building, straight into the arms of the woman she loved, the woman who was her mother. They clung together, crying and laughing, both talking at once. Happiness filled their hearts, as well as those of the two women behind Ruby and the officers all around. Lucretia Lucinda Sawyer did not think she could ever be happier than she was at that moment.

# Chapter 85

Devereux LaClaire conceived a plan so simple that it could not fail. He would wait a couple of days to give the women time to settle in at the mansion Lucretia owned. He did not care about the old black woman, or even Fat Whore whom he had twice seen together in the old wagon, unless he came across them. He certainly was not going to hunt for either of them. All her wanted was his revenge. Lucretia would feel his manhood and watch as he gave the bitch a few more cuts. Then they would feed the alligators.

He was sure Lucretia would have money at her home. She was big on tipping everyone, dumb bitch. Maybe he could hold her hostage for a couple of days and ransom her. Yes, that would work. He even composed a note in his head. "If you want to see the women alive again, put $10,000 in a carpetbag and leave it…" Well, he would work on that later. Hell, he might even have the fat whore do the pickup. He knew where he could find her. Oh, he was going to have some great fun before this was over. The pictures in his head hardened his cock. He closed his eyes and put his hand around it, pretending it was Lucretia.

At that moment, Lucretia and the three other women sat in her kitchen, sipping tea while Peg and Sam stood aside, grinning as they served them. "Now, you two, stop all that and sit down with us," Lulu ordered.

"No, ma'am, ain't right fer servants ta sit wif white folk," replied Sam.

"What am I, you old buck, da Queen of France?" Old Betty shook her finger at him. "Get your butts o'er here like da lady say."

Everyone laughed as he acquiesced. "Ain't nobody argue wit Old Betty," said Claralee.

"I know you are all tired, and the police will be here later to ask you some questions, so would you like to wash up and rest awhile?" Lucretia rose and poured more tea in the pot.

"Here? We wash up and rest here?" Claralee seemed stunned at the idea.

"Of course, here. Where did you think I meant?"

"Well, I ain't ne'er been in a place like dis afore. What if'n I break somethin'?"

"Then we will throw it out. Probably don't need it anyway." Ruby smiled.

They chatted on and on until Old Betty rose, nodded to Lucretia, and bent to hug Claralee and Ruby. "I bes' be goin' now. Ya can tell da policeman dat I donna know nothin' but dat I drive ya round. Thank ya, Miss Lucretia, fer tea an' vittles."

She could not be persuaded to stay or let Sam drive her home. "I drive me here, I drive me da utter way." With that, she opened the door and walked painfully down the long flight of stairs and around the house to where her old wagon and ancient pair of horses waited.

Lucretia led the two women up the wide staircase to the second floor and turned to the left. "This will be your room, Claralee, if you like it." She opened the door on the right.

"My room? I havin' a room here?" Her eyes widened so much that they seemed too big for her gigantic face. She could not comprehend that all this was for her. Even for one day, she thought, it was like heaven. The bed was covered with a pink comforter with white rosebuds that matched the wallpaper and the rugs. A fireplace was laid, but unlit, on the outside wall. The wall was so long, it had a large window that looked out over the back garden. Along another wall was a dressing table and matching bureau. A closet with two doors took most of another wall. A settee with matching chairs and tables completed the décor. Sparkling sconces reflected the light from all around the room.

Their sparkle could not compete with the glittering in the eyes of the woman. "I ain't ne'er seed nothin' like dis in ma life. I canna stay here. It belons ta a high lady, na a fat ol' whore."

Ruby pulled her into her arms. "Claralee, you are the highest lady in the world to me. If not for you, some gnarly old gator would have eaten me alive. You are here with me and you will stay as long as you want." Lucretia moved to join them, spreading her arms as wide as she could to take Claralee into her arms as well. They cried together, out of happiness.

A sweet-faced young woman, small and cocoa-colored, waited outside the door until they noticed her. "Oh, Teresa, come in and meet Miss Claralee. Claralee, this is Teresa. She will be here to help you in any way you like. She will draw your bath now and when you are asleep, she will go to town and purchase some clothes for you. Now, if you need anything else, just pull this cord here and Sam or Peg will come."

"Wait, Miss Lucretia. I canna have a maid. I jist a fat ol' whore and whore's dunna have maids."

Ruby took both Claralee's hands in hers. "Listen, and listen good, Claralee. From now on, you are not a whore. You are a permanent guest in our house and our guests all have maids. Teresa will be your friend, too, if you let her. One of her first tasks is to teach you to speak properly and show you how a lady acts. Oh, that is, if you want to learn."

Claralee shouted. "Damn hell, shits afire. I gonna be a lady."

Teresa spoke as Ruby and Lucretia left the room. "Well, for one thing, Miss Claralee, ladies do not say 'damn hell, shits afire.' Nor do they say 'gonna.' They say 'going to.' Now, you try it."

The smile faded from her fat face as Claralee looked at the young woman. "Well, if ya thin you is gonna tell me whatta do, well, den you is right." She grinned again, pulling the other into her overly ample arms. "Going to. How was that? Ya *going to* learn me to get skinny, too?"

Old Betty would have been furious to know that she had been followed by a couple of her neighbors, who took turns watching out for their wonderful matriarch. The next morning, one of them returned to Lucretia's, asking for Scar. They huddled for a few minutes, whispering, and then the man left.

She had tears in her eyes as she returned to the breakfast table. "I have sad news. Old Betty passed last night, sitting on her porch, smoking her pipe. Cassius said she just closed her eyes and was gone. He said he was sure I would want to know, and he is right But, we were asked not to come to the village or attend the funeral. It is, as he said, 'jist fer home folk.'"

# Chapter 86

The trio of women was so happy, getting to know one another and shopping. If you had asked Sam, he would have told you he got tired just driving them, so he could not understand how they could spend all morning shopping, have lunch, then shop some more. He waited outside the businesses, taking their parcels to load in the carriage, and watched shaking his head, as they moved on to another establishment. More often than not, one parcel always contained a small thing for Peg and him. A scarf for her head, as the law required her to wear, a pair of stockings for him, a lap robe for cool evenings, even silly, nonsensical doodads to make them laugh.

A few blocks away, in the stone and brick courthouse, Devereaux Benoit LaClaire forced himself to vomit, deliberately missing the bedpan. He wanted the guards to see that he really was sick. After the first time, it was easy. All he had to do was smell the odor permeating his cell, and up more would come. He dropped to the floor, moaning as he held his stomach, making sure his nose was firmly pressed into his armpit until he needed to upchuck again.

Three guards conferred before sending a message to the captain that they had a really sick man. There was no way the captain was going near any sick man. He lived in fear of catching something. He even covered his nose and mouth when his own children sneezed or coughed.

He sent for a doctor, who took one look at the man who feigned semi-consciousness with his low moaning, and decided to have him moved to the hospital. LaClaire's simple plan was working just the way he had hoped it would. By dark, he would be inside the bitch's mansion and by morning, she and her aunt would both be missing.

He had not foreseen being strapped to his bed. He fought the two large orderlies as they removed his restraints in the wagon and moved him to a wheeled cot. He forced himself to calm down, hoping they would forego the straps, but one man grabbed each arm and before he could flex a muscle, he was tied down. He knew that if he was quiet, they would not fasten his legs, so he remained still but for moaning and making his stomach bounce up and down.

In a room with five other men, he saw his chances of escaping dwindling away. He might be able to handle one or two, but five—that was another story. *Think, think, think, think.* However, his luck turned. Three of the five were old and unconscious. *Die, you bastards,* he thought. All right, two then. And a nurse, probably.

He waited until the hospital quieted. No doctor or anyone else came to see him. He concluded that he had been brought here to die. Well, he would show them. Finally a young female nurse came in and leaned over him.

"Mr. LaClaire, can you hear me?"

He moaned and made his voice sound thin and strangled. "Hurt, hurt, so bad, sister." He kept up the charade until she saw his hand motion. His wrist was bleeding from the abrasion he had done himself to make it appear the strap was too tight.

She smiled at him, taking a small knife from her pocket, and cut him loose. As she straightened, his hand came up to encircle her neck and pull her down, pressing her face into his chest. His cock came to full attention as she gasped for breath. He knew he did not have the time to spread her legs and give her what all women wanted, as much as his need pained him. When she stopped struggling, the rest was easy. He blew out the lantern, put the woman's body in his bed, and covered her. All was well in the terminal men's dorm.

Back at the mansion, Judge Franklyn Mountebank and his wife and Banker Melvin Charles Duval, Esq. were dining with the three ladies. It was a gala affair. Even Claralee made every attempt to curtail her language and said very little, but smiled continually. Ruby had covered her face again with a veil and loved the small talk, although she, too, said little. Lucretia led the conversation from one subject to another as a good hostess might. From the cellar below, an unwanted guest listened and hated. It had been so easy to break a window that went unheard under the laughter above. He recognized the voices of the judge and banker. Could he be that lucky? Yes, he could and he was. His grin was so grim that even the devil might have hesitated accepting him. Oh yes, his time was coming and coming soon.

# Chapter 87

The servants moved in and out of the kitchen while Devereaux watched them from a slightly ajar door that led to the cellar. It was not a cellar in the true sense of the word, because no digging was done anywhere in New Orleans. The water level was so low that even a small downpour would bring up little floods here and there. Under the Sawyer home, a latticework allowed water to run where it would and at the same time allowed air movement to cut down on the rot and mold so prevalent in the south. Under the Sawyer home, the stairway led to a floating platform that allowed the servants to hang bags of onions, potatoes, and the like. Rats might find them, but the city offered so much for the rodents, they seldom bothered with things they had to work at reaching.

As Sam and Peg filled and lifted the trays of food, Devereaux took the opportunity to run into the kitchen, grabbing two long knives and a loaf of bread. He was hungry after the strain of repeated vomiting, but forced himself to eat small bites until his stomach settled.

From that point, it was simple. Banker Duval left the party first, looking forward to a visit with his delectable mistress on Bourbon Street. He was thinking of her as he walked to his carriage; then the man walked boldly up behind him and quickly sliced his throat. Devereaux pulled the body back under the house and waited.

The judge's carriage held a driver who had died easily in his sleep. The Mountebanks departed soon after the banker, and the killer was ready. He held a string he had tied to a shrub and stretched it across the walkway. Mrs. Mountebank tripped on it and fell forward. Her husband bent to help her up, but never had a chance to complete his sentence of concern before his blood spurted down on his wife. Devereaux hit her hard where she lay before dragging them both under the house. Mrs. Devereaux moaned and begged but he calmly cut her throat.

The night was his. He could do anything and everything he wanted to anyone he chose. The sense of power was exhilarating. He was omnipotent.

He waited for the servants to finish cleaning up the kitchen and dining room. Waiting gave him a chance to rest and relive the rape of the judge's wife under the house. Remembering the pain he caused often gave him enough to masturbate himself to a climax. In jail, he did that every night. He had often wondered if sodomizing might give the same relief, but since he was by himself, that was not an option. Besides, the others in jail would have wanted to do it to him instead and he did not want to be on the receiving end of the pain.

When the house was silent, he went back outside to see if any lights showed in any room. Upstairs to the left, he saw one in front and two in back. He went back inside and moved quietly into the kitchen and through the house. He had not been inside before, but a quick search of the main floor, just to be sure, showed no bedrooms. The broad, carpeted stairs offered silence as he climbed them.

He listened outside the door that had shown light—the one closest to the middle of the house. He heard throaty snores that were definitely not from his fair Lucretia. He guessed it was the fat whore. After all, he had shared a bed with her in a different lifetime, he thought. Filthy bitch was not worth his time now.

Now it was a toss-up. Front room or the room in the back? The back one overlooked a rose garden with fountains and shaded walks, elegant, with an ambience Lucretia might like. The front overlooked a grassy lawn, terraces with blooming flowers and shrubs, and a view of the river and part of the city, which he knew she had enjoyed from the hotel. Damn her! All that money for her suite and what did he get in return? A jail cell! Oh, she must pay and pay dearly.

He decided the rose garden view was more like her. He carefully turned the doorknob and peeked inside. He saw a form on the bed, but could not tell in the dim light who it was. He removed his shoes and walked carefully to the bed. It was the bitch. He hated her. He picked up a pillow and pressed it over her head. She made small noises and began kicking as he struggled with her. She was stronger than he thought. She managed to push him away, forcing him to hit her hard enough to knock her out, but not before she emitted a yell loud enough to be heard if anyone was awake to hear it.

His manhood stood out against his pants as it responded to the violence it needed. He debated whether or not to use her still body or wait. The choice was made for him as the door opened.

# Chapter 88

Lucretia heard a stifled voice. At first, she thought she might have imagined it or dreamed it, but some intuition made her rise and investigate. She opened the door to Ruby's room. There was a figure standing by the bed. Without thinking, she ran as fast as she could, head down, and hit the shadowy shape like a battering ram, knocking the figure down across the bed. She jumped on it, not thinking of Ruby, now unconscious under two people's weight.

She pummeled the figure with her little fists, but was no match for his superior size and strength. He rolled her off and sprung to his feet. "Well, well, if it isn't Mrs. Mills or Mrs. Sawyer or whatever you call yourself these days. You are just the person I am looking for." He caught her hands, holding them in one of his as he fondled her through her thin nightgown. "If you scream, I swear that I will kill the bitch right where she lies." She saw the knife as he dropped her hands and pulled it from behind him. "Nice little trick I learned in jail. Never go to a kidnapping without a weapon."

He laughed. "You, my dear, and I are going for a little ride. Oh, yes, and when we get there, I am going for a long, deep ride on you." His laugh was as evil as she had ever heard. "It would have been so much simpler if you had agreed to marry me. I had it all worked out in my mind. After all, as my wife, I could not hurt you every time I wanted to fuck you, so I planned to have Fat Whore join us on our marriage bed. I would hurt her and shove it to you. See what a thoughtful husband I would have been?

"But no…you ruined everything. So now, I have no choice but to hurt you and fuck you until you give in and marry me. I want you and your money. I will be the perfect gentleman to share all this with you. The kind, gentile folks of this fair city who have looked down their patrician noses at me, the assholes. Now they will see who is the patrician when you give extravagant soirees and elaborate parties. You can afford it!"

"You are crazy." Lucretia kept her voice low, almost a whisper, as he had done, even in his tirade. "You can kill me, but I will never marry you. You can rape me, but I will never give myself freely to you. You can hurt me as much as you want, but I will never be *your* woman."

He ignored her and rambled on and on as he tied her hands behind her back with a robe belt. He ran his hands inside her nightgown and pinched her breasts, hurting her. He rubbed her mound, even so far as sticking his gown-covered finger inside her softness, deliberately causing her pain. He pushed his tongue into her mouth as he sucked her lips, feeling them cracking under his teeth.

"Oh, yes, we are going to have such a good time. Come now, sweet bride-to-be, we are going to take your carriage to my house. The bank took it and locked it, but we will get inside. It will be a little dark, but we will have no trouble doing what I want. Now, not a sound or I will come back up and kill the bitch." He insured her silence by shoving a kerchief in her mouth.

Ruby heard voices, but in her semi-conscious state could not react. She drifted in and out, thinking she was dreaming, until her pain reminded her of what had happened. She heard the carriage leave, as had Sam and Peg.

Sam was bewildered that anyone had gone out this late at night without calling him to drive. He arose and looked out just in time to see the carriage turn the corner and head north. A sense of dread filled his head. He drew on his pants and padded barefoot down from the third floor where he and Peg shared a room. From the end of the hall, he heard a groan. He ran to see Miss Ruby trying to stand. At the same time, he noticed that Miss Lucretia's bedroom door was open.

Ruby saw him. "Sam, go for the police. Devereaux has taken Lulu. Hurry. He plans to kill her at his house."

# Chapter 89

The train ride from Cottonwood Creek to New Orleans was on time, which seldom happened, but for the two men watching the landscape go by, it was slower than the proverbial snail. They did not talk. Each was lost in his own world and memories, but the same sweet face filled both minds.

Jed Dryer remembered every minute of the ride from the depot to the fort. Lord, how he envied the man into whose arms she threw herself. He remembered her smile every time she looked at her husband. He remembered thinking she had a halo over her head the evening she led them in the Lord's Prayer. But mostly, he remembered her smooth skin, soft breasts, and legs wrapped around him. He tried to forget that she had only done what the devil forced her to do, but to him it was the most wonderful thing that had ever happened. He had loved her from the first moment he laid eyes on her, and that night only cemented how he felt. He would die for her, of that there was no doubt.

Black Eagle Grant tried to think of other women. Anything to put her out of his mind. Then what the hell was he doing on this damn train to New Orleans? As much as he tried to deny it, even to himself, he knew why. Because someone said Lucretia needed him, and he knew down in his very soul that he would follow her to the ends of the earth, if she needed him.

Eagle had not loved her from the first moment. He thought her to be another spoiled rich girl, and about that, he was right. What he did not think was that she had spunk and could handle herself, at least in a verbal bout, as she had shown him in the officers' office. She was white…no, she was yellow and pink, as he later found out.

She showed strength that he could not have imagined any white woman having. She did not scream and wail as he had expected, but remained calm and strong, just as she had been assisting him in surgery. But the memory that always won out was of her locking the door to her cabin, dropping her clothes, and moving into his arms. The sex that night was more than sex…it was love. He loved her, even as he hated her. She asked for nothing from him but what he offered and gave so freely.

He tried to forget how he had humiliated her and his young troopers by forcing them together, thinking they were going to die the next day. The cruelty of it was to punish her somehow for making him love her. It was the ultimate punishment, knowing that he had lied to them…telling them that they were not going to die. He could still see in his mind the pure hate she poured from her body and soul over him. He knew he deserved it, and more.

When the train finally arrived, it was well after dark. By the time they retrieved their horses, it was near midnight. Jed asked for directions to the bank, but it was closed, so he asked how to get to the police station. At the station, Jed was unable to obtain any information as to where Lucretia Sawyer and her companion might live. He turned, frustrated, and shrugged at Eagle.

The officer at the desk looked up as the taciturn man moved to stare down at him. In a voice so quiet it was hard to hear, he spoke. "My friend here asked you a question. It was not a hard question, so I will not have to repeat it to you, now will I? Where can I find Mrs. Sawyer?"

"I am not at liberty to give out such information to anyone who asks. Ladies living alone are entitled to protection and we do our best to see that they are protected. That includes divulging their addresses. Come back tomorrow and talk to the chief. Maybe he will help you."

The words were hardly out of his mouth when he found himself dangling from the hand that held him aloft. "You have one more second to tell me or I will beat it out of you."

Jed smiled. "You better listen, 'cause he can beat an answer out of a dead man. Seen him do it couple times."

"Six blocks east, then four blocks north. Big house with four stories, on the northeast corner." He dropped to the floor and waited until they were leaving before continuing. "I will be filing charges for assaulting an officer. You will go to jail…" He was talking to air.

The sound of their horses' hooves on the cobblestone streets echoed from building to building. An elderly black man was running barefoot toward them, yelling, "Police! Police!"

Eagle pulled his horse to an abrupt stop. "Tell me, old man, what is wrong?"

"He done take Miss Lucretia. He gonna kill her."

"Where did he take her? Can you show me?" The man nodded as Black Eagle pulled him up behind him. "Which way?" Sam gave him directions and hung on for dear life, afraid he would fall under the thundering feet of the two horses. When they were a short distance away, they stopped and followed Sam on foot as he led them into the overgrown yard of the dilapidated LaClaire house.

No one knew the grounds or house the way he did. Sam had worked his entire life there until the past few weeks. Motioning them to follow him, he shoved through a hedge that grew so high along one side of the structure that the windows were nearly covered with foliage. At the base of the hedge, he pushed against a door that swung open on rusty hinges.

Once inside, he lit a lantern by the door. "We is in da cellar now. Stairs goes to kitchen o'er dere. Right round the corner in a kitchen is more stairs, go up to 'nother floor. Bedrooms is dere. Mr. Devereaux is in corner o'er udder end of house from da kitchen. Dat be where he prob'ly take her."

He led the way up the steps and opened the kitchen door. He showed them the second set of stairs and moved out of their way. Eagle blew out the lantern. “Stay here, old man. We will call when it is safe.”

They slipped off their shoes. “Damn it, Jed, if you can’t walk quieter than that, just stay here. You sound like a herd of buffalo stampeding. No, I mean it. Stay here and do not move again until you hear something.”

Jed swore under his breath, but understood when Eagle disappeared into the black and he could hear not so much as a whisper of movement. *Damn Indian,* he thought.

Eagle heard a voice as he neared a close door. “All of them, Lucretia. Take it all off and lie down on that bed. You can see it, same as I can. I am going to hurt you, then fuck you to death. Bitch.”

Black Eagle heard the sound of a fist hitting skin. He pushed through the door, knife drawn. In the shadowy room, he could see white skin on the bed and the form of a man hovered over her. Without another thought, he released the knife and the man fell sideways to the floor. He ran to the bed, scooped up the wet-faced little woman, and held her close.

Jed heard Eagle’s voice and raced to the open door. He saw and heard what Eagle and Lucretia said to each other in the following moment. It was as if a knife cut through him, but he had known this was true since the night before their rescue. She was not his and never would be.

“Lulu, you are safe now. I swear to God, no one will ever hurt you again as long as I am alive.”

It was too dark to see, but she knew who it was. No other arms in the world could feel like this. No other man had his smell or the body that held her to him. He kissed her eyes and felt the cloth in her mouth as he touched his lips to hers. He pulled it out and kissed her torn lips gently. “I love you, Lucretia Lucinda Sawyer. Now and forever.”

“And I love you, Black Eagle Grant. Now and forever.”

# THE END

**www.simsbooks.com**

# ABOUT THE AUTHOR

Beverly grew up on the Oregon Coast where the stormy surf and rugged cliffs made perfect backgrounds for her first few novels. Her move to Central Florida, where she now lives with her husband, opened a new world of bayous and critters that live in them, and set the scene for another novel.

She and her husband love traveling this great country in their motor home. You never know what might be around the next bend.

To love to write is to love to read.

www.simsbooks.com
beverly@simsbooks.com

## *Also by Beverly Sims*

The Lust Collection 1: *Blizzard of Lust*
The Lust Collection 2: *Plantation of Lust*
The Lust Collection 3: *Oasis of Lust*
*Caroline's House*
*Black Bayou*
Witness Tree 1: *The Legend of Summer Swan*

**Siren Publishing, Inc.**
**www.SirenPublishing.com**

CPSIA information can be obtained at www.ICGtesting.com
232706LV00002B/264/P

9 781606 017180